THE CHAMPIONS

THE CHAM

Writers: Tony Isabella, Bill Mantlo
& Chris Claremont
Pencilers: Don Heck, George Tuska,
Bob Hall & John Byrne
Inkers: Mike Esposito, John Tartaglione,
Vince Colletta, Bruce D. Patterson, Bob Layton & Frank Giacoia
Colors: Petra Goldberg, Phil Rachelson, George Roussos,
Janice Cohen & Don Warfield
Letters: Dave Hunt, Irving Watanabe, Karen Mantlo,
John Costanza, Ray Holloway & Bruce D. Patterson
Editors: Marv Wolfman & Archie Goodwin

PIONS

Cover Art: Gil Kane & Dan Adkins
Cover Colors: Tom Smith
Color Reconstruction: Jerron Quality Color

Senior Editor, Special Projects: Jeff Youngquist
Associate Editors: Jennifer Grünwald & Mark D. Beazley
Assistant Editor: Michael Short
Vice President of Sales: David Gabriel
Production: Jerron Quality Color
Book Designer: Jhonson Eteng
Vice President of Creative: Tom Marvelli

Editor in Chief: Joe Quesada
Publisher: Dan Buckley

THE CHAMPIONS **MARVEL COMICS GROUP**™

25¢ 1 OCT 02112

HERCULES! BLACK WIDOW! ANGEL! GHOST RIDER! ICEMAN!

THE CHAMPIONS™

ACTION-PACKED FIRST ISSUE!

ONWARD, MY COMRADES! THE TIME HAS COME TO FACE OUR **GREATEST FOES!**

KANE ADKINS

Stan Lee PRESENTS:
THE MOST POWER-PACKED PREMIERE OF ALL IN THIS-- THE MIGHTY MARVEL RENAISSANCE!
THE WORLD STILL NEEDS...
THE CHAMPIONS!
STARRING THE AVENGING ANGEL! THE DEADLY BLACK WIDOW! THE DOOM-DEFYING GHOST RIDER!
STARRING HERCULES, PRINCE OF POWER! THE INDOMITABLE ICEMAN! --AND GUEST-STARRING-- THE ASTOUNDING VENUS!
SERIES CONCEIVED AND WRITTEN BY TONY ISABELLA• PENCILLED BY DON HECK• INKED BY MIKE ESPOSITO• LETTERED BY DAVE HUNT• COLORED BY PETRA G.• EDITED BY MARV WOLFMAN

TWO YOUNG MEN STROLL THE U.C.L.A. CAMPUS THIS SUNNY AUTUMN MORNING. IN THE PAST, THE WORLD HAS KNOWN THEM AS MUTANTS. OR FREAKS. OR RENEGADES. OR, ON RARE OCCASIONS, AS WORLD-SAVERS. BUT WE HAVE SEEN THEM IN ALL THOSE ROLES BEFORE. TODAY, THEY ARE MERELY... TWO CONFUSED YOUNG MEN.
IT'S NOT WORKING FOR YOU EITHER, IS IT, BOBBY?

GOOD SHOT, WARREN. PROF X WAS GREAT-- GETTIN' ME A SCHOLARSHIP HERE AND ALL--
--BUT I GUESS COLLEGE ISN'T WHAT THIS LITTLE MU-TANT IS LOOKIN' FOR.
I'D GO BACK TO THE X-MEN...
...EXCEPT THEY AREN'T THE SAME X-MEN THAT WE GREW UP WITH. I KNOW.

I READ IN THE PAPER HOW HANK* IS MAKIN' IT BIG IN THE AVENGERS. MAYBE...
COME ON, LITTLE BUDDY. DO YOU REALLY THINK WE'D FIT IN WITH THAT GROUP?
*HANK McCOY, A.K.A. THE BEAST--MARV.

FACE IT-- THIS FLYBOY-POPSICLE COMBINATION JUST ISN'T CUT OUT TO DO SOMEBODY ELSE'S THING. I...
HOLY HANNAH!

I SEE IT TOO, WARREN!
IT'S SOME KIND OF--

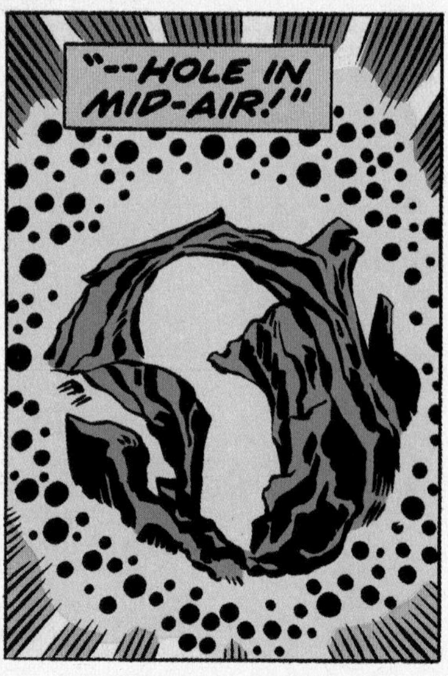
"--HOLE IN MID-AIR!"

"AND LOOK WHAT'S POURING OUT OF IT!"
THE GODDESS, MORTALS!
HAND OVER VENUS--
--OR FACE THE WRATH OF THE HARPIES!

WHERE IS SHE, MAN-CHILD?
ANSWER --OR DIE!

THRUD!

BOBBY! YOU SAVED THAT STUDENT, BUT YOU CAN'T FIGHT THEM IN YOUR CIVILIAN IDENTITY! WHAT IF SOMEBODY SEES YOU?
WHAT ABOUT YOUR PARENTS?
NO SWEAT, MR. WORTHINGTON.

BY THE TIME ANYBODY FIGURES OUT WHERE THAT ICEBOLT CAME FROM, THEY WON'T SEE BOBBY DRAKE...
THEY'LL SEE--

THE ICEMAN!
WHOOPS! SCRATCH ONE SET OF FREEZE-DRIED CLOTHES!
HOLD 'EM, PAL--WHILE I GET INTO COSTUME!

MOVE IT, WINGS!
'CAUSE IT LOOKS LIKE ICEMAN AND THE ANGEL ARE BACK ON THE CHARTS!

DESTROY THE ICY ONE!

SORRY, LADY! BUT AS FAST AS YOU GALS ARE--

--MY ICE-SLED IS FASTER!
KLUG!

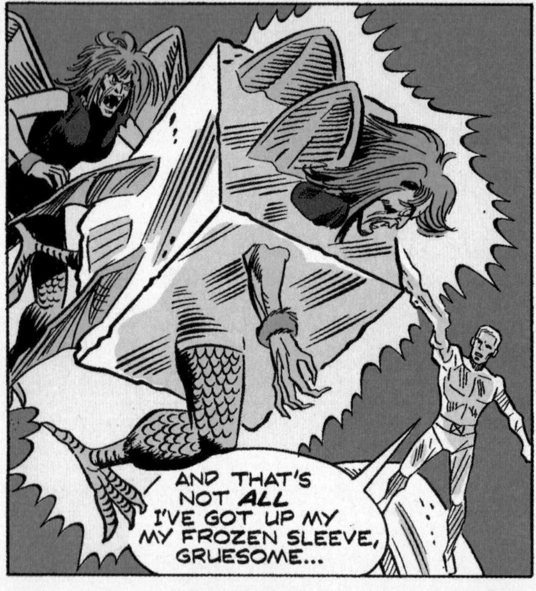
AND THAT'S NOT ALL I'VE GOT UP MY MY FROZEN SLEEVE, GRUESOME...

CATCH MY SNOW DRIFT?
KWUNK!
YOU BOAST TOO MUCH, YOUTH!

AT HIM, SISTERS!
WHAM!
YUGH!
OUR CLAWS WILL SLICE HIM TO RIBBONS!

LIKE BLAZES THEY WILL, UGLY!
NOT WITH THE ANGEL ON THE SCENE!
HUH? WARREN'S NOT WEARING HIS MASK!

"SOMEBODY'S BOUND TO RECOGNIZE HIM!"
CHOK!

YOU OKAY, TIGER?
YEAH... BUT LET'S GET OUT OF HERE BEFORE YOUR COVER IS BLOWN!
NO WAY, FRIEND. THIS IS A DECISION I MADE AFTER MOM DIED. NO MORE HIDING! FOR BETTER OR FOR WORSE, FROM HERE ON IN--
--THE ANGEL GOES PUBLIC!

BESIDES...
OUR FANS OVER THERE ARE MAKING RETREAT A DECIDEDLY DIFFICULT VENTURE!
KILL THEM! KILL THEM!

A VERY WEARY WOMAN GAZES OUT OVER THE UCLA CAMPUS THIS SUNNY AUTUMN MORNING. IN THE PAST, SHE HAS BEEN KNOWN AS A SPY, A JET-SETTER, AND A SUPER-HEROINE. TODAY, HOWEVER, SHE ASSAYS A NEW ROLE:
HONESTY-TIME, IVAN. WHAT DO YOU THINK MY CHANCES ARE?
JOB APPLICANT.

SHE WAITS PATIENTLY FOR HER INTERVIEW, TRYING TO PUSH FROM HER MIND THE KNOWLEDGE THAT, ONCE AGAIN, SHE HAS BEEN FORCED... BY WHAT AND WHO SHE IS... TO LEAVE A MAN SHE LOVED.*
* DAREDEVIL # 124. --MARV.
RELAX, SWEETHEART. THE AD SAID THEY NEEDED SOMEONE TO TEACH RUSSIAN TO THE KIDDIES. AN' UNLESS YOU'VE FORGOTTEN OUR MOTHER TONGUE, YOU'RE A SHOE-IN FOR THE JOB.
I HOPE YOU'RE RIGHT, OLD FRIEND. WE NEED THIS JOB. WE'RE JUST ABOUT BROKE.
MORE THAN THAT-- I NEED THIS JOB BADLY.
WHAT SHE IS-- IS A HIGHLY CAPABLE INDIVIDUALIST WHO HAS NEVER REALLY FOUND HER PLACE IN THE SUN.
WHO SHE IS--IS... THE BLACK WIDOW!

WHY, 'TASH? TO HELP YOU FORGET MATT?
THAT'S NOT IT, IVAN. I DON'T WANT TO FORGET MATT MURDOCK. WHAT WE HAD WAS GOOD-- WHILE IT LASTED.
WE PUSHED OUR LUCK, THAT'S ALL. KEPT THE GAME GOING TOO LONG.

I WOULDN'T CALL IT A GAME, KID.
'CAUSE EVEN THIS OLD FOGEY CAN SEE THAT YOU'RE STILL IN LOVE WITH HORN-HEAD. MAYBE...
WHERE'S THIS UNEARTHLY GLOW COMING FROM?
HUH?
IVAN! THERE'S SOME KIND OF PORTAL APPEARING IN THIS VERY ROOM!

AND ARMORED WOMEN ARE CHARGING FORTH FROM IT.
WE HAVE COME FOR VENUS! WOMAN!
WE KNOW SHE IS NEAR. CONCEAL HER ONLY AT THE COST OF YOUR OWN MORTAL LIFE!

I DON'T LIKE THE WAY YOU'RE WAVIN' THAT PIG-STICKER AROUND, BEAUTIFUL!
SO HERE'S LOOKIN' AT YOU!
THOP!
'TASH! STRIP FOR ACTION!

I'LL HOLD THEM OFF UNTIL YOU--
URGH!
GOOD WORK, WARRIOR!

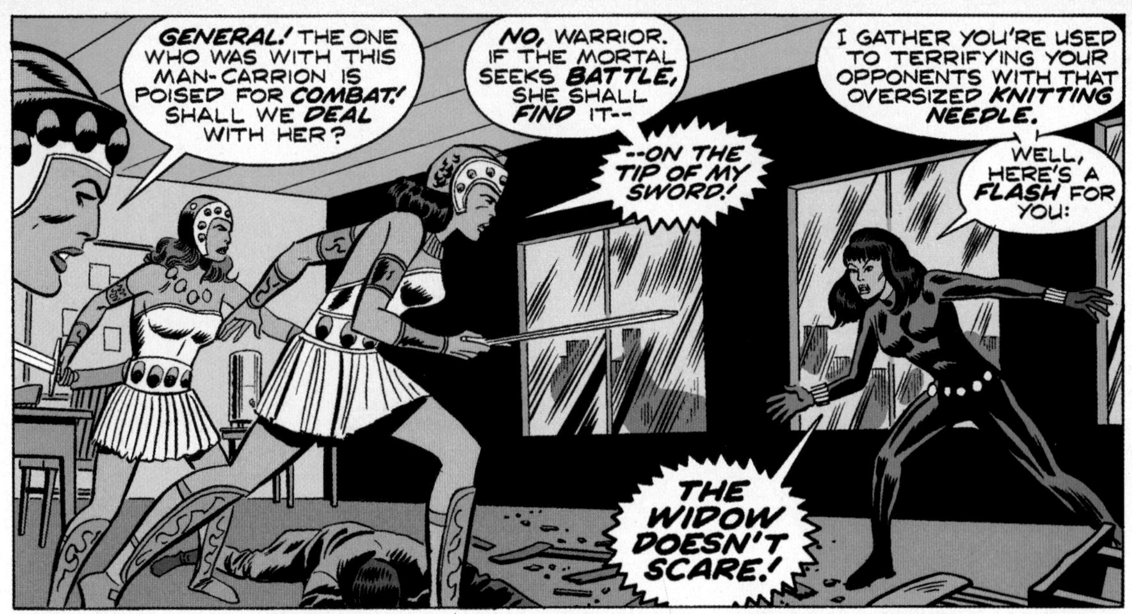

GENERAL! THE ONE WHO WAS WITH THIS MAN-CARRION IS POISED FOR COMBAT! SHALL WE DEAL WITH HER?
NO, WARRIOR. IF THE MORTAL SEEKS BATTLE, SHE SHALL FIND IT--
--ON THE TIP OF MY SWORD!
I GATHER YOU'RE USED TO TERRIFYING YOUR OPPONENTS WITH THAT OVERSIZED KNITTING NEEDLE.
WELL, HERE'S A FLASH FOR YOU:
THE WIDOW DOESN'T SCARE!

WELCOMING PROSPECTIVE RUSSIAN TEACHERS ISN'T REALLY A JOB FOR UCLA'S NEWEST HUMANITIES PROFESSOR--
--BUT I WANT TO MEET THE FAMOUS NATASHA ROMANOFF.
I SEEM TO HAVE ACQUIRED AN ALMOST HUMAN CURIOSITY IN MY MORTAL GUISE AS DR. VICTORIA STARR.

GENERAL! THE GODDESS IS HERE!
THIS CAN'T BE!
WHAT ARE HIPPOLYTA'S AMAZONS DOING HERE?
SEIZE HER!

UUNNNNNN!
ZAT!
APPARENTLY, OUR NEW ARRIVAL IS THE REASON FOR YOUR VISIT HERE, LADIES--
ZAT!
--AND, AS SUCH, SHE'S JUST GAINED THE PROTECTION OF THE BLACK WIDOW--
--AND MY WIDOW'S BITE!

YOU CAN'T FIGHT THEM! THEY'RE THE MOST FIERCELY-TRAINED WARRIORS IN OLYM--THEIR WORLD!
I DOUBT MY K.G.B. TASKMASTERS WERE LESS DEMANDING IN PREPARING MY CURRICULUM. STILL...
ZAT!

IT MIGHT INDEED BEHOOVE US TO SEEK A--
CHUK
--STRATEGIC WITHDRAWAL.
BUT WHERE DOES THAT LEAVE IVAN?

YOU NEEDN'T CONCERN YOURSELF ABOUT HIM, MS. ROMANOFF. THOUGH THE AMAZONS ARE INTERESTED SOLELY IN MY DEMISE--
--I HAVE NEVERTHELESS, ARRANGED HIS SAFETY.
HOW--
I THINK, MY FRIEND--

--YOU HAD BEST EXPLAIN JUST WHO YOU ARE AND WHY THESE WARRIOR-WOMEN PURSUE YOU.
I DON'T FACE DEATH WITHOUT GOOD REASON!

AN APPREHENSIVE CYCLIST TRAVERSES THE UCLA CAMPUS THIS SUNNY AUTUMN MORNING. IN THE PAST, HE WAS A PAWN... NO, A VICTIM ...OF SATAN. TODAY, HE IS A FREE MAN.
WHAT'S GOING ON HERE?
THESE KIDS LOOK TERRIFIED!

YET HIS FREEDOM HAS MADE HIS LIFE INCREASINGLY COMPLICATED AND HE WONDERS WHY THIS SHOULD BE SO.
TURN AROUND, PAL! THERE'S SOME KIND OF THING BACK THERE!
HE WILL FIND NO RELIEF FOR HIS PUZZLEMENT HERE...

...ONLY DANGER!
WHOA!
NOW THAT WAS JUST A MITE TOO CLOSE!

THEN AGAIN...

STAND FAST, BE YE MORTAL OR DEMON! BY COMMAND OF MY MASTER, NO ONE MUST PASS CERBERUS, GUARDIAN OF THE DEPTHS!

FOR MY MASTER WILL BROOK NO INTERFERENCE WITH HIS PLAN TO CRUSH THE MAN-GOD!

YOUR "MASTER" APPEARS TO BE A MEMBER OF THE SAME CLUB AS AN OLD ACQUAINTANCE OF MINE, FELLA.

AND THAT BEING THE CASE--

HE CAN TAKE HIS PLAN AND STUFF IT!
FWOOSH!
YRRGH!
THE MAN-DEMON STRIKES WITH A FLAME THAT BURNS EVEN ONE SUCH AS I!*
*HELLFIRE, BY TRADE-NAME--MARV.

BUT CERBERUS WAS CREATED TO BE MANY GUARDIANS.
AND WHAT ONE IS ILL-EQUIPPED TO BATTLE--
--ANOTHER CAN DESTROY!
OHHH, BOY. NOW I GET IT!
CERBERUS: THE GUARDIAN OF HADES IN ROMAN MYTHOLOGY.
A.K.A. BOWSER HERE.

RRRRR
AND JUDGING FROM THE WAY HE'S FLASHIN' HIS PEARLY WHITES AT ME--

--HIS BARK ISN'T EVEN IN THE SAME BALLPARK AS HIS BITE!
I THINK I'D BETTER VAMOOSE--
VROOOOMMMM

RRRRR
--LEASTWISE UNTIL I CAN COME UP WITH SOME WAY OF CORRALLIN' THIS CRITTER!
ONE THING'S FOR CERTAIN--

THIS IS THE LAST TIME I PLAY ERRAND BOY --EVEN FOR A FELLOW STUNT-PERSON!*
* SEE GHOST RIDER #14, NOW ON (HINT! HINT!) SALE--MARV.

A SOMEWHAT UNIQUE LECTURER HAS COME TO THE U.C.L.A. CAMPUS THIS SUNNY AUTUMN MORNING. HIS SUBJECT: "MYTHOLOGY: WHAT IT MEANS TO YOU."
AND HOW THE HEAVENS MUST ROCK WITH LAUGHTER AT THE MONUMENTAL JEST. FOR THE SPEAKER IS NONE OTHER THAN--
--HERCULES, PRINCE OF POWER!
THOU SEEM TROUBLED, RICHARD FENSTER.

IS THERE ANY WAY HERCULES MIGHT EASE THY CONCERN?
JUST "WOW" THE AUDIENCE TONIGHT, HERCULES. I NEED TO SCORE A FEW POINTS WITH THE CAMPUS BRASS--
--OR I COULD LOSE MY "THANKLESS BUT SO NECESSARY" JOB AS LECTURE AGENT.

THOU HAST NOTHING TO FEAR THERE.
WHEN I TELL YOUR YOUNG PEOPLE OF THE GLORIES OF OLYMPUS, THEY WILT VERILY SWOON WITH WONDERMENT.
I HOPE SO. THE LAST OFF-BEAT SPEAKER I HIRED DIDN'T WORK OUT TOO WELL. A REAL HITCHCOCK TYPE.

PICTURE A SCRAWNY MOP-HAIRED NEW YORK WRITER --WHO SPENDS ALL HIS TIME WRITING ABOUT SOME BLOOD-THIRSTY BARBARIAN HE CALLED CO- ULP!
MORTAL! WHAT IS IT? WHY DOTH FEAR CROSS YOUR FACE LIKE A BLEAK SHADOW?
PERHAPS BECAUSE HE SEES--

--US!
ZEUS! WHAT MANNER OF CREATURES ART THOU?
MUTATES, MAN-GOD! DESTINED TO RULE THIS PLANET IN EONS TO COME!

BUT NOW, MERELY--
--YOUR CONQUERORS!

CONQUERORS?
YOU PRESUME TOO MUCH, FUTURE MEN!

AWAY, O IGNOMINIOUS FLEAS!
NONE MAY HOLD THE PRINCE OF POWER THUS!

THERE SHALL BE PAYMENT EXTRACTED FOR THIS FOUL DEED YOU HAVE ATTEMPTED, MUTATES.
RENCH

PAYMENT IN FULL!

SPAK!

YOU MAY HAVE FELLED MY MEN, HERCULES...
WAK!
BUT YOU HAVE YET TO FACE THE MOST SAVAGE MUTATE OF ALL!

FOR YEARS I HAVE RULED THEM. AND IN THOSE YEARS, ONLY THE MIGHTY THOR HAS EVER DEFEATED ME!*
THOUGH HERCULES BE SWORN FRIEND OF THE THUNDER GOD, KNOW YOU THIS:
* THOR #163--MARV.

WHATEVER THOR CANST DO--
SPRAK!

BRAKK!
--HERCULES CANST ACCOMPLISH MORE MIGHTILY!

THOR HAD ALLIES WHEN HE FOUGHT US, HERCULES!
YOU STAND ALONE!
AND THAT IS WHY YOU MUST FALL--
--BEFORE THE FULL, UNSTOPPABLE POWER OF--
--THE MUTATES UNLEASHED!
WHAM!

YE GODS!
CRACK!
THE FORCE OF THEIR CHARGE DOTH DRIVE BOTH MYSELF AND MINE FOEMEN THROUGH THE WALL!
BUT 'TWILL TAKE MORE THAN THIS MERE PLUNGE TO STILL HERCULES' RAGE! UNTIL THESE BASE ONES HAVE BEEN DEFEATED--

THE PRINCE OF POWER FIGHTS ON!
SMASH!

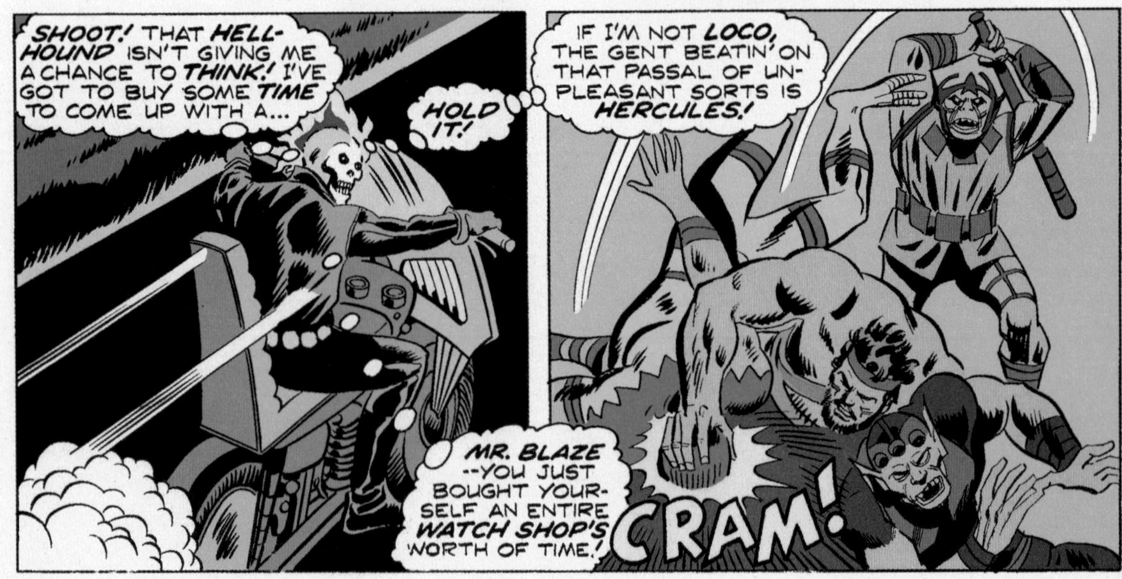
SHOOT! THAT HELL-HOUND ISN'T GIVING ME A CHANCE TO THINK! I'VE GOT TO BUY SOME TIME TO COME UP WITH A...
HOLD IT!
IF I'M NOT LOCO, THE GENT BEATIN' ON THAT PASSAL OF UNPLEASANT SORTS IS HERCULES!
MR. BLAZE --YOU JUST BOUGHT YOURSELF AN ENTIRE WATCH SHOP'S WORTH OF TIME!
CRAM!

TITAN'S BLOOD!
WHAT NEW ENEMY DOTH DARE TO LAY HAND UPON HERCULES IN THE MIDST OF BATTLE?
WAIT A MINUTE, PARTNER! I'M ON YOUR SIDE!
JUST SWING UP AND GRAB A SEAT ON MY SKULL CYCLE AND I'LL CLUE YOU IN!
BUT TO GIVE YOU A QUICK IDEA OF WHAT I'VE SEEN WHILE BEING CHASED BY BOWSER BACK THERE: ALL HELL'S EXPLODING 'ROUND HERE-- AND I CAN'T STOP IT ALONE!

YOUR VOICE REEKS WITH EVIL, MORTAL--
--YET HERCULES DOTH SENSE THE TRUE VALOR THAT UNDERLIES THY TONE AND THE URGENCY IN THY REQUEST.
I'M GLAD OF THAT, BIG FELLA.
'CAUSE OUR HASSLES GO WAY BEYOND AN OVERGROWN MUTT AND SOME ASSORTED UGLIES.

THIS WHOLE CAMPUS IS GOING CRAZY!
LOOK!
BY THE CLOVEN HOOVES OF PAN!
AMAZON WARRIORS AND HARPIES--HERE ON EARTH!

AND AMONG THOSE THEY PURSUE: SHE WHO HERCULES DOTH KNOW AS THE BLACK WIDOW AND ANOTHER WOMAN WHO DOTH LOOK STRANGELY FAMILIAR.
"I'M GLAD YOU RECOGNIZED THE LADIES, HERK. I CAN PUT NAMES TO THE GENTS: THE ANGEL AND THE ICE-MAN-- TWO OF THE X-MEN!"

DO WHAT YOU CAN FOR THEM, MORTAL!
HERCULES SHALL DEAL WITH YON DEVIL-HOUND.
MUCH OBLIGED, PARTNER.
LET'S SEE HOW THOSE WINGED TERRORS REACT OF A SUDDEN BURST OF--
--HELL-FIRE!

AYIEEEEEEEE!
FLEE, MY SISTERS!
THIS UN-NATURAL FIRE CAN DESTROY US!

HO! CERBERUS! THOUGH IT HATH BEEN AGES SINCE I DIDST VANQUISH YOU AND DRAG YOU FROM THE PITS OF HADES--
SPANG!
--STILL DOTH HERCULES REMAIN THY MASTER!

HEY! THE CAVALRY'S ARRIVED--AND THAT'S THE ONLY BREAK WE'VE GOTTEN SINCE FLYBOY AND I RAN INTO YOU LADIES.
FRIZZZZZ
AND IT LOOKS LIKE THE ODDS HAVE BEEN ADJUSTED JUST ENOUGH--
--FOR YOURS TRULY TO CUT LOOSE!

GENERAL! WE --CAN'T MOVE!
USE YOUR SWORDS TO HACK YOURSELVES FREE MY WARRIORS!
AND THEN TURN THEIR SHARP STEEL ON THOSE WHO ATTEMPT TO KEEP THE GODDESS FROM US!

OH, NO! THE AMAZONS AND THE HARPIES ARE RECOVERING--AND HERE COMES A NEW GROUP OF PLAYMATES!
NO, WARREN, I THINK IT'S TIME I LENT A HAND HERE.
MS. ROMANOFF--CAN YOU DELAY THEM FOR A MOMENT?
DR. STARR, MAKE A RUN FOR IT AND--
WARREN, FLY ME ABOVE OUR ATTACKERS.
UGHN!
YOU'RE THE BOSS, DOC.
YOU'RE NOT THE ONLY ONE HARBORING A SECRET IDENTITY, WARREN. THE WOMAN YOU KNOW AS VICTORIA STARR IS REALLY--

--THE GODDESS MEN CALL VENUS!
AND WITH THE GOLDEN GIRDLE, CESTUS, AROUND MY WAIST, I HAVE THE POWER OF LOVE OVER MAN OR GOD!
THOUGH IT APPEARS MY POWER AFFECTS THESE STRANGE CREATURES DIFFERENTLY THAN I HAD ANTICIPATED.

THAT SHINING LIGHT! IT CAUSES MY MIND TO REEL!
I CANNOT STAND!
OHHHHHH

WELL DONE, MY COUSIN. THY POWER HATH RENDERED ALL OUR ENEMIES IMMOBILE.
THOUGH, GIVEN TIME, I WOULD HAVE ACCOMPLISHED THE SAME END.
AND ART THOU UNHARMED, FAIR NATASHA?
UNHARMED, BUT INCREDIBLY CONFUSED, HERCULES.
WHAT'S GOING ON HERE?
APPARENTLY, OUR FOES WERE SEEKING TO CAPTURE ME FOR SOME REASON.
YOU CAN'T HARDLY BLAME THEM FOR THAT!
BUT THE GHOST GUY SAID CERBERUS AND THE MUTATES WERE AFTER HERK!
DO YOU THINK THERE'S SOMEBODY ELSE INVOLVED IN THIS?
SOMEBODY RUNNING THE WHOLE MAGILLA?

ZAT!
THOU ART INDEED A BASE FOOL, WINGED ONE. OF COURSE, THERE BE SOMEONE BEHIND THE WEAVING OF THIS DAY'S EVENTS! SOMEONE WITH POWER ENON TO SMITE YOU ALL WITH BUT A SINGLE BLAST!
UHN!
YRRGH!

THAT BLAST WAS POWERFUL ENOUGH TO DROP ALL OF US! I FEEL LIKE ALL MY STRENGTH HAS BEEN DRAINED OUT OF ME!
YOU'RE NOT KIDDIN' LADY! I FEEL LIKE I'VE BEEN RUN OVER BY A MACK TRUCK!
LOOK! THERE'S ANOTHER OF THOSE "HOLES" APPEARING --JUST LIKE THE ONE THE AMAZONS CHARGED OUT OF! AND INSIDE...

IT CAN'T BE!
AND WHY NOT, VENUS? ART NOT THOU, A GOD-DESS OF OLYMPUS, HERE ON EARTH? WOULDST THOU DENY THE SAME TO THY FELLOW...
VILLAINS! THOU HAST PERPETRATED THY FINAL SCHEME UPON THE PRINCE OF POWER! THOU WILT BE...
SILENCE, THOU PRAT-TLING MAN-GOD! FOR, THIS DAY, I BRING THEE A DECREE FROM THY OWN FATHER, OUR LORD ZEUS!

HEED THE WORDS OF PLUTO, HERCULES. FOR THE DREAD RULER OF THE UNDERWORLD DOTH MERELY ECHO THE WORDS OF ZEUS:
BEFORE THIS DAY IS DONE, THOU SHALT WED HIPPOLYTA, QUEEN OF THE AMAZONS, AND SERVE LOYALLY AS HER PRINCE CONSORT.
AND THOU, MY DEAR VENUS, WILT LIKEWISE BECOME THE SPOUSE OF THE WAR-GOD ARES!
AND BEFORE THY SHOCKED COUNTENANCES FAIN LEAP FROM THY FACES, KNOW YE THIS:
SHOULDST EITHER OF YOU RESIST THESE MATCHES--
--THE UNIVERSE DIES!
NEXT: WHOM THE GODS HAVE JOINED TOGETHER...!

THE CHAMPIONS **MARVEL COMICS GROUP**™

APPROVED BY THE COMICS CODE AUTHORITY

25¢ | 2 DEC 02112

HERCULES! BLACK WIDOW! ANGEL! GHOST RIDER! ICEMAN!

THE CHAMPIONS

YOUR COMRADES CANNOT *HELP* YOU, HERCULES!

Stan Lee PRESENTS: THE CHAMPIONS™
CHAOS REIGNS ON THE CAMPUS OF U.C.L.A. FOR IN THE PAST HOUR, ITS SCHOLARLY CONFINES HAVE BEEN RENT BY CREATURES FROM BEYOND TIME. HERCULES AND HIS NEW-FOUND COMRADES--THE ANGEL, THE BLACK WIDOW, THE GHOST RIDER, THE ICEMAN, AND VENUS--HAVE VALIANTLY DEFEATED THESE CREATURES...ONLY TO LEARN THAT THE PERIL HAS BARELY BEGUN!
WHOM THE GODS WOULD JOIN...
WHAT MADNESS IS THIS?
TONY ISABELLA WRITER
DON HECK ARTIST
JOHN TARTAG INKER
PHIL RACHE, Colorist IRV WATANABE, Letterer
MARV WOLFMAN EDITOR

DEEM IT WHAT THOU WILT, MAN-GOD, BUT THY BLUSTEROUS OUTRAGE CANNOT ALTER THE DECREE OF OUR LORD ZEUS.
BEFORE THIS DAY IS DONE: THOU SHALT WED HIPPOLYTA, QUEEN OF THE AMAZONS, FOREVER-MORE TO SERVE HER.
AND THOU, MY DEAR VENUS, WILL LIKEWISE BECOME THE SPOUSE OF THE WAR GOD ARES.
FOR, AS ZEUS DOTH KNOW FULL WELL, SHOULDST EITHER OF THEE RESIST THESE MATCHES--
--THE UNIVERSE DIES!
HERCULES, CAN THE DEATH-GOD SPEAK TRULY?
NO!
NEVER WOULD MY FATHER ZEUS CONDEMN HIS SON AND LOYAL NIECE TO SUCH FATES!
PLUTO DOTH LIE--

--BUT HE WILL LIE NO MORE!
WILT THOU NEVER LEARN, HERCULES?
ARES...

UGHN!
HIS HUMAN HALF, PLUTO. ALWAYS HATH IT CAUSED THIS MONGREL TO ACT THUS TOWARDS HIS BETTERS.
ELSE HOW COULD HE THINK ARES TO STAND IDLE WHILE HE DOTH ATTACK?
WHUMP!

WAR-GOD, HERCULES DID BUT THINK--
--OF THY PAST DEFEATS AT HIS HANDS.
SPAK!
PITY THY MEMORY DIDST FAIL THEE!

HOLD, PRINCE OF POWER!
HE WHO STRIKES MY ALLY MUST FACE MY SWORD AS WELL, AND I HAVE NO WISH TO INJURE--
--MY HUSBAND-TO-BE.

HUSBAND-TO-BE!
WOMAN...

CHOOM!
I WOULD SOONER MARRY ALL THREE OF THE GORGONS!

NOW, PLUTO!
NOW IT IS JUST WE TWO WHO BATTLE!
BATTLE, HERCULES?

DOTH THE HAWK BATTLE THE SPARROW?
DOTH THE LION BATTLE THE LAMB?
THY GRIP! NEVER HAVE I FELT ITS LIKE!

WE DO NOT BATTLE, HERCULES.
BATTLE IS BETWIXT EQUALS.

AND THOU CANST NEVER BE--

--PLUTO'S EQUAL!
STARS! HERCULES' STRENGTH DOTH FADE AT THY MEREST TOUCH!

THAT CREEP IS KILLIN' HERK!
THEN MAYBE IT'S TIME WE STOPPED STANDING AROUND STARING LIKE A BUNCH OF GOGGEL-EYED GROUPIES!
WE'VE GOT TO STOP PLUTO!
OR DIE TRYING, ANGEL?

WE CAN'T FIGHT POWER LIKE HIS-- NOT EVEN WITH VENUS ON OUR SIDE!
THERE'S ONLY ONE WAY TO SAVE HERCULES...

BUT EVEN AS NATASHA ROMANOFF, A.K.A. THE BLACK WIDOW, OUTLINES HER PLAN...
HAH! THOUGH THOU DIDST CHIDE ARES FOR HIS LACK OF MEMORY, THOU--THOU HALF-MORTAL BRAGGART--ART NO LESS FORGETFUL!

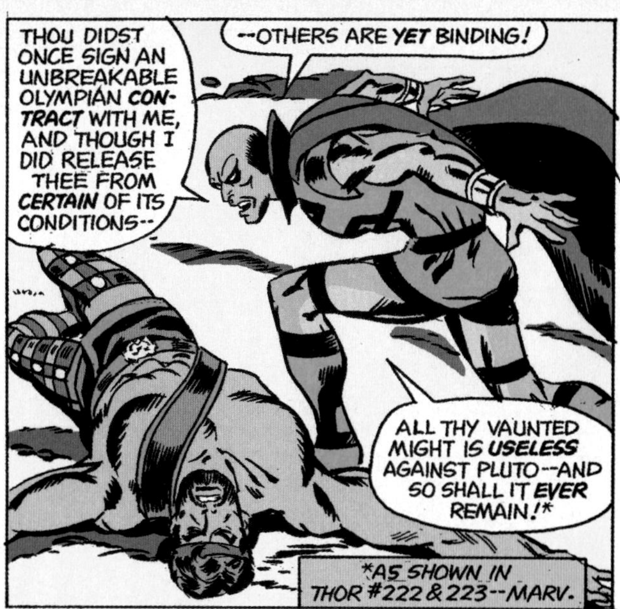
THOU DIDST ONCE SIGN AN UNBREAKABLE OLYMPIAN CONTRACT WITH ME, AND THOUGH I DID RELEASE THEE FROM CERTAIN OF ITS CONDITIONS--
--OTHERS ARE YET BINDING!
ALL THY VAUNTED MIGHT IS USELESS AGAINST PLUTO--AND SO SHALL IT EVER REMAIN!*
*AS SHOWN IN THOR #222 & 223--MARV.

SORRY TO SHAKE UP THE STATUS QUO, MISTER--
--BUT THAT'S OUR FRIEND YOU'VE BEEN BEATING ON!
WE TEND TO GET A MITE UPSET OVER THAT SORT OF THING.

WHAT?
YOU DARE ATTACK ME?
FOOLS! I AM THY FINAL MASTER!

I AM PLUTO!
FAAKKK!
LORD OF THE DEAD!

IT WORKED! WARREN AND THE GHOST RIDER HAVE DRAWN PLUTO'S ATTENTION AWAY FROM HERCULES SO WE CAN DRAG MY COUSIN TO SAFETY.
WE'RE ONLY HALFWAY HOME, VENUS.
THE REST IS UP TO THE ICEMAN.

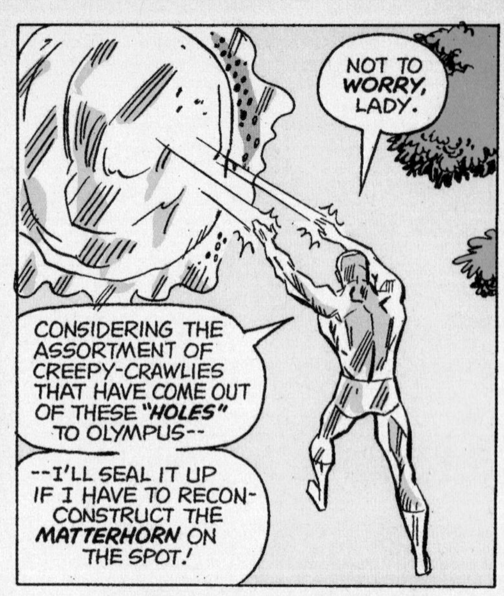
NOT TO WORRY, LADY.
CONSIDERING THE ASSORTMENT OF CREEPY-CRAWLIES THAT HAVE COME OUT OF THESE "HOLES" TO OLYMPUS--
--I'LL SEAL IT UP IF I HAVE TO RECON-CONSTRUCT THE MATTERHORN ON THE SPOT!

EVEN THAT MOUNTAIN OF ICE WON'T HOLD PLUTO AND THE OTHERS FOR LONG.
THEN I SUGGEST WE VACATE THIS AREA UNTIL HERCULES RECOVERS.
YOU CALLED IT, WIDOW.
I'LL GIVE A LIFT TO MY HUMANITIES PROFESSOR NÉE GODDESS OF LOVE--
--WHILE YOU SLIDE THE FRIENDLY SKIES.
THE GHOST RIDER IS GOING TO DO A LITTLE ADVANCE SCOUTING.
IF WE'RE GOING TO FACE THAT TRIO AGAIN, I'D PREFER HE WERE AT FULL STRENGTH.
I'LL BE DARNED! IN SPITE OF ALL WE'VE JUST GONE THOUGH, WARREN SEEMS MORE TOGETHER THAN HE'S BEEN IN MONTHS!
MAYBE THIS IMPROMPTU COFFEE KLATCH IS AGREEING WITH HIM.

WHILE, ON THE OTHER SIDE OF THE INQUISITIVE BOBBY DRAKE'S HANDIWORK...
PLUTO, IF YON BARRIER REMAINS UNSHATTERED, WE CANNOT PURSUE OUR FOES.
SO WHY DOST THOU WITH-HOLD THY POWER FROM THIS TASK?
BECAUSE, O QUEEN, I PERCEIVE 'TIS UNNECESSARY.
SO UNNECESSARY THAT I HAVE ALREADY RETURNED OUR DEFEATED WARRIORS TO OLYMPUS.

HERCULES AND VENUS WILL NEVER SUBMIT TO US.
BUT THERE BE ONE WHO CAN COMPEL THEIR OBEDIENCE.

AND SINCE IT BE "HIS" WISH THAT THOU WED OUR MOST UNCOOPERATIVE GODLINGS--

--LET US TAKE LEAVE OF THIS PLACE AND SEEK AUDIENCE WITH--

--ZEUS!
PLUTO, THOU BASEST OF VILLAINS!
THOU DAREST TO FOUL THIS HALLOWED AIR WITH THINE STYGIAN PRESENCE?

"--REALIZING THAT THERE BE OTHER RULERS OF THE DEAD THROUGHOUT THE DIMENSIONS WHO MIGHT ALSO FEEL THE UNJUST PERSECUTION OF THEIR PEERS, SOUGHT OUT THESE GODS TO FORM AN ALLIANCE FOR OUR MUTUAL PROTECTION.

"THOUGH SOME REFUSED MOST HAUGHTILY--

"--THE MAJORITY WERE...RECEPTIVE.

"WE SEEK ONLY PEACE AND SECURITY FOR OUR DARK REALMS, MY LORD, AND SO IT GRIEVES ME TO REMIND THEE THAT NOT EVEN FABLED OLYMPUS COULD LONG WITHSTAND AN ASSAULT BY SUCH AN ALLIANCE.

"NOT THAT SUCH A TRAGIC CONFLAGRATION WOULD EVER COME TO PASS."

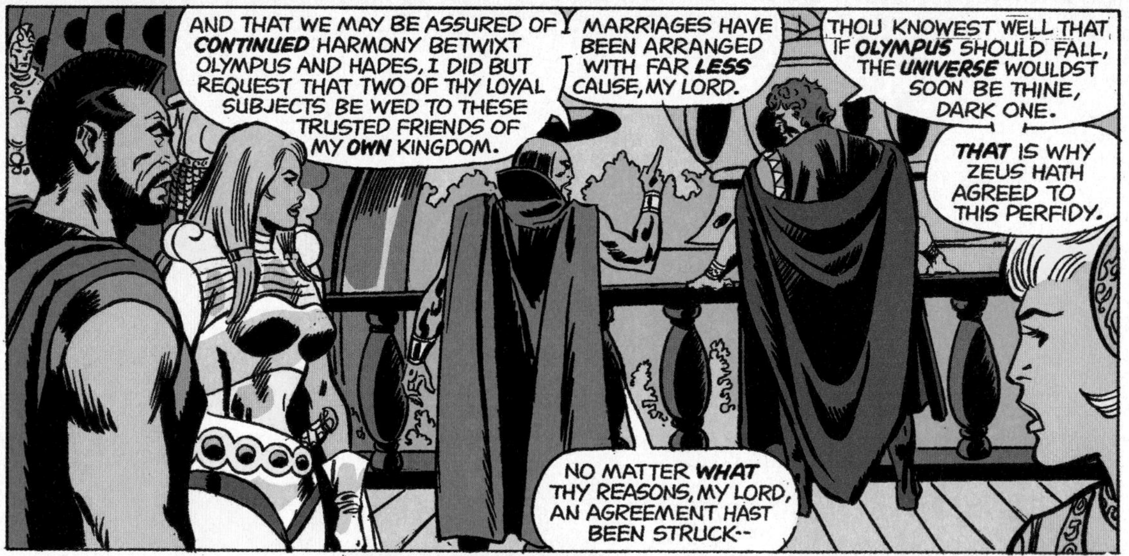
AND THAT WE MAY BE ASSURED OF CONTINUED HARMONY BETWIXT OLYMPUS AND HADES, I DID BUT REQUEST THAT TWO OF THY LOYAL SUBJECTS BE WED TO THESE TRUSTED FRIENDS OF MY OWN KINGDOM.
MARRIAGES HAVE BEEN ARRANGED WITH FAR LESS CAUSE, MY LORD.
THOU KNOWEST WELL THAT IF OLYMPUS SHOULD FALL, THE UNIVERSE WOULDST SOON BE THINE, DARK ONE.
THAT IS WHY ZEUS HATH AGREED TO THIS PERFIDY.
NO MATTER WHAT THY REASONS, MY LORD, AN AGREEMENT HAST BEEN STRUCK--

AN AGREEMENT HERCULES AND VENUS APPEAR LOATHE TO HONOR. I INSIST THEY BE MADE TO ABIDE BY THY COMMANDS.
THEY--
--SHALL--
KREEE...

..RAKK
--ABIDE!

BUT I WARN THEE, PLUTO:
IF THIS BE BUT FURTHER DECEIT ON THY PART--
--THOU SHALT FEEL THE AWESOME VENGEANCE OF ZEUS AS NO MAN OR GOD HATH FELT IT BEFORE!

HE IS AS MUCH THE FOOL AS HIS SON.
THINK HE THAT THESE MARRIAGES ARE ALL I DESIRE?
HATH HE FORGOTTEN THE SACRED LAWS OF THIS LAND--LAWS HE HIMSELF DID ENSCRIBE FOR ALL TO OBEY?

AYE! FOR IN THE LORD OF OLYMPUS' OWN HAND IS IT WRITTEN THAT WIFE MAY NOT OPPOSE HUSBAND--
--NOR HUSBAND WIFE!
WITH THESE MARRIAGES, WE DO BIND THE ONLY TWO OLYMPIANS WHO COULD PREVENT THE OVERTHROW OF ZEUS!
THE UNIVERSE BECKONS, MY FRIENDS.
SOON, OLYMPUS WILL FALL!
THERE WILL BE NO ZEUS!
THERE SHALL ONLY BE PLUTO!
THE SOVEREIGN SUPREME!

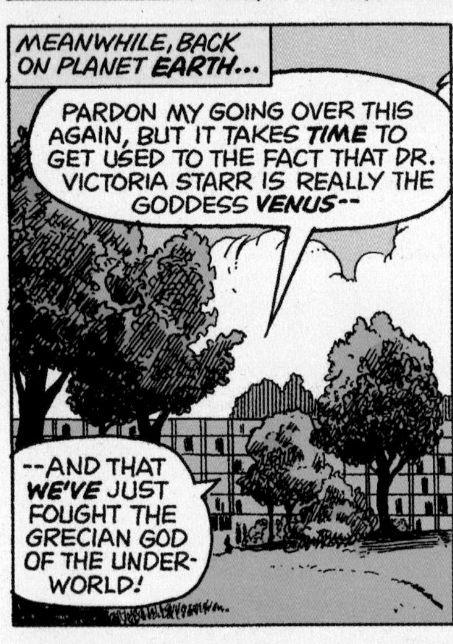
MEANWHILE, BACK ON PLANET EARTH...
PARDON MY GOING OVER THIS AGAIN, BUT IT TAKES TIME TO GET USED TO THE FACT THAT DR. VICTORIA STARR IS REALLY THE GODDESS VENUS--
--AND THAT WE'VE JUST FOUGHT THE GRECIAN GOD OF THE UNDER-WORLD!

I KNOW WHAT YOU MEAN, WINGS.
IT'S TOUGH GETTING YOUR TAILS KICKED BY SOMETHING OUT OF BULLFINCH'S MYTHOLOGY!
WE HARDLY GOT OUR TAILS KICKED, ICEMAN.

TELL IT TO THE GHOST RIDER, WIDOW.
PLUTO BLASTED HIM AND THAT SKULL-CYCLE NEAR THIRTY YARDS WITH HIS PARTING SHOT.
I'M SURPRISED THEY'RE BOTH STILL RUNNING.

WHAT HAST THOU DISCOVERED, MORTAL?
MY FRIENDS CALL ME JOHNNY BLAZE, BIG FELLA. BUT ON THE NEWS FRONT:
THE VARIOUS CRITTERS WE TANGLED WITH HAVE ALL DIS-APPEARED... ALONG WITH THOSE BLASTED "HOLES".

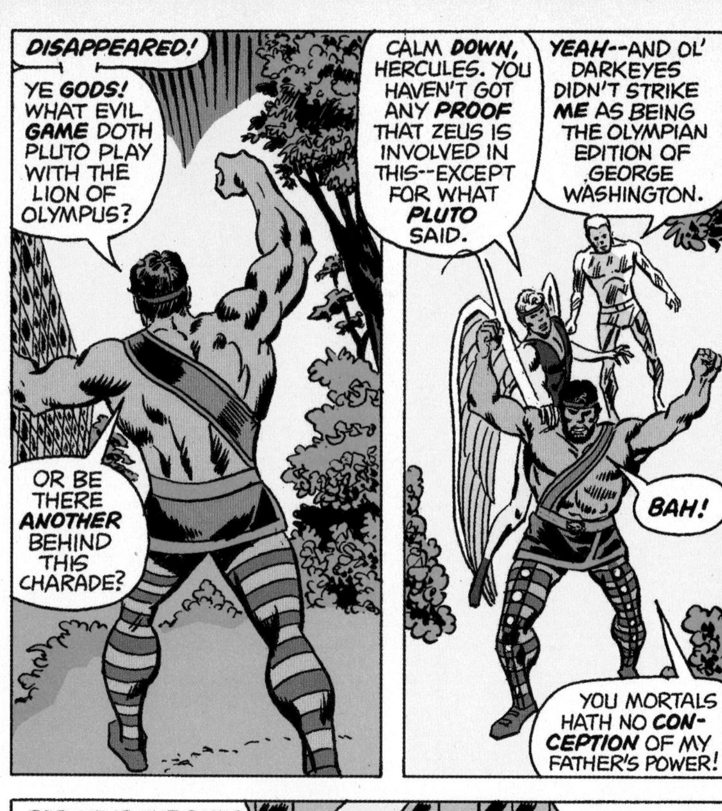

FOR HE IS THE ONLY BEING IN ALL THE COSMOS TO BE ENDOWED WITH A FRACTION OF THY FATHER'S MATCHLESS ENERGY!

THE HUNTSMAN!*

THE ONE CREATURE NO OLYMPIAN CAN CONQUER!

HUH? THAT SKINNY GUY?

DISPARAGE NOT MY PHYSICAL APPEARANCE, WHELP.

FOR BESIDES MY ZEUS-GIVEN ABILITY, I CAN NOW COMMAND THE FLAMING WEAPONS OF PLUTO AS WELL!

*SEE SUB-MARINER #29--MARV.

CONSIDER THIS SPEAR OF FIRE--
--WHICH POSSESSES THE UNUSUAL PROPERTY--

--OF PARALYZING THOSE IT STRIKES!
ZZAZKK!

THOUGH PERHAPS NOT ALL THOSE IT STRIKES!
THE OTHERS ARE ROOTED TO THE SPOT!
BUT MY SATANIC POWER IS PROTECTING ME!

SO LET'S STRETCH THE OL' BLAZE LUCK--
--AND PRAY THE REVERSE DOESN'T HOLD TRUE!

SKRAK!
BINGO! MY HELLFIRE BOLT HIT HIM DEAD CENTER--

--AND BLASTED HIM PLUMB OUT OF THE SKY!
WONDER WHAT EFFECT THAT'LL HAVE ON THE REST OF THE GOOD GUYS...

AND, BY WAY OF ANSWER...
THEY'RE UNCONSCIOUS! APPARENTLY, OUR FOE'S WEAPONS ARE MORE EFFECTIVE AGAINST OLYMPIANS.

GREAT.
'CAUSE JUDGING FROM THE WAY THE HUNTSMAN BLINKED OUT BEFORE HE HIT THE GROUND--
--WE'VE STILL GOT A FIGHT ON OUR HANDS!

I CAN'T REVIVE THEM WITH MY HOME-GROWN COLD COMPRESSES, WARREN. THEY'RE OUT FOR THE COUNT--
--AND THEN SOME.
THEN IT'S JUST THE FOUR OF US.
THE THREE OF US, ANGEL.
JOHNNY, ONLY YOU CAN WITHSTAND THOSE SPEARS. CAN YOU STAY HERE AND GUARD THEM?
CAN'T SAY I LIKE THAT, BUT I CAN SEE YOU'RE RIGHT.

WELL, IT LOOKS LIKE YOU'VE BECOME THE LEADER OF OUR LITTLE GROUP IN RECORD TIME.
IS THAT AN OBJECTION, YOUNG MAN?

HECK, NO!
YOU'RE A DARNED SIGHT MORE ATTRACTIVE THAN THE LAST TEAM LEADER I WORKED WITH!*
*HERE, NOW!--CHRIS CLAREMONT.

THEN LET'S FIND THE HUNTSMAN BEFORE HE FINDS US!
OR TO PUT IT AS CYCLOPS--THE PREVIOUSLY-REFERRED-TO LEADER--MIGHT HAVE PUT IT:
LET'S GO!

THE MORTALS DO PURSUE ME!
I WAS A FOOL TO TRUST IN PLUTO'S DEVICES!

BUT I NEED ONLY MY ZEUS-CREATED STAFF TO DESTROY THESE FOES--
--THAT AND THIS REFRAIN:
SLAIN BY ZEUS' DREAD THUNDERFIRE --REBEL THOU WERE AND SO THOU DIED--

BUT NOW, O TITAN FROM HADES' MIRE-- ARISE TO DO BATTLE AT MY SIDE!
HIS NAME IS MENOETIUS: AND IN THE EARLY DAYS OF ZEUS' REIGN, HE JOINED WITH HIS FELLOW TITANS IN A RASH WAR AGAINST OLYMPUS.
IN THAT EPIC COMBAT OF EONS PAST, MENOETIUS WAS FELLED BY ONE OF THE THUNDERER'S AWESOME BOLTS.
SO AWESOME, INDEED, THAT IT TRANSFORMED PORTIONS OF THE GIANT'S OWN FLESH INTO LIVING ENERGY!
THIS THEN IS THE CREATURE THAT THE HUNTSMAN HAS SUMMONED TO FIGHT IN HIS BEHALF.
THIS IS THE CREATURE WHO NOW HEARS AND OBEYS A SHRILL COMMAND TO--
ATTACK!

ARRRRRR
SO MUCH FOR THE ADVANTAGES OF HAVING BIG, WHITE WINGS!
LOOKS LIKE OL' KING KILO-WATT HAS SPOTTED ME--
--AND OBVIOUSLY SELECTED ME AS HIS FIRST ATTACKEE!
HEY, FROST BITE!
HOW ABOUT LENDING A HAND?

ARRRR?
ARRRR!
ZRASP!
SURE THING, FEATHERS!
LET'S SEE HOW HE REACTS TO A SUB-ZERO BLAST!
SPRACT!
CRIPES! HE SHATTERED MY ICE-SLIDE WITHOUT EVEN MISSIN' AN "ARRR"!
BUT THIS LITTLE MUTANT HAS DONE ENOUGH TIME IN PROF X'S DANGER ROOM--
--TO BE ABLE TO RE-FORM SAID SLIDE IN SECONDS--
ZOOSH!
--AND COME BACK FIGHTING!

EVEN THOUGH THAT BEHEMOTH IS UNABLE TO REGAIN HIS **FOOTING**--
--HIS INTENSE ENERGY IS ACTUALLY **MELTING** THE ICE SLICK!

BUT I'VE HAD **EXPERIENCE** BATTLING LIVING LIGHTNING BOLTS!*
SO LET'S SEE WHAT HAPPENS WHEN I THROW **ONE** END OF MY SPARE WEB-LINE AROUND THAT STEEL **FLAGPOLE**--
*ELECTRO, IN DAREDEVIL #89--MARV.

--AND TOSS THE **OTHER** END INTO THAT SMOULDERING MIXTURE OF FURY AND **ICE!**

WHAT **HAPPENS** IS THAT THE WHOLE THING GOES:
KRAAACCKKK!
NO, NO!
MENOETIUS HATH BEEN STRUCK **DOWN!**

FOLLOWED **DIRECTLY** BY:
ZAK!
FOR THE HUNTSMAN'S **STAFF**--WHICH SUMMONED THAT LATE TITAN TO EARTH --IS MADE OF WOOD NATIVE TO **OLYMPUS**--
--WOOD THAT IS, AGAINST ALL **MORTAL** LOGIC--
--**CONDUCTIVE!**

MY **STAFF!**
I **MUST** REGAIN IT!

CAN'T LET YOU **DO** THAT, FELLA.
IT'S **NOT** SO MUCH THAT WE'RE WORRIED YOU'LL CONJURE UP ANOTHER **MONSTER**--
IT'S JUST THAT YOUR **POETRY** IS SO BAD.

BUT IF YOU REALLY WANT IT, YOU'LL GET YOUR STAFF BACK FRIEND--
--WRAPPED AROUND YOUR SCRAWNY NECK!
WITLESS MORTALS!

THINK'ST THOU THAT THE HUNTSMAN HATH NO POWERS OF HIS OWN?
THINK'ST HE CANNOT CALL UPON--

--THE POWER TO BYPASS TIME AND SPACE--
--AND SEND THEE ELSEWHERE?

ELSEWHERE: WHERE AN ANXIOUS JOHNNY BLAZE GIVES STRENUOUS TEST TO THE THEORY THAT "THEY ALSO SERVE WHO ONLY STAND AND WAIT."
I'M GETTING A MITE FIDGETY WAITING FOR THE OTHERS TO RETURN. I HOPE THEY'RE...
HUH?

THAT STRANGE GLOW--
--AND CHARGING FROM ITS CENTER--

--ARES, PLUTO AND HIPPOLYTA!
WHAT HAPPENED TO THE HUNTSMAN?
WE'RE BACK WHERE WE LEFT THE GHOST RIDER!
BUT WHY IS HE LOOKING AT US SO STRANGELY?
THEY'RE MAKING ANOTHER GRAB FOR HERCULES AND VENUS!

BUT IT AIN'T THAT EASY!
YRRGGH!
WHAT'S THAT CRAZY JERK DO--
UHNN!
FKOOOM!
I GOT 'EM ALL WITH ONE BLAST! THEY'RE--

--CHANGING?
OH, MY LORD!
I JUST MURDERED MY OWN FRIENDS!
NOT QUITE, THOU FLAMING FOOL!
BUT 'TIS ENOUGH, 'TWILL SERVE!
WAP!

'TWAS SIMPLICITY ITSELF TO CREATE THE ILLUSION THAT THY FRIENDS WERE THINE MORTAL ENEMIES!
AND NOW THAT I HAVE REGAINED MY STAFF--
--I SHALL PART THIS VEIL OF TEARS--
--WITH MY SLUMBERING CHARGES!

REJOICE, O' HUMANS!
THIS DAY THERE BE WEDDINGS MOST AUSPICIOUS IN FABLED OLYMPUS!

THEY'RE GONE!
THE HUNTSMAN HAS TAKEN THEM!
AND IT'S YOUR FAULT!

BOBBY!
WHERE ARE YOUR GHOST TRICKS NOW, BLAZE?
NOW THAT YOU'VE SCREWED IT UP FOR HERCULES AND VENUS?
I--I ONLY TURN INTO THE GHOST RIDER WHEN THERE'S SOME DANGER PRESENT.
WELL, THERE SURE ISN'T ANY DANGER AROUND HERE!

PLUTO'S GOT WHAT HE WANTS!
DON'T BLAME YOURSELF, JOHNNY. THIS AFFAIR ISN'T ENDED YET.
WE'LL TRACK DOWN THE HUNTSMAN AND RESCUE THEM.

TRACK DOWN THE HUNTSMAN?
TELL ME HOW, WIDOW.
TELL ME HOW FOUR MORTALS TRACK SOMEBODY TO OLYMPUS?

THERE ARE MANY PATHS A MAN MAY TAKE, AND MANY THE PATHS OF OTHERS HE WILL CROSS IN A LIFETIME.
BUT THERE ARE TIMES WHEN ALL PATHS SEEM TO LEAD TO BUT ONE DESTINATION.
AND WHEN THAT DESTINATION IS DESPAIR--
--SOMETHING WITHIN THE HUMAN SOUL DIES.

NEXT:
THE ASSAULT ON OLYMPUS!

THE CHAMPIONS **MARVEL COMICS GROUP**™

25¢ 3 FEB 02112

HERCULES! BLACK WIDOW! ANGEL! GHOST RIDER! ICEMAN!

THE CHAMPIONS

TM

EVEN IF THY SON AND HIS COMRADES *SURVIVE* THIS COMBAT, ZEUS--

--STILL ARE THEY CONDEMNED TO *HELL!*

AND I AM *POWERLESS* TO AID THEM!

ADKINS

ASSAULT ON OLYMPUS!

Stan Lee PRESENTS: THE CHAMPIONS™

Plot TONY ISABELLA / Script BILL MANTLO / Pencils GEORGE TUSKA / Inks VINCE COLLETTA / Letters KAREN MANTLO / Colors GEORGE ROUSSOS / Editor MARV WOLFMAN

HE JUST DOESN'T SHOW IT LIKE NORMAL PEOPLE, THAT'S ALL!
BUT THEN, WE MUTANTS AREN'T SUPPOSED TO ACT LIKE "NORMAL PEOPLE."
I SENSE THE SAME ...BITTERNESS IN YOUR VOICE THAT I HAVE HEARD FROM OTHERS MADE OUT-CASTS BY THIS SOCIETY, ANGEL--
--WOMEN, FOR INSTANCE --AND EX-RUSSIANS!

RIGHT ON, LADY! BUT SAYING IT DOESN'T CHANGE ANYTHING!
WE'RE FAILURES ALL THE WAY DOWN THE LINE!

WE BLEW IT WITH HERC AND VENUS JUST LIKE I'VE MESSED THINGS UP AS FAR BACK AS I CAN REMEMBER!
AND IT SHOWS, MR. DRAKE! IT SHOWS!

SCOTTY AND THE NEW X-MEN SOUND LIKE THEY'RE DOING JUST FINE WITHOUT ME AND WARREN--

-- HANK'S GOT IT MADE WITH THE AVENGERS--
--AND THE GIRL I LOVED, LORNA DANE, HAS FORGOTTEN ALL ABOUT ME! THE ONLY THING THAT MATTERS TO HER THESE DAYS... IS ALEX SUMMERS!

BUT THE THING THAT TOPS IT ALL OFF IS THAT THE WORLD MAY BE RIGHT! MUTANTS MAY BE DANGEROUS!

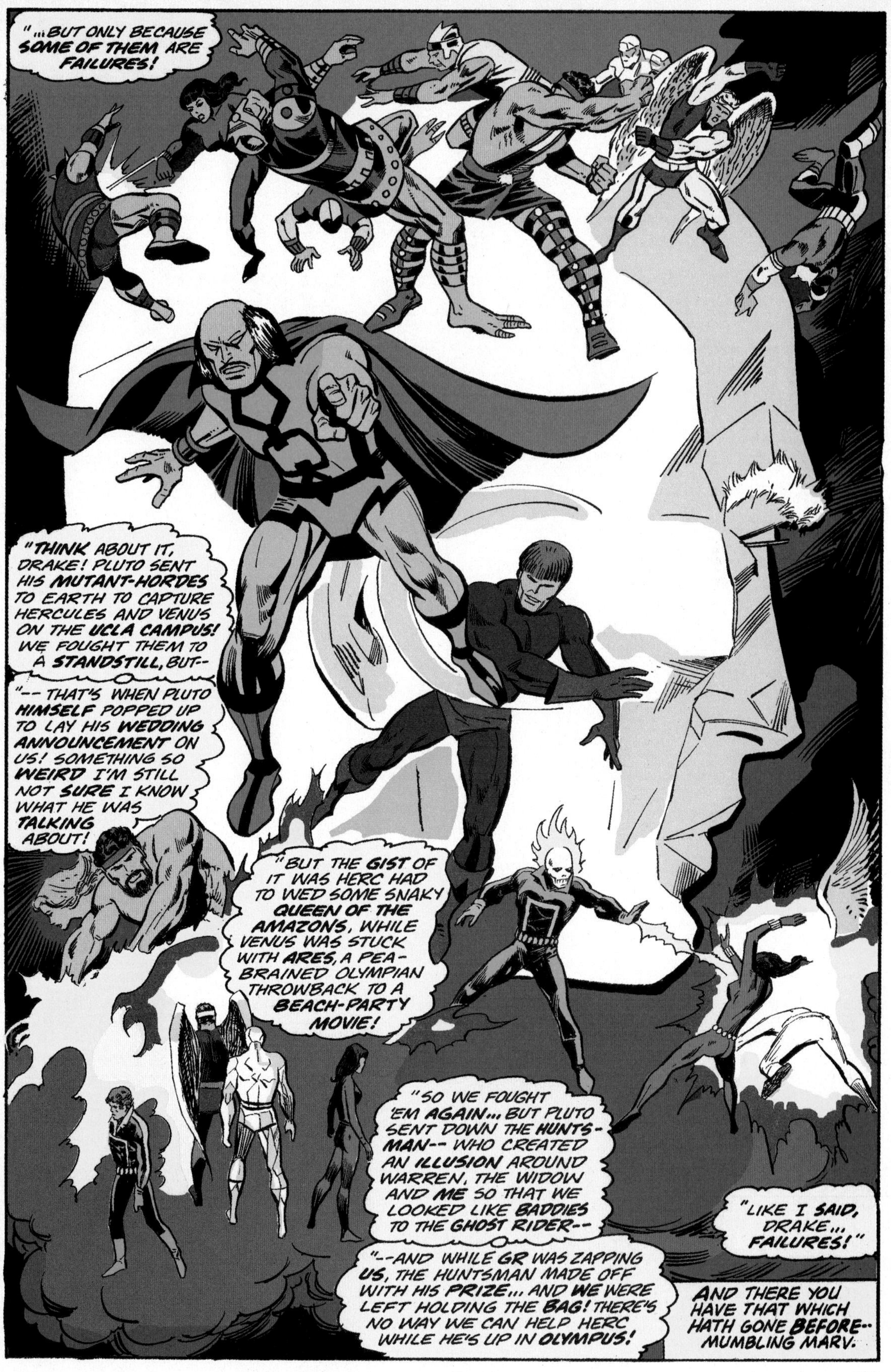
"...BUT ONLY BECAUSE SOME OF THEM ARE FAILURES!
"THINK ABOUT IT, DRAKE! PLUTO SENT HIS MUTANT-HORDES TO EARTH TO CAPTURE HERCULES AND VENUS ON THE UCLA CAMPUS! WE FOUGHT THEM TO A STANDSTILL, BUT--
"-- THAT'S WHEN PLUTO HIMSELF POPPED UP TO LAY HIS WEDDING ANNOUNCEMENT ON US! SOMETHING SO WEIRD I'M STILL NOT SURE I KNOW WHAT HE WAS TALKING ABOUT!
"BUT THE GIST OF IT WAS HERC HAD TO WED SOME SNAKY QUEEN OF THE AMAZONS, WHILE VENUS WAS STUCK WITH ARES, A PEA-BRAINED OLYMPIAN THROWBACK TO A BEACH-PARTY MOVIE!
"SO WE FOUGHT 'EM AGAIN... BUT PLUTO SENT DOWN THE HUNTS-MAN-- WHO CREATED AN ILLUSION AROUND WARREN, THE WIDOW AND ME SO THAT WE LOOKED LIKE BADDIES TO THE GHOST RIDER--
"--AND WHILE GR WAS ZAPPING US, THE HUNTSMAN MADE OFF WITH HIS PRIZE... AND WE WERE LEFT HOLDING THE BAG! THERE'S NO WAY WE CAN HELP HERC WHILE HE'S UP IN OLYMPUS!
"LIKE I SAID, DRAKE... FAILURES!"
AND THERE YOU HAVE THAT WHICH HATH GONE BEFORE-- MUMBLING MARV.

DRAKE, YOU PETULANT POPSICKLE! SNAP OUT OF IT, PARDNER--
--WE'VE GOT WORK TO DO!
BLAZE! WHAT ARE YOU DOING HERE!

AH, WHAT A WELCOME! WELL, POUT IF YOU WANT TO--
-- BUT YOU'LL NEVER FIND OUT HOW WE'RE GOING TO GET HERCULES BACK IF YOU DO!
WHAT??

WELL, WELL! LOOKS LIKE OUR OUT-OF-FAVOR STUNT-RIDER HAS PULLED THE BAD-PENNY ACT!
HE'S TURNED UP AGAIN!
THEY LOOK EXCITED ABOUT SOMETHING!

YOU'D BETTER BET I'M EXCITED, LADY!
IT'S NOT EVERY DAY THAT A MERE MORTAL FIGURES OUT A WAY TO GET HIMSELF AND HIS BUDDIES--

-- TO OLYMPUS!
IF THIS IS A JOKE, BLAZE--!
NO JOKE, FROSTY! FACT!
I SUGGEST YOU CALM YOURSELF AND BEGIN EXPLAINING, JOHNNY!

"YOUR WISH IS MY ETC., WIDOW!
"ANYWAY... AFTER OUR LITTLE ALTERCATION, I RODE OFF BACK TOWARDS UCLA...

"... AND THERE I OVERHEARD A BUNCH OF STUDENTS JAWING ABOUT A MOUNTAIN OR SOMETHIN' ON CAMPUS!"
I'M TELLING YOU, MAN! I SAW IT!
ASK
BEFORE OR AFTER YOU SAW THE UFO?

"I DUG RIGHT AWAY JUST WHAT THE GUY WAS TALKING ABOUT! IT WAS A 'SOUVENIR' OF YESTERDAY'S BATTLE...
"... ONE ALL OF US HAD FORGOTTEN ENTIRELY ABOUT.

"SOMETHING THAT SEEMED ALMOST MEANINGLESS...
HOLY COW!
"... UNTIL I SAW IT STARTING ME IN THE FACE!"

THE MOUNTAIN!
ICEMAN'S MOUNTAIN!!
"AND THERE IT WAS! BIG AND HARD AND FROZEN AS EVER! THE ONE DRAKE FORMED TO PREVENT PLUTO FROM FOLLOWING AFTER US WHILE WE LUGGED AN UNCONSCIOUS HERC AND VENUS OUT OF HARM'S WAY!"

NOW DO YOU GET WHAT I'M TALKING ABOUT?
SURE WE DO, PAL! YOU'RE SICK!
IT WAS A POOR JOKE, JOHNNY!

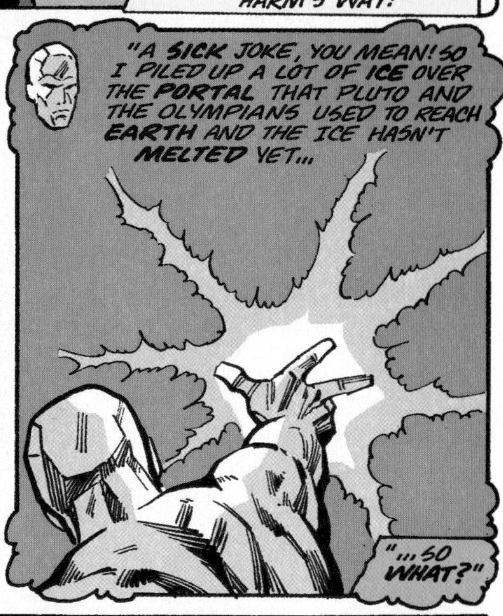

"A SICK JOKE, YOU MEAN! SO I PILED UP A LOT OF ICE OVER THE PORTAL THAT PLUTO AND THE OLYMPIANS USED TO REACH EARTH AND THE ICE HASN'T MELTED YET...
"...SO WHAT?"

WAIT! DON'T YOU SEE, BOBBY!
SEE WHAT?
ALL THE OTHER PORTALS TO OLYMPUS WERE CLOSED BY THE OLYMPIANS--BEHIND THEM, BEFORE WE COULD GET THROUGH!
BUT NOT THIS ONE! YOUR MOUNTAIN BLOCKED PLUTO FROM CLOSING IT! IT'S STILL THERE!

WHICH MEANS WE'VE GOT A WAY TO FOLLOW THEM AND RESCUE HERCULES!
KICK ME, SOMEBODY! KICK ME!
LATER, BOBBY, RIGHT NOW--

"-- WE'RE BACK IN BUSINESS!"
OLYMPUS. HOME OF THE IMMORTAL GODS...

... AND THE SCENE, THIS DAY...

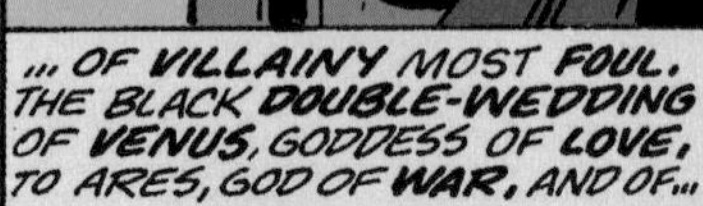
... OF VILLAINY MOST FOUL. THE BLACK DOUBLE-WEDDING OF VENUS, GODDESS OF LOVE, TO ARES, GOD OF WAR, AND OF...

HERCULES! MY SON--!
-- FOREVER WED TO THAT WITCH, HIPPOLYTA!
SAY IT IS NOT SO, DIONYSIUS! TELL ME 'TIS A LIE!

'TIS NO LIE, MILORD ZEUS! 'TIS AS IT MUST BE IF HALLOWED OLYMPUS IS TO SURVIVE!
THOU KNOWEST, MY LORD, THE WHY AND THE WHEREFORE OF THE DECREE!

I KNOW, DIONYSIUS!
I KNOW THAT 'TWAS REPREHENSIBLE PLUTO THAT DID CONSPIRE WITH THE LORDS OF OTHER HELLS TO UNITE AGAINST OLYMPUS--
--AND THAT 'TIS ONLY THIS MOCKERY OF A WEDDING WILL HOLD SUCH AN ALLIANCE AT BAY!
YET, HERCULES IS MY SON, DIONYSIUS! MY SON!
I KNOW, MY LORD!
I KNOW!

GAZE ON THE KING OF THE GODS, MY FRIENDS! LOOK YE ON THE END OF OLYMPUS!
HE BELIEVES THIS MARRIAGE WILL END THE THREAT AGAINST HIM! THE FOOL!
DOES HE NOT KNOW THAT HE IS BOUND BY HIS OWN SACRED LAWS? THAT HUSBAND MAY NOT OPPOSE WIFE-- NOR WIFE GO AGAINST HER HUSBAND!
AND THAT BY WEDDING HERCULES AND VENUS HE HAS BOUND THE ONLY TWO OLYMPIANS WHO COULD HAVE PREVENTED THE OVERTHROW OF ZEUS!

"THE TASTE OF VICTORY IS SWEET, ARES! AND IT IS PLUTO'S... NOW AND FOREVERMORE!"
AWAY, THOU VILE, BASE-BORN, MINDLESS SLAVES TO THE GOD OF DEATH!
HERCULES MAY BE FORCED TO SUCCUMB TO SUCH AS THEE--
--BUT NEVER WILL THE PRINCE OF POWER ALLOW THEE TO TAUNT HIM!
LIST' TO THE GODLING CROW, MY FELLOW MUTANTS!
LIST' WELL TO THE CRIES OF THE GROOM--CONDEMNED BEFORE HIS WEDDING TO ETERNAL HELPLESSNESS!

I CAN DO NOTHING, MY SON...
...NOTHING!
THEN THY SON CALLS THEE COWARD, FATHER! COWARD AND CUR!

HERCULES! NO!
WHATEVER PASSES HERE... WHATEVER EVIL MAY BEFALL US--
--THE FAULT IS NOT YOUR FATHER'S --BUT PLUTO'S!
THOU ART EVER READY TO SPARE ANOTHER HURT, LOVE-GODDESS! EVEN IF THOU MUST SHOULDER THE PAIN THYSELF!

"THAT IS LOVE, HERCULES. I AM BUT WHAT I MUST BE!
"AS ARE YOU ...AND YOUR FATHER!"

CUT: TO THE WOODED SLOPES SURROUNDING OLYMPUS...
BAH! WHAT USE HAS THE HUNTSMAN FOR WEDDINGS OR MACHIAVELLIAN SCHEMINGS?
MY PURPOSE IS THE HUNT! MY PREY, ERRANT OLYMPIANS!
I AGREED TO HELP PLUTO ONLY BECAUSE HIS ENDS AND MINE ARE THE SAME!

A RULE OF DEATH WILL PROVIDE DEATH'S HUNTER WITH SPORT FOR ALL ETERNITY!
BUT HOLD! WHAT MADNESS IS THIS?

'TIS THE MOUNTAIN OF ICE ONE OF THE MORTAL WARRIORS DID TRAP US WITH IN HIS VAIN DEFENSE OF HERCULES!
YET IT DOES SEEM TO WARM ITSELF FROM WITHIN!

ALMOST AS IF IT DID...
...BURN?

THAT'S THE TICKET, HUNTSMAN! IT'S CALLED HELLFIRE--
--AND IT'S TIME YOU ANSWERED TO THE GHOST RIDER!
I'LL BET I'M THE FIRST ANGEL WHO EVER HAD TO BUST INTO HEAVEN!
I APOLOGIZE, BLAZE! WE DID IT!
WE'VE REACHED OLYMPUS!
CAREFUL, COMRADES! THE HUNTSMAN HAS PROVEN HIMSELF A MOST FORMIDABLE FOE!
AND WE MUST PASS HIM TO REACH HERCULES!

HEADS UP, GROUP!
SKINNY JUST MATERIALIZED AN ARMY FROM OUT OF NOWHERE!

HERCULES IS OUR MAIN CONCERN, ANGEL! BATTLE WITH SUCH AS THESE MEANS DELAY WE CANNOT AFFORD!
LEAVE THEM TO MYSELF AND ICEMAN--

"-- YOU AND THE GHOST RIDER KEEP GOING!"
WELL, I ACCEPTED YOU AS TEAM-LEADER, YESTERDAY, WIDOW--
--I GUESS I CAN DO THE SAME TODAY!

STRAM!
BUT BEFORE I GO, LET ME AT LEAST LEAVE MY CALLING CARD!
JUST SO THESE CLOWNS KNOW THAT THE ANGEL WAS HERE!

AND HERE'S ONE FOR THE ROAD FROM THE GROUP SPOOK, TROOPS!
REMEMBER IT WHEN YOU THINK OF ME!
YAARRR!

THEY'RE GONE, ICEMAN!
LEAVING THE TWO OF US TO FACE AN ARMY!
YOU WANT TO KNOW SOMETHING, LADY?
WITH YOU AT MY BACK--

MEANWHILE, A SHORT ETERNITY AWAY...

MAKE THY PROCLAMATION, FATHER! THY SON WILL DEFY THEE TO THE LAST!

SILENCE, HERCULES! TEMPT NOT MY WRATH, SON OF MY HEART! THAT WHICH MUST BE--

--WILL BE!

SPOKEN LIKE A TRUE-KING, ALL-FATHER!

THE WEDDING WILL BE PERFORMED--THOUGH ZEUS' HEART DOTH BREAK!

I PRAY THAT IT RAINS!

I CAN THINK OF WORSE FATES THAN BEING WED TO VENUS, HIPPOLYTA! YOUR FATE, FOR INSTANCE!

YOU ARE NOT A GODDESS, ARES, AND YOU SEE NOT AS A GODDESS SEES!

MY FUTURE HUSBAND IS NO GIFT OF ILL-FATE!

HAVE COURAGE, LOVE-GODDESS! WE ARE NOT WED YET!
I HAVE NO FEAR, HERCULES! I--
MY LORD PLUTO! WE ARE UNDONE!
WHAT?? GET THEE GONE, HUNTSMAN! THE CEREMONY MUST CONTINUE BEFORE--
BEFORE WHAT, DEATH-GOD?

BEFORE SALVATION IS VISITED UPON US, MY FRIEND!
THOUGH ALL HEARTS IN OLYMPUS STAND UNWILLING TO HELP ME--
--THE MORTALS HAVE NOT FORGOTTEN ME!

'TIS STILL NOT YET TOO LATE TO STOP THEM!
ANOTHER RHYME WILL CONJURE FORTH--
NOTHING, PAL!

YOUR DAYS OF CONJURING ARE DECIDEDLY DONE FOR!
NOW, ARE YOU GOING TO GIVE ME THAT STAFF--
--OR AM I GOING TO HAVE TO TAKE IT?

NO! THE STAFF IS MY POWER! THOU MUST NOT--
ARE YOU KIDDING, FRIEND? DO THEY REALLY GIVE THE SAME CORNY VILLAIN SPEECHES UP HERE--

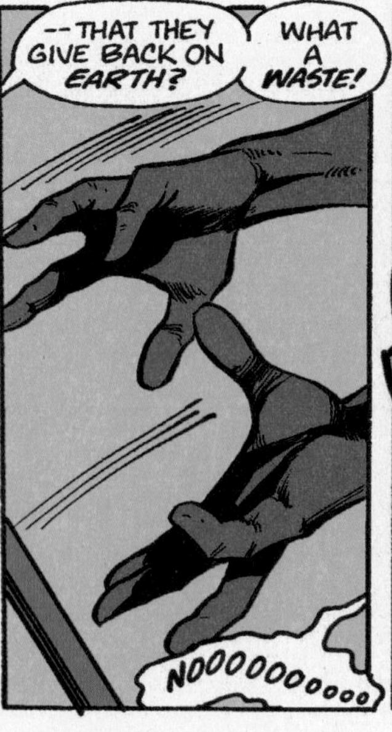

--THAT THEY GIVE BACK ON EARTH?
WHAT A WASTE!
NOOOOOOOooo

BUT YES!
CRACK!
OLYMPIAN OR MORTAL, A HEAD IS BUT A HEAD... AND A STONE WALL IS JUST AS HARD ON OLYMPUS AS IT IS ON EARTH.

ARES! ARE YOU NOT THE WAR-GOD? STOP THEM, YOU FOOL-- ERE ARE WE UNDONE!
BUT ZEUS--?
ZEUS WILL NOT HELP THEM! HE STILL BELIEVES THIS UNION MUST COME TO PASS IF OLYMPUS IS TO BE SAVED!

THOU DAREST TO FACE ME IN OPEN COMBAT, ARES?
I AM YOUR MATCH, DEMI-GOD--!
--AS LONG AS THE POWER OF ZEUS ENTRAPS YOUR RAGE!

COWARD! WERE MY HAND NOT HELD--
BUT IT IS, BRAGGART!
YOU ARE HELPLESS, HERCULES! HELPLESS!

THOU DOST TAUNT ME, WAR-GOD? THOU DOST DARE TO MAKE A MOCKERY OF THE PRINCE OF POWER?!
THOU HAST PRESUMED TOO MUCH, ARES--

--AND THOU MUST ANSWER FOR IT!
HERCULES' FIST SCREAMS THROUGH THE ZEUS-IMPOSED BARRIER... CONNECTING BEAUTIFULLY WITH THE CHIN OF THE GOD OF WAR.
AND FROM BEHIND HERCULES COMES A LOW CHUCKLE... THE LAUGHTER OF ZEUS... FATHER OF THE GODS!

WE ARE LOST! 'TIS CLEAR TO THE QUEEN OF THE AMAZONS!
BUT IF HERCULES IS NOT TO BE MINE, VENUS--
--HE WILL NOT BE YOURS!

I HAVE NO CLAIM ON HERCULES, SAVE IN YOUR UNSETTLED MIND, HIPPOLYTA!
AND YET, I AM THREATENED WITH VIOLENCE!
THAT SHALL NEVER BE--

--FOR MINE IS THE POWER OF LOVE, AMAZON!
MY SWORD!

THE POWER TO ALTER THE WEAPONS OF WAR--
--INTO THE GENTLE TOOLS OF PEACE!
THE AMAZON QUEEN'S WEAPON IS TRANSFORMED...

...AND SHE IS NEGATED BY HER OWN VIOLENCE ...FOR THE PRESENT.
SUCH IS THE POWER OF LOVE, HIPPOLYTA!

THY COURAGE HAS MADE MY HEART REJOICE, FAIR VENUS--
--A JOY THAT IS BOUNDLESS AS MINE EYES PERCEIVE A REUNION OF ALL THE MORTALS THAT DID ALLY THEMSELVES WITH OUR JUST CAUSE!
IF THAT MEAMS YOU'RE GLAD TO SEE US, HERC--
--THEN IT'S DITTO! THE FEELING'S MUTUAL!

UNNNH! FEEL LIKE I'M BEING KILLED AND ALLOWED TO WATCH IT HAPPEN!
NO! THIS WILL NOT BE!

SO YOU ARE, MORTAL! TWICE HAVE YOU DARED THE WRATH OF DEATH! TWICE HAVE YOU DEFIED ME!
THERE WILL BE NO THIRD TIME!

GET THEE BEHIND ME, MORTALS! YOUR STRENGTH IS NO MATCH FOR PLUTO!
NOR IS YOURS, HERCULES! YOU WILL BE SLAIN!
AS WOULD ANY OF US!

WE CANNOT HOPE TO WIN OVER PLUTO! THAT IS FOR ANOTHER POWER, ANOTHER STRENGTH!
WIDOW, YOU'RE COMIN' IN LOUD AND CLEAR!

BLAZE! WHAT--?
PLUTO'S GOTTA BE STOPPED, ANGEL!
ONE WAY OR ANOTHER!
YOU FOOL, HE'LL KILL YOU!
THINE ALLY SPEAKS TRUTH, MORTAL!

I'LL BET HE DOES, PLUTO! BUT I'M NOT STUPID ENOUGH TO TAKE ON ONE LORD OF HELL--NOT AFTER WHAT I WENT THROUGH TANGLING WITH ANOTHER!
WHAT? YOU PASS ME BY?
YOU GOT IT, DEATH-GOD!

THERE'S ONLY ONE DUDE THAT CAN TAKE YOU ON AND COME AWAY CLEAN--
--AND NONE OF US--NOT EVEN HERCULES--ARE IN HIS LEAGUE!

YOUR LEAGUE, ZEUS!
YOU ARE THE ONLY ONE WHO CAN STAND AGAINST PLUTO!
AND YOU COPPED OUT! WAS IT EASY TO SELL YOUR SON TO DEATH, PAL?

BY CHRONUS, MORTAL, THOU DOST TOY WITH DOOM!
ALL MY LIFE, ZEUS... SINCE I THOUGHT I COULDN'T MAKE IT ON MY OWN! SINCE I ASKED THE DEVIL FOR HELP--
--AND ACCEPTED IT!

THE WAY YOU ARE ACCEPTING PLUTO'S LIES!
LIES?
SURE! WHAT DO YOU THINK HE HAD TO PROMISE THOSE OTHER DEATH-GODS IN ORDER TO GET THEIR UNITY? DIDN'T IT OCCUR TO YOU THAT IT MIGHT BE YOUR HEAD ON A PLATTER?

PLUTO!!
I ALLOWED A MORTAL WEAKNESS TO POSSESS ME SO THAT I DID NOT SEE THY DUPLICITY!
GET THEE GONE, DEATH-GOD! ZEUS WILL DEAL WITH THEE LATER!
I--
--I GO, MY LORD ZEUS!

MY SON... VENUS! 'TWAS AGAINST THEE THAT I DID ERR! YOURS IS THE CHOICE OF PUNISHMENT!
NAME WHAT THOU WOULDST SEE DONE TO THE MISCREANTS AND IT SHALL BE THINE!
WE ASK--

--FORGIVENESS, MY LORD!
FORGIVE THOSE THAT DID STRIKE AT US!
GODDESS! ARE YE--?
WHAT??

I BEG THEE NOT TO LET THEIR MADNESS RULE OUR SENSE OF LOVE, MY LORD!
WOULD MEN SAY WE WERE ANY BETTER WERE WE TO TAKE VENGEANCE UPON THOSE THAT SOUGHT TO HURT US?

PLUTO! ARES! HIPPOLYTA! THESE THREE ARE DOOMED, TO A HELL OF THEIR OWN MAKING!
A HELL OF PETTY PLOTS AND SCHEMINGS ...INTO WHICH NO LIGHT, NOR PURITY MAY EVER REACH!

IS THAT NOT PUNISHMENT ENOUGH, MY LORD?
IF YOU SAY IT... THEN 'TIS SO, GODDESS!
THE CHOICE WAS YOURS... AND I CONCUR!
IT WILL BE AS YOU SAY!

THERE GOES ONE VERY FINE WOMAN, GROUP!
AND I THINK UCLA'S JUST LOST A DEPARTMENT-HEAD!
VENUS, I--
AYE! VENUS HATH DONE WITH HER MORTAL GUISE FOR THE NONCE! SHE HATH LEARNED THAT SHE IS EVER A GODDESS--
--AND THAT LOVE IS NEEDED IN HEAVEN AS WELL AS EARTH!

HERCULES... MY SON, I--
FATHER, WE ARE IMMORTALS-- RULED BY IMMORTAL PASSIONS!
THOUGH THOU KNOWEST ALL--THERE IS STILL MUCH FOR US BOTH TO LEARN!
I, FROM THE MORTALS, FROM WHENCE CAME MY MOTHER--

AND I FROM MY SON, WHO GOES WITH MY BLESSING!
THANK YOU, FATHER!
HERCULES THANKS THEE!

IT IS TIME, MY FATHER! I MUST GO-- BACK TO EARTH!
I HAVE LEFT MUCH UNDONE--
--INCLUDING A LECTURE ON THYSELF AS A MYTH!
I WOULD GREATLY LIKE TO HEAR IT, MY SON!
'TWOULD FILL ALL OLYMPUS WITH LAUGHTER!

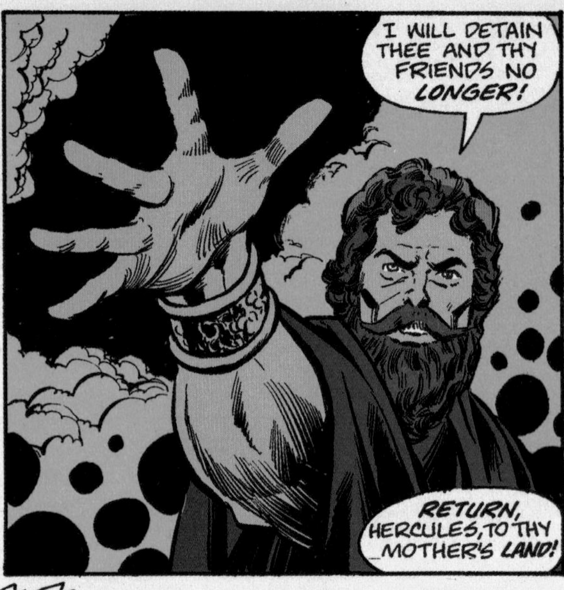
I WILL DETAIN THEE AND THY FRIENDS NO LONGER!
RETURN, HERCULES, TO THY MOTHER'S LAND!

THOU GOEST WITH THE LOVE OF ZEUS!
COME, MY FRIENDS--
--TO EARTH!
THEY GO, MY LORD!

THEY ARE GONE, DIONYSIUS!
MY LORD, DOST THOU RECALL THAT ENCHANTED MEAD I DID BREW A FORTNIGHT PAST?
AYE, DIONYSIUS! BE THERE ANY LEFT?
WITHOUT A DOUBT, MY LORD ZEUS!

EARTH!
YES, MY FRIENDS! WE ARE BACK!
BACK! BUT WHAT HAPPENS NEXT?
THAT WILL BE REVEALED IN A MERE SIXTY DAYS, TRUE BELIEVER, IN A TALE WE CALL--
MURDER AT MALIBU!

THE CHAMPIONS
MARVEL COMICS GROUP
APPROVED BY THE COMICS CODE AUTHORITY
25¢
4
MAR
02112
HERCULES! BLACK WIDOW! ANGEL! GHOST RIDER! ICEMAN!
THE CHAMPIONS
IT'S CHAMPION VERSUS CHAMPION IN A BATTLE TO THE DEATH!
THE SLUGFEST YOU DARE NOT MISS!
MURDER AT MALIBU!

Stan Lee PRESENTS:
THE CHAMPIONS™
CHRIS CLAREMONT GUEST WRITER * GEORGE TUSKA ARTIST * VINCE COLLETTA INKER * I. WATANABE, LETTERER P. RACHE, COLORIST * MARY WOLFMAN EDITOR
MURDER AT MALIBU!
IT BEGINS WITH A WALK ON THE BEACH...
IT'S A RARE BEAUTIFUL MORNING FOR IT--THE AIR CRISP AND COOL WITH THE BITE OF WINTER, THE SKY CLEAR AS CUT CRYSTAL AND AZURE-BLUE FROM HORIZON TO HORIZON...
...IT'S A ONCE-IN-A-LIFETIME DAY, ONE THAT'S MEANT TO BE SAVORED AND REMEMBERED --OR SO THE BLACK WIDOW THINKS.
ONE EVEN A GOD COULD APRECIATE...
...IF HE'D ONLY CARE TO NOTICE.
I TELL THEE, WIDOW, THAT IT DOTH PAIN MY HEART TO SEE PLUTO TURN AGAINST MY FATHER, ZEUS...
...AND YET GO UNPUNISHED FOR HIS TREACHERY!*
THE WAR IS OVER, HERCULES --GIVE IT A REST!
PLUTO GAMBLED AND HE LOST--AND THERE'S THE END OF IT.*
*A BRIEF REFERENCE TO LAST ISSUE'S AWESOME OLYMPIAN CLIMAX--MARV.
JV 217

AND YET, AMID THE SILENCE AND THE BEAUTY, SOMETHING... MOVES...
THE END--? I THINK NOT, MILADY...
THERE'LL BE NO ENDING SO LONG AS PLUTO LIVES TO COVET MY FATHER'S THRONE.

...SLIPPING STEATHILY FROM DUNE TO DUNE... WAITING... WATCHING... STALKING...
AN ARMISTICE, THEN--A PAUSE FOR BREATH-- ISN'T THAT WORTH SOMETHING?
THOU SPEAKEST A'RIGHT... BUT IT WOULD HAVE BEEN A GLORIOUS WAR.

...UNTIL THE MAN-FIGURE SEES ITS CHANCE... AND STRIKES!
YOU WANTED A WAR, HERCULES?
WELL-- HERE IT COMES!
KILLL--!!

SQWARK!
FTHOM!
BY ALL THE GODS--!
MILADY, WE ARE ATTACKED!

WHOEVER HE IS, HE CHOSE A PERFECT SITE FOR HIS AMBUSH...
TOO MUCH LOOSE SAND TO SEE WHO HE IS, AND THERE'S NO WAY TO DEFEND MY-SELF ON THIS DUNE SLOPE.
...BUT FIRST THINGS FIRST, NATASHA--GET RID OF YOUR COAT...

...SO THAT WHEN WE REACH THE BEACH PROPER, YOU'LL BE ABLE TO MOVE...
...LIKE SO!
WHUK
HAIII--!

I DON'T BELIEVE IT-- I HIT HIM WITH A NEAR-KILLING BLOW...
...AND THE MAN IS STILL COMING!
HE'S FAST, TOO...

...BUT, MY FRIEND, THE BLACK WIDOW IS FASTER.
INCREDIBLE--HE JUST RAN INTO MY KICK--THE MAN HAS ABSOLUTELY NO KNOWLEDGE OF THE MARTIAL ARTS...
KRAK!

ALL THE BETTER, THEN...
...THIS BATTLE WILL BE QUICKLY ENDED.

WHA--!?
THAT WAVE-- I DIDN'T SEE IT COMING...
...IT'S THROWING ME OFF-BALANCE!

TOSSING ME RIGHT INTO THE MAN'S ARMS--!
THINGS MOVE IN A BLUR NOW, THE MAN-FIGURE GRABBING NATASHA IN HANDS LIKE STEEL VISES...
...LIFTING HER HIGH BEFORE SHE CAN BREAK FREE...

...ONLY TO SMASH HER DOWN!
NO TIME TO ROLL WITH THE PUNCH... NO TIME...
UNNHHH!
BROW!

INDEED, WIDOW, IT SEEMS THAT NOW, THERE IS ONLY TIME FOR YOU TO...
...DIE!
BILLY'S GONNA KILL YOU, LADY-- BILLY'S GONNA KILL YOU BAD!
KILLYOUKILLYOUKILLYOU--!

AND PERHAPS YOU WOULD HAVE DIED...
...HAD YOU BEEN ALONE.
THE BLACK WIDOW--THE VILLAIN HAS HER HELP-LESS...
...AND THERE BE NO WAY FOR HERCULES TO REACH HER IN TIME...!

BUT HERCULES IS EVER THE PRINCE OF POWER...
...AND THE BLACK WIDOW IS HIS FRIEND...
...THUS, SHE WILL NOT DIE!
SHOCK WAVES RIPPLE THE GROUND LIKE JELLY...
...AND THE MAN-FIGURE STAGGERS, CRY-ING OUT IN STRANGE, UNREA-SONING PANIC AT THE GOD-BORN TREMOR.
BWHOMM!

A PANIC THAT QUICKLY FADES AS HERCULES APPROACHES...
...TO BE REPLACED BY ANGER...AND HATRED...
YOU TRIED TO HURT BILLY...
...BILLY'S GONNA MAKE YOU PAY FOR THAT, MISTER!

BILLY'S GONNA MAKE YOU PAY GOOD!
BY ARES, MORTAL--THE FORCE OF THY BLOW WOULD DO AN OLYMPIAN PROUD--!
BRAK!

BUT A THOUSAND SUCH WOULD DO THEE NO GOOD--
--FOR THIS DAY, THOU DOST FACE POWER INCARNATE!
THOU DOST FACE HERCULES!
PTOW!

IN TRUTH, E'EN THIS BRIEF COMBAT HATH EASED THE BLEAKNESS IN MY SOUL...
THOU ART WELL, WIDOW?
I'M FINE, HERCULES, BUT WHAT ABOUT...
OH MY GOD.
FATHER ZEUS, THIS CANNOT BE--! THIS IS MADNESS! MADNESS!

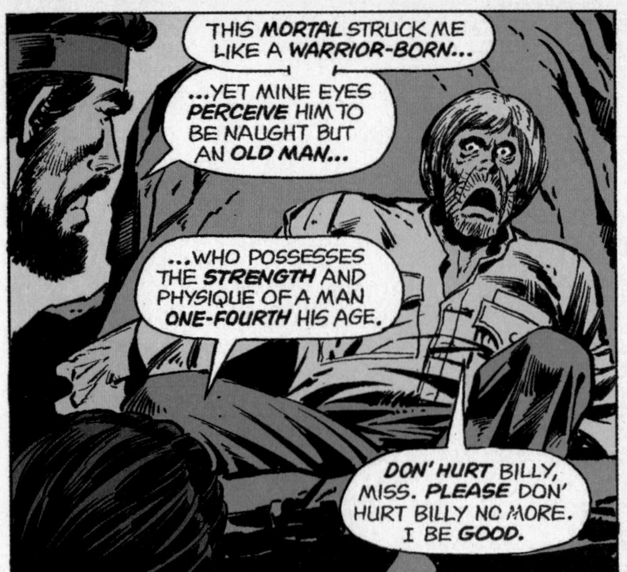
THIS MORTAL STRUCK ME LIKE A WARRIOR-BORN...
...YET MINE EYES PERCEIVE HIM TO BE NAUGHT BUT AN OLD MAN...
...WHO POSSESSES THE STRENGTH AND PHYSIQUE OF A MAN ONE-FOURTH HIS AGE.
DON' HURT BILLY, MISS. PLEASE DON' HURT BILLY NO MORE. I BE GOOD.

NO ONE'S GOING TO HURT YOU, OLD ONE.
HERCULES--GET BACK TO THE ANGEL'S HOUSE--HAVE IVAN PHONE FOR AN AMBULANCE.
SAN MARI
STATE HOS
THAT WON'T BE NECESSARY, MISS...

...OLD BILLY HERE IS IN OUR CHARGE.
WE'LL TAKE CARE OF HIM, IF YOU DON'T MIND.
CURIOUSER AND CURIOUSER. SIX ARMED MERCENARIES TO DEAL WITH ONE OLD MAN?
BELIEVE IT OR NOT, LADY--HE'S COMING WITH US!
I FIND THAT SOMEWHAT HARD TO BELIEVE.

HOLD THY TONGUE, MORTAL!
THIS GREYBEARD IS UNDER THE PROTECTION OF HERCULES...
...THOU WOULDST HARM HIM AT THY PERIL.

NO WAY, OLYMPIAN--IF YOU WANT TO GET INVOLVED...
...THEN YOU'VE GOT TO PAY THE PRICE.
DIE HAPPY, FOLKS!
ZRAK!
MILADY, BEWARE--THE MORTAL'S WEAPON--
--AAARRGH!

TIME...
...PART OF IT IS LOST IN DARKNESS, THE REST SHROUDED IN GRAY, FOG-LIKE IMAGES AS ELUSIVE AS WOOD SPRITES...
SAN MARINO
STATE HOSPITAL
SAN MARINO, CALIFORNIA
...A BUILDING, OLD, WORN DOWN BY AGE AND NEGLECT, ITS OUTER WALLS TOPPED BY JAGGED SHARDS OF GLASS, ITS INNER ONES PAINTED INSTITUTION GREEN.

A BUILDING...
...AND A MAN.
AH, YOU'RE AWAKE, I SEE.
WELCOME TO SAN MARINO, MR. HERCULES. OH, YES, I KNOW YOUR NAME--YOURS AND MADAME ROMANOFF'S--FROM THE NEWSPAPERS.
I'M HONORED TO HAVE YOU AS MY GUESTS.
GUESTS?
THOU DAREST TO NAME US GUESTS?!

THOU DOST NOT BIND THY GUESTS, VILLAIN--
--AND THOU WILT NEVER BIND HERCULES!!
ZZKAK!

STOP HIM, YOU FOOLS-- AAARRGH--
AND HOW WILT THOU STOP ME, THOU SPAWN OF THE JACKAL?
BRAM
THOU COULDST AS SOON STOP THE ALL-FATHER ZEUS HIMSELF!

I BEG TO DIFFER, OLYMPIAN--
--FOR IF YOU DO NOT YIELD--NOW!--YOUR BEAUTEOUS COMPANION DIES!

THOU HAST THE UPPER HAND, MORTAL--FOR THE NONCE--
--I'LL DO NAUGHT THAT WOULD THREATEN THE BLACK WIDOW'S LIFE.
BUT IF HERCULES MUST NEEDS BE CAGED, I WOULD KNOW THE NAME OF THE CUR WHO HOLDS THE KEY.
HIS NAME IS LANSING, MY FRIEND. DR. EDWARD LANSING...
...AND HE IS INSANE.

"YOU SEE, MY FRIEND, EDWARD LANSING WAS NOT ALWAYS AS YOU SEE HIM NOW, DIRECTOR OF A TENTH-RATE WELFARE HOSPITAL...

RESEARCH DEPT.

"...OH NO, ONCE I HELD A FULL PROFESSORSHIP AT A GREAT TEACHING HOSPITAL. BUT THE ADMINISTRATION... DISAPPROVED OF MY THEORIES, MY METHODS--THE FOOLS!--AND I WAS DISMISSED.

"SO, I CAME TO SAN MARINO, THIS DUMPING GROUND FOR THOSE SOCIETY WISHES TO IGNORE...OR FORGET...THE OLD POOR, THE SICK, THE MENTALLY INFIRM...

"AND HERE AT SAN MARINO, I EXPERIMENTED ON MY POPULATION OF OUTCASTS--NO ONE INTERESTED IN THEIR FATE, NO ONE CARING--AND AFTER YEARS OF FAILURE, YEARS OF DEATHS RECORDED AS 'ACCIDENT' OR 'NATURAL CAUSES'...

"MY DREAM WAS TO RECREATE THE LEGENDARY SUPER-SOLDIER SERUM, TO CREATE A RACE OF INVINCIBLE WARRIORS...

"I SUCCEEDED--I CREATED MY MUTATE--MY WARRIOR SUPREME--!"

YOU FOUGHT MY PROTOTYPE--OLD BILLY--ON THE BEACH, AFTER HE'D MANAGED TO ESCAPE...
UNFORTUNATELY, THE PROCESS SEEMS TO AFFECT THE MEN MENTALLY. IT TENDS TO TURN THEM INTO CHILDLIKE SIMPLETONS OR MINDLESS BEASTS --BUT I'LL WORK THAT OUT IN TIME...

I HAVE HEARD ENOW!!
BUTCHER IS TOO KIND A WORD FOR THEE, MORTAL, FOR SURELY THOU ART THE GREATEST MONSTER TO EVER WALK THIS EARTH...
AT THE COST OF THE BLACK WIDOW'S LIFE, IMMORTAL?!?
...AND BOUND OR NO, I'LL SEE THEE DAMNED ERE THOU DOST TORMENT ANOTHER IN THIS PLACE!
KTAM!

I THOUGHT NOT.
I'M GLAD YOU HAVE SOME FEELING FOR THE WOMAN, HERCULES. IT MAKES MY JOB THAT MUCH EASIER.
ENJOY THY TRIUMPH WHILST THOU CAN, DOG--
--THOU HAST WON ONLY A BATTLE, NOT THE WAR!

I--I'M SORRY, HERCULES...
THERE IS NO NEED, MILADY...
...WE ARE STILL ALIVE, AND WE WILL YET PREVAIL.
HAH!
YOU HAVE THE RIGHT IDEA, OLYMPIAN, BUT THE WRONG MAN, FOR IT IS I WHO WILL PREVAIL...
...BECAUSE WHEN I'VE FINISHED WITH YOU TWO, YOU'LL TELL ME YOUR INNERMOST SECRETS...
...AND SERVE ME AS BLINDLY, AS LOYALLY, AS ANY OF MY MUTATES!

TIME: AN HOUR PAST SUNSET, AT THE BEACH HOUSE OF WARREN WORTHINGTON III, A.K.A. THE ANGEL...
...A PLACE WHERE THINGS ARE ABOUT TO HAPPEN.
I TELL YA, ANGEL, I'M WORRIED ABOUT NATASHA--SHE'S BEEN GONE ALL DAY WITHOUT A MESSAGE, A PHONE CALL, NOTHIN'!..
SHE'S NOT A KID, IVAN. SHE CAN TAKE CARE OF HERSELF.
YEAH--AN' BESIDES, SHE'S OUT WITH HERCULES. THE BEST SPY IN THE WHOLE WORLD TEAMED UP WITH AN OLYMPIAN DEMI-GOD...
...FOR CRYIN' OUT LOUD, WHAT COULD HAPPEN TO THEM?
X-MEN
YOU HAD TO ASK, BOBBY DRAKE?
FROOM!
IN THE NAME OF THE MASTER...
...ALL WITHIN THESE WALLS MUST DIE!!
X-MEN
HEY, MAN, WHAT'S GOIN' ON HERE--?! IS THIS SOME KINDA JOKE--?!
TAKE A LOOK IN HIS EYES PAL--THIS IS NO JOKE!
THEY'RE OUR FRIENDS--AND THEY WANT US DEAD!!

I DON'T KNOW WHAT'S GOIN' DOWN, LADY...
...BUT IF YOU WANT TO CLIP THIS MUTANT'S WINGS...
...YOU'RE GONNA HAVE TO DO A WHOLE LOT BETTER THAN THAT!

AND THE SAME GOES FOR ICEMAN, OLYMPIAN!
LET'S SEE YOU TRY AND PUNCH ME OUT ON ONE OF MY PATENTED ICE SLIDES...

SKROM!
I DIDN'T THINK YOU COULD DO IT, BIG MAN.

NICE TALK, MR. DRAKE-- BUT THAT LITTLE NUMBER JUST LEFT YOU WIDE-OPEN FOR HERC'S HAIRY PLAYMATES...

...AND THESE CLOWNS ARE DEFINITELY OUT FOR BLOOD!
SLAY HIM--
--SLAY THE BEARDLESS YOUTH!!

HOLD ON, KID-- FOR GOD'S SAKE, HOLD ON!!
I'LL GET YOU OUTTA THERE!
SOK!
BUT HOW, IVAN, HOW--? THESE HAIRIES'RE SWARMIN' ALL OVER THE HOUSE...
...KNOCK ONE DOWN, TWO MORE JUMP TO TAKE HIS PLACE.

DON'T SWEAT IT, IVAN--
--IT'LL TAKE A LOT MORE THAN THESE DODOS TO WHOMP THE ICEMAN--!
HECK, MAN, I KNEW A DANGER ROOM ONCE THAT WAS MORE HASSLE THAN THIS!

WAY TO GO, FELLA--IT SHOULDN'T TAKE MORE'N A COUPLE OF ICE BLASTS TO PUT THESE HAIRES TO BED.
THOU STILL MUST DEAL WITH ME, YOUTH!
HUH--?!

AND THOU CANST NOT!
PAKOW!
HERCULES--! DIDN'T SEE HIM COMING--!

EXCELLENT, MY BRAIN-SCRAMBLED IMMORTAL, EXCELLENT.
YOU AND THE WIDOW ARE PERFORMING BETTER THAN I'D HOPED...
FEEL LIKE MUSH INSIDE...MUZZY...BUT I CAN'T GIVE UP NOW ...I...CAN'T...

HOLD THE YOUTH, MY MUTATES--LET HERCULES ADMINISTER THE COUP DE GRÂCE...
...FOR THE MOMENT HERCULES AND THE BLACK WIDOW KILL THEIR FRIENDS...THEN, WILL MY CONDITIONING BE COMPLETE...
...AND THEY WILL BE MY SLAVES FOREVER--EH??!
VVMM
THAT NOISE--COMING FROM BEYOND THE DUNE--!

THE MAN'S NAME IS BLAZE, JOHNNY BLAZE...
...BETTER KNOWN, PERHAPS, AS...THE GHOST RIDER!
VVRRMMM

WITH GOOD REASON.
WHAT THE--?!
THOSE MEN--THINGS--GATHERED OUTSIDE ANGEL'S HOUSE...
WHATEVER THIS IS, IT MUST BE BAD NEWS, 'CAUSE I CAN FEEL MY-SELF STARTIN' TO CHANGE--!

IF IT'S A FIGHT YOU CREEPS WANT...
...THEN THE GHOST RIDER'LL BE GLAD TO GIVE YOU ONE!

NICE TALK, BLAZE--
--BUT HOW 'BOUT PUTTIN' YOUR MONEY WHERE YOUR MOUTH IS FOR ONCE, BEFORE WE ALL GET CREAMED?
BROOM!
HUH? THE ANGEL AN' ICEMAN TACKLIN' HERCULES...?
WHAT IS GOING ON HERE, COWBOY?
THY COURAGE IS GREAT, MORTAL...

...BUT THEE AND THY COMPANIONS DOST FACE ONE WHO HAS STOOD BLOW-TO-BLOW WITH THOR!
LORD ABOVE-- HE TOOK MY STRONGEST BOLTS OF HELLFIRE...
...AND SHRUGGED THEM OFF AS IF THEY WERE NOTHIN'!
TRAKK!

FOR I AM HERCULES, PRINCE OF POWER!
AND THERE IS NO MORTAL BORN WHO CAN STAND AGAINST ME!!
HE'S RIGHT, BLAST IT--!
SKRATAM!
THIS LANSING DUDE'S GOT HIM BRAINWASHED INTO BELIEVING WE'RE THE BAD GUYS...
...AND HERC ISN'T GONNA LET UP UNTIL ALL OF US ARE STONE COLD DEAD!

MAYBE SO, ICEMAN--BUT IF THIS IS THE NIGHT WE'RE GONNA DIE..
LET'S MAKE SURE WE DIE LIKE HEROES!
PICTURE IT: THE SCION OF ZEUS TURNED AGAINST HIS FRIENDS, FACING FIRE ON ONE HAND, ICE ON THE OTHER, FACING ATTACK FROM THE AIR...
...FACING MEN WHO HAVE BEATEN SOME OF THE MOST DEADLY VILLAINS IN HISTORY...
...FACING ALMOST INDESCRIBABLE LEVELS OF RAW, UNBRIDLED POWER...
...AND STANDING TRIUMPHANT AGAINST THEM ALL.
IT'S A BATTLE OUT OF LEGEND FOUGHT THIS EVEN-TIDE ON A CHILL, WINTRY MALIBU BEACH ...A BATTLE FOR THE LIVES OF MAN, AND THE SOUL OF ONE...A BATTLE THAT CAN ONLY END IN TRAGEDY...

AS MIGHT THIS ONE...
GOT YOU, YA FUZZY-FACED TERROR...
BAK!
...AN', AS FAR AS I CAN TELL, YOU'RE THE LAST!

NOT THE LAST, MY FRIEND...
...YOU FORGOT THE BLACK WIDOW!
NATASHA--!
WHUK!

LITTLE TSARINA, IT'S ME, IVAN!
NO USE-- SHE DON'T KNOW ME. AN' THAT LIGHT-NING KICK'LL TAKE MY HEAD OFF IF IT CONNECTS...

...IF IT CONNECTS.
SCORE ONE FOR THE OLD GUY!

NO! SHE TURNED MY PARRY AGAINST ME...
...SHE'S COMIN' IN TOO FAST TO BLOCK--!
THOK!

THE MASTER WANTS YOU DEAD, FRIEND...
KRAK!

...AND THE BLACK WIDOW IS HERE TO SEE THAT THE MASTER GETS WHAT HE WANTS!
NATASHA... LITTLE TSARINA ...DON'T DO THIS... CHOKING ME... I BEG... YOU...
'TASHA... PLEASE...

NOTHING PERSONAL, FRIEND...
...FRIEND...?
YOU... ARE A FRIEND... MY MIND, BURNING AS IF IT'S ON FIRE INSIDE... CAN'T... THINK...

BUT I KNOW YOU, DON'T I? YOU... YOU'RE...
...IVAN...?
OH MY GOD, WHAT HAVE I DONE?

IVAN... FORGIVE ME, IVAN, I...ALMOST... I COULD HAVE...
KILL HIM!!
YOU HAVE HIM AT YOUR MERCY, WIDOW-- KILL HIM!!
LANSING!

OF COURSE IT'S ME --I'M YOUR MASTER, WIDOW--
--AND I ORDER YOU TO KILL HIM!
I'D WORRY MORE ABOUT YOUR OWN LIFE, "MASTER," IF I WERE YOU!

BECAUSE I'M COMING FOR YOU, LANSING...
...AND NOTHING ON EARTH IS GOING TO STOP ME!
REBELLION, EH? WELL, THAT'S EASILY DEALT WITH!
SHPREEZ!

WITH THAT TOY, LANSING?
SHPREEZ!
THIS IS NO TOY, WOMAN --THIS NEURAL DISRUPTOR WILL FRY YOUR NERVOUS SYSTEM IN AN INSTANT!

ONLY IF IT HITS ME, LITTLE MAN!
AND HITTING THE WIDOW IS VERY HARD TO DO...

...IN FACT, IT'S NEXT-TO IMPOSSIBLE!
HAAIII--!!

NO, I CAN'T LOSE NOW, NOT WHEN I'VE WORKED SO HARD--!
WHOOMFF!
PHLOP!

AND I WON'T LOSE...
WHAT DOES IT MATTER THAT THE WIDOW'S BROKEN MY CONDI-TIONING...
...COME ON, BOX--WHERE ARE YOU, BOX!!

I STILL CONTROL HERCULES--
--AND I'LL KEEP CONTROLLING HIM SO LONG AS THE BOX REMAINS INTACT--!
GOT IT!

NO!!
SKRUNCH!

IT'S JUST YOU AND ME NOW, LANSING...
...YOU... AND ME!

NO!
I CAN STILL ESCAPE, RALLY MY MERCENARIES, RALLY MY MUTATES...!
OH MY LORD, THE MUTATES...I ...FORGOT...

THEY'RE ANIMALS NOW, HELD IN CHECK ONLY BY MY CONTROL BOX--AND WITH IT DESTROYED...
...THEY'LL BE HUNTING... ME...
MERCY--ALL OF YOU! HAVE PITY! IN GOD'S NAME-- MERCY!!

AAAAGGH!

DAWN: AND LITTLE HAS CHANGED...
THERE'S A NEW CORPSE ON THE BEACH, WAITING FOR THE POLICE TO COME CART IT AWAY...
...A CORPSE SURROUNDED BY A HALF-DOZEN AIMLESS, SHUFFLING...THINGS...THAT HAD ONCE BEEN BORN HUMAN!

HERCULES, YOU ALL RIGHT, MAN? YOU'VE BEEN OUT HERE ALL NIGHT.
I AM...WELL, MORTAL. MY BRAIN-SICKNESS IS PAST.
THE COPS WILL BE HERE SOON--THEY'LL SEE THAT LANSING'S... MUTATES...WILL BE WELL LOOKED-AFTER...

LOOKED AFTER, AYE-- BUT THEY CAN NEVER BE CURED! THEY CAN NEVER REGAIN THE HUMANITY LANSING STOLE FROM THEM!
THEY WERE INNOCENTS, BOY, AND THEY TRUSTED LANSING TO CARE FOR THEM--AND HE REPAID THEIR TRUST BY DESTROYING THEIR SOULS!

ALL RIGHT!
THERE IS EVIL IN THE WORLD, HERCULES--AND LANSING WAS A PART OF IT.
BUT THERE'S GOOD AS WELL--AND WE'RE A PART OF THAT!
THE QUESTION IS: DO WE DO ANYTHING ABOUT IT--OR DO WE SIT AROUND CRYING IN OUR BEER?

LIKE IT OR NOT, FOLKS, WE'RE UNIQUE, WE'VE GOT POWER--AND I HOPE THE RESPONSIBILITY--THE DUTY TO USE IT WISELY...
TO HELP THOSE WHO CAN'T HELP THEMSELVES, THE INNOCENTS, THE VICTIMS OF PEOPLE LIKE LANSING.
BECAUSE...THE WORLD STILL NEEDS... CHAMPIONS...
NEXT: LOS ANGELES FACES ITS WORST THREAT SINCE EARTHQUAKE: AND ONLY THE CHAMPIONS CAN SAVE IT FROM THE MADMAN KNOWN ONLY AS: RAMPAGE!

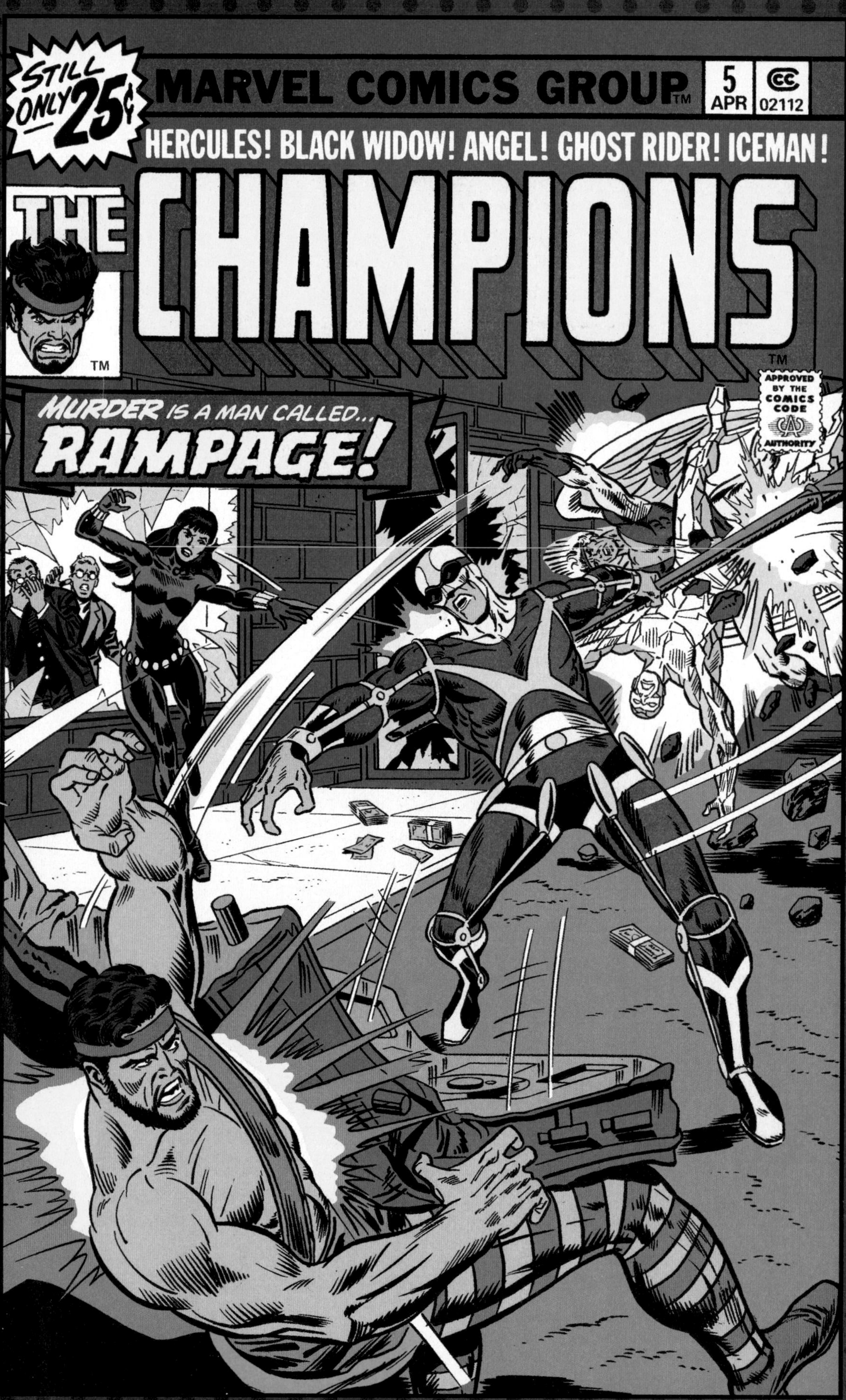
STILL ONLY 25¢
MARVEL COMICS GROUP™
5 APR
CC 02112
HERCULES! BLACK WIDOW! ANGEL! GHOST RIDER! ICEMAN!
THE CHAMPIONS™
APPROVED BY THE COMICS CODE AUTHORITY
MURDER IS A MAN CALLED... RAMPAGE!

HERCULES, Prince of Power! **THE BLACK WIDOW,** beautiful but deadly! **THE GHOST RIDER,** the most super-natural super-hero of them all! **THE ANGEL** and **ICEMAN,** two former X-Men, each seeking a life of his own! They are brought together to fight mankind's greatest foes... because the world still needs heroes!

Stan Lee PRESENTS:

THE CHAMPIONS™

BACK TO THRILL MARVELDOM ANEW... TONY ISABELLA, WRITER • DON HECK & JOHN TARTAG, ARTISTS • J. COSTANZA, letterer • J. COHEN, colorist • MARV WOLFMAN, EDITOR

EMERSON BALE IS ONE OF THE WORLD'S FINEST LEGAL MINDS. HIS CASES ARE LANDMARK, HIS COMMENTS, HEADLINES. AND EMERSON BALE BOASTS A CLIENTELE ENCOMPASSING SENATORS AND SPORTS STARS, MILLIONAIRES AND MILITANTS...
...AND ONE MUTANT!
I APPRECIATE EVERYTHING YOU'RE DOING FOR ME, MR. BALE. I'VE NEVER BEEN INVOLVED IN THE FAMILY FINANCES BEFORE THIS. I WOULDN'T KNOW WHERE TO BEGIN.
WARREN, YOUR PARENTS WERE MY DEAREST FRIENDS. I'M NOT ABOUT TO ALLOW THEIR SON TO BE CHEATED OUT OF HIS INHERITANCE.
NOT BY THOSE HUMAN SHARKS YOU CALL RELATIVES.

THEIR CLAIMS THAT YOUR PARENTS WOULDN'T HAVE MADE YOU SOLE BENEFICIARY IF THEY'D HAVE KNOWN YOU'RE THE ANGEL* ARE SHEER POPPYCOCK! THEY'LL BE LAUGHED OUT OF COURT!
I'VE FOLLOWED YOUR EXPLOITS WITH THE X-MEN, MY BOY. I SUSPECT THE WORTHINGTON FORTUNE WILL BE PUT TO FAR BETTER USE IN YOUR HANDS.
*WARREN'S MUTANT IDENTITY BECAME PUBLIC KNOWLEDGE IN OUR FIRST ISSUE-- MARV.

YOU MAKE IT SOUND LIKE I'D JUST INHERITED FORT KNOX. I KNOW MY FOLKS HAD MONEY, BUT IT'S HARDLY A...
BEFORE YOU FINISH THAT SENTENCE, MAYBE YOU SHOULD SEE THIS PARTIAL LIST OF THEIR HOLDINGS.

MIND IF I TAKE A LOOK, WARREN? AFTER WORKING IN MY PARENT'S CORNER STORE ALL THOSE SUMMERS, IT'D BE INTERESTING TO GET A GANDER AT THE WORLD OF BIG BUSINESS.

GANDER AWAY, FROSTBITE. BUT I THINK YOU'LL BE DISAPPOIN... ULP!
WARREN...

...THAT'S MORE MONEY THAN GOD MAKES!

WOW!
I'M RICH!
I'M RICH!
THAT YOU ARE, MY BOY. THAT YOU ARE.

CUT TO:
AND WHAT DO YOU FIGURE TO GAIN FROM THIS CHILDISH DISPLAY, CLARKE? THROWING YOUR UNPAID BILLS IN THE AIR WON'T SOLVE YOUR PROBLEMS--ONLY PAYING THEM WILL!

YOU OWE, MISTER--THE GOVERNMENT, YOUR SUB-CONTRACTORS--EVEN ME, YOUR LAWYER!
IF YOU'D SOLD OUT TWO YEARS AGO, YOU COULD HAVE BEEN A RICH MAN TODAY. BUT NOW--
--YOU'VE GOT TO DECLARE BANKRUPTCY!

DECLARE BANKRUPTCY!
YOU SPINELESS WORM! DO YOU KNOW WHAT CLARKE FUTURISTICS MEANS TO ME?
I PUT MY SOUL INTO THAT COMPANY, CRAWLEY!
HOW COULD I SELL MY SOUL TO SOME CORPORATION?

YOU WERE HANDLING MY FINANCES, CRAWLEY! YOU'RE TO BLAME FOR THIS!
STUART, PLEASE...

WHY DIDN'T YOU PLAN FOR THIS BLASTED RECESSION? IT WAS TOUGH ENOUGH COMPETING WITH ALL THE BIG OUTFITS BEFORE THOSE IDIOTS IN WASHINGTON STARTED RUNNING THE ECONOMY INTO THE GROUND!
WHY DIDN'T YOU PLAN?
I...

CONSIDER YOURSELF FIRED, CRAWLEY!
UGHN!
I'LL GET IN TOUCH WITH YOU THE NEXT TIME I WANT A DREAM DESTROYED!

AND DON'T WORRY ABOUT MY CREDITORS.
I'LL FIND A WAY TO PAY THEM BACK.

I'LL FIND A WAY TO PAY THEM ALL BACK!
THERE GOES ANOTHER ONE!
BETWEEN L.A.'S SMOG AND THE REPUBLICANS, WE'RE ALL GONNA FLIP OUT BEFORE LONG.
STUART CLARKE IS ONE OF THE WORLD'S FINEST SCIENTIFIC MINDS. THIS MORNING, THAT MIND HAS SNAPPED.

IT IS A LOSS THAT WILL DIRECTLY AFFECT TWO PEOPLE WE'VE COME TO KNOW QUITE WELL...
...THE BLACK WIDOW AND IVAN!
OUT WITH IT, IVAN.
ALL MORNING YOU'VE BEEN POUTING LIKE GARY COOPER IN "HIGH NOON."

OR IS THAT TOO RECENT A REFERENCE FOR YOU?
IT'S THAT CALL YOU GOT FROM THE WORTHINGTON KID. IT SOUNDS LIKE BAD NEWS TO ME.
BAD--? WARREN'S IDEAS FOR THE CHAMPIONS...

...AIN'T THAT MUCH DIFFERENT FROM THE AVENGERS OR EVEN YOUR PARTNERSHIP WITH DAREDEVIL-- NOT WHERE IT COUNTS!
BECAUSE EVERY TIME YOU EVER TIED UP WITH ANYBODY, YOU GOT BURNED-- INSIDE-- WHERE IT REALLY HURTS!
WHAT MAKES YOU THINK IT'LL BE DIFFERENT THIS TIME, MY LITTLE TSARINA?
WHAT MAKES YOU THINK YOU WON'T GET HURT AGAIN?

IT'S NOTHING THAT MAKES ANY LOGICAL SENSE, OLD FRIEND. JUST A FEELING. YOU KNOW, THE CHAMPIONS ARE REALLY A LOT LIKE US. LONERS.
TAKE THE ANGEL AND THE ICEMAN. I DON'T BE-LIEVE THEY EVER FELT TRULY COM-FORTABLE IN THE X-MEN. A GROUP CONSIST-ING SOLELY OF MUTANTS PROBABLY DIDN'T ALLOW FOR MUCH INDIVIDUAL GROWTH.

JOHNNY BLAZE IS EASY TO FIGURE OUT. HE BELONGS TO A WEST THAT DOESN'T EXIST ANYMORE. AND HERCULES...
WHAT CAN IT BE LIKE TO BELONG NOWHERE? IN OLYMPUS, HE'S A MAN AMONG GODS. ON EARTH, A GOD AMONG MEN.
IVAN... I THINK IT MIGHT WORK THIS TIME.
OKAY, KID. I'LL PLAY IT YOUR WAY.
AND PRAY I CAN PICK UP THE PIECES LATER.

IN TRUTH, YOUNG MORTAL, HERCULES IS STILL UNSURE AS TO THE PURPOSE OF THIS AIR-FILLED BAG.
NOTHING TO IT, MR. HERCULES. I'LL RUN THROUGH IT ONE MORE TIME.
13

THE IDEA IS TO CARRY THIS FOOT... ERR, AIR-FILLED BAG... ACROSS THE GOAL LINE--
13

--WHILE THOSE MEN TRY TO STOP YOU.
GET READY, BOYS. YOU'RE ABOUT TO BECOME THE FIRST TEAM IN UCLA HISTORY TO TACKLE A MYTHOLOGICAL GOD!
64
86
73
THE ELEVEN OF US'LL TURN THAT GUY INTO AN OLYMPIAN PANCAKE!

HERCULES WILT DO AS THOU DOST REQUEST, MORTAL. BUT I DO NOT FATHOM THE IMPOR-TANCE OF REACHING YON "GOAL LINE."

GOOD LORD! DO THOSE COLLEGE STUDENTS HAVE ANY INKLING OF WHAT THEY'RE GETTING THEMSELVES INTO?
IT LOOKS LIKE THEY'RE GONNA FIND OUT, SWEETHEART--
--RIGHT ABOUT NOW.
SEE?

I HAVE MADE MY WAY TO THE GOAL LINE AS WAS REQUESTED.
COULDST THOU ENLIGHTEN ME FURTHER, YOUNG ONES?
GROAN...
OHHH...
I WONDER IF IT'S TOO LATE TO TRY OUT FOR THE DEBATING TEAM.
AND WHILE THE UCLA BRUINS HAVE SECOND THOUGHTS ABOUT THEIR CHOSEN FIELD OF ATHLETIC ENDEAVOR...

...ANOTHER MEMBER OF OUR EVER-BURGEONING CAST IS LIKEWISE CONTEMPLATING HIS FUTURE ACTIVITIES.
FIRED!
THEY FIRED ME!
AS IF I'M TO BLAME FOR THE DAMAGE PLUTO'S ARMY DID TO THE CAMPUS! *
*CHAMPIONS #1 --MARV.
BUT THAT'S NOT THE HALF OF IT!
I HAVE TO TELL HERCULES AND THE WIDOW THAT THE UNIVERSITY HAS NO FURTHER NEED OF THEIR SERVICES, EITHER.
WELL, RICHARD FENSTER, EX-LECTURE AGENT, WHAT NEXT?

HOW ABOUT BUSINESS MANAGER OF "CHAMPIONS, INC."?
WHA--?

THE ICEMAN'LL GIVE YOU THE DETAILS, PAL.
YOUR FIRST JOB IS TO FIND US SUITABLE HEADQUARTERS. NOTHING TOO BIG. TWENTY OR THIRTY FLOORS OUGHT TO DO IT.
WHAT'S THE MATTER, FENSTER?
COLD FEET?
I...I... OH, WHAT THE HEY!
I ACCEPT.

THE BALANCE OF LIFE: ONE MAN RISES ON THE VERY WINGS OF HOPE WHILE HIS FELLOW SINKS DEEPER INTO THE BITTER MORASS OF DESPAIR.
THEY STACKED THE DECK AGAINST ME FROM THE VERY BEGINNING. EVEN WHEN I WAS FIRST WITH A PRODUCT--
RKE
STICS
--I COULD NEVER SUPPLY IT AS ECONOMICALLY OR AS RAPIDLY AS BIG OUTFITS LIKE STARK OR ROXXON.

I HAD HIGH HOPES FOR THIS EXO-SKELETON UNIFORM.
IT COULD HAVE REVOLUTIONIZED MODERN POLICE WORK.
BUT WHEN STARK'S L.A. OPERATION STARTED WORKING ON A SIMILAR PROJECT, IT GOT THE FAT GOVERNMENT CONTRACTS, NOT ME.

MAYBE THERE'S ANOTHER WAY I CAN UTILIZE MY INVEST-MENT, THOUGH.
MAYBE...

IT HAD TO HAPPEN EVENTUALLY.

THE LAW OF AVERAGES DEMANDED IT.
CLICK!

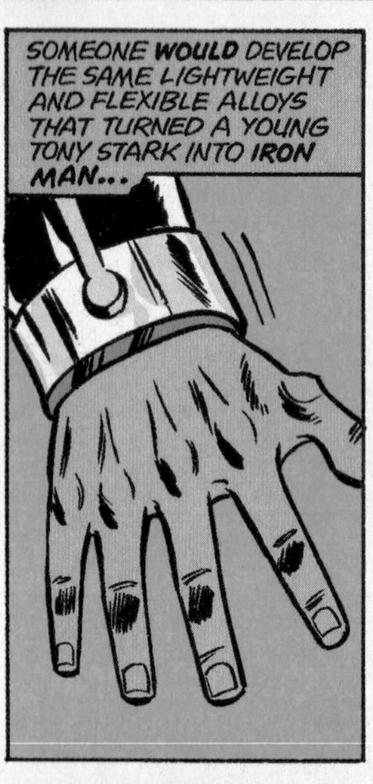
SOMEONE WOULD DEVELOP THE SAME LIGHTWEIGHT AND FLEXIBLE ALLOYS THAT TURNED A YOUNG TONY STARK INTO IRON MAN...

...AND THEN MASTER THE POWERFUL MAG-NETIC FORCES NECESSARY...

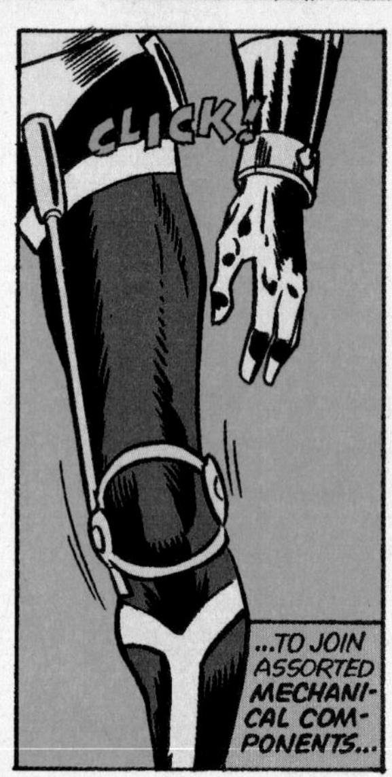
CLICK!
...TO JOIN ASSORTED MECHANI-CAL COM-PONENTS...

...INTO AN INVINCIBLE SUIT OF ARMOR!
CLICK!
CLICK

STUART CLARKE IS NOT AN INHERENTLY EVIL MAN.
HE HAS BEEN BENT, TWISTED, AND FINALLY CRUSHED BY THE TIMES IN WHICH HE LIVES.

EVEN SO, HE TAKES PAUSE BE-FORE EMBARKING ON AN INSANE PLAN TO SAVE HIS FAIL-ING BUSINESS.
BUT TIME IS MONEY, SAYETH THE WORLD OF 1976...

...AND THE PAUSE IS REGRETTABLY BRIEF...
I'LL DO IT!

MINIATURE GENERATORS CHARGE THE EXO-SKELETON COSTUME. BOOT JETS FLARE INTO LIFE.
STUART CLARKE SMILES INWARDLY AT THIS GUT-LEVEL JUSTICE HIS SCHEME OFFERS.

HE PLANS TO TAKE WHAT HE NEEDS TO REVIVE CLARKE FUTURISTIC FROM F.D.I.C.*-PROTECTED BANKS.
THAT WAY--OR SO HE THINKS--NO REAL PEOPLE WILL SUFFER LOSS.
THE BANK'S LOSSES WILL BE COVERED BY THE GOVERNMENT...
*FEDERAL DEPOSIT INSURANCE CORPORATION--MARV.

...THE VERY GOVERNMENT WHOSE ILL-CONCEIVED POLICIES CAUSED THE RECESSION WHICH HAS PUT HIS BUSINESS IN SUCH DIRE STRAITS.
HE THINKS THIS POETIC.
IN ONE HOUR, THIS HUMBLE "POET" (WHOM THE AUTHORITIES WILL DUB "RAMPAGE") WILL BECOME THE MOST WANTED MAN IN LOS ANGELES.

ELSEWHERE...
I HAVEN'T BEEN ABLE TO CONTACT THE GHOST RIDER*, AND THE ICEMAN IS STILL WITH FENSTER, BUT THERE'S NO REASON WE...
THOU SEEKEST TO INCLUDE HERCULES TOO SWIFTLY, ANGEL.
THOUGH I HAVE COME HERE AT THE BEHEST OF THE BEAUTEOUS NATASHA, I CARE NOT FOR THY DESIRE TO PLACE THE LION OF OLYMPUS AT THE COMMAND OF MERE MORTALS.
I'LL GET MY VIOLIN.
THAT'S NOT EXACTLY WHAT WARREN HAS IN MIND BY THE CHAMPIONS BECOMING "STORE-FRONT SUPERHEROES", HERCULES.
*AND IF YOU PICK UP ON JOHNNY BLAZE'S OWN MAG, NOW ON SALE, YOU'LL FIND OUT WHY!--MARV.

YOU'VE PALLED AROUND WITH ENOUGH OTHER SUPERHERO TYPES TO KNOW MOST ARE TOO INVOLVED IN THEIR OWN AFFAIRS--VITAL AS THOSE MAY BE--TO BE OF MUCH HELP TO THE AVERAGE MAN.
I THINK WE-- THE CHAMPIONS-- CAN CHANGE THAT.

"I'M TALKING ABOUT EXTENDING A NEEDED HAND WHEN ORDINARY PEOPLE FACE OUT-OF-THE-ORDINARY PROBLEMS. LIKE THOSE PATIENTS DR. LANSING TURNED INTO MONSTERS.*"
*LAST ISSUE--MARV.

WE'VE GOT POWER, MISTER--AND THAT EQUALS HEAVY RESPONSIBILITY IN MY BOOK. CAN YOU WALK AWAY FROM THAT?
YOU TELL 'IM, KID.
THOU DOST SPEAK WITH CONVICTION, ANGEL.
FOR THE NONCE, HERCULES WILL JOIN THEE.

THE BALANCE: ONE DECIDES, ANOTHER PONDERS.
I HOPE WARREN SELLS THE OTHERS ON THIS GROUP. THE MORE MAN-POWER HE'S GOT--
--THE EASIER IT'LL BE FOR ME WHEN I DECIDE TO SPLIT.

I'M NOT LIKE WARREN. IF I GO PUBLIC, I RISK LOSING MY SECRET IDENTITY.
WHAT EFFECT WOULD THAT HAVE ON THE REST OF THE DRAKE FAMILY?

WHAT'S WRONG, ROSE? YOU'RE SHIVERING!
I DON'T KNOW, ANNA. ALL OF A SUDDEN, THIS STRANGE CHILL CAME OVER ME.
BESIDES, I MAY WANT TO CHUCK THIS WHOLE ICEMAN BIT SOMEDAY--
--AND LIVE A NORMAL LIFE.
UH-OH!
I GUESS "SOMEDAY" IS STILL A WAYS OFF.
'CAUSE UNLESS THIS BANK GOES IN FOR WAY-OUT PROMOTIONS--
ATIO
BANK

--IT'S BEING ROBBED!
NOT CLEVER, MISTER. TIME LOCK OR NOT, NO BANK IS GOING TO LEAVE ITSELF UNABLE TO OPEN ITS VAULT DURING BUSINESS HOURS.
PLEASE. I...
SKIP IT, FRIEND. IT'S PROBABLY JUST AS WELL I SHOW THIS CITY WHAT I CAN DO NOW.

CRUNCH
OTHERWISE, THE NEXT TIME I GET LIED TO, I MIGHT JUST LOSE MY TEMPER--

--AND HURT SOMEBODY!
RIPPPPP

WELL, IT DOES LOOK LIKE TIME FOR THE ICEMAN TO COMETH ONCE AGAIN, SO...
HMM... WONDER IF THE CHAMPS WILL PAY FOR ALL THE THREADS I'VE FREEZE-DRIED OUT OF EXISTENCE WITH THIS QUICK CHANGE NUMBER.
HAVE TO TALK TO WINGS ABOUT THAT. BUT IN THE PROVERBIAL MEANTIME...
GANGWAY, FOLKS!
THE ICEMAN EXPRESS WILL STOP HIM COLD!

NOT LIKELY, PUNK!
WROP!
UGHN!

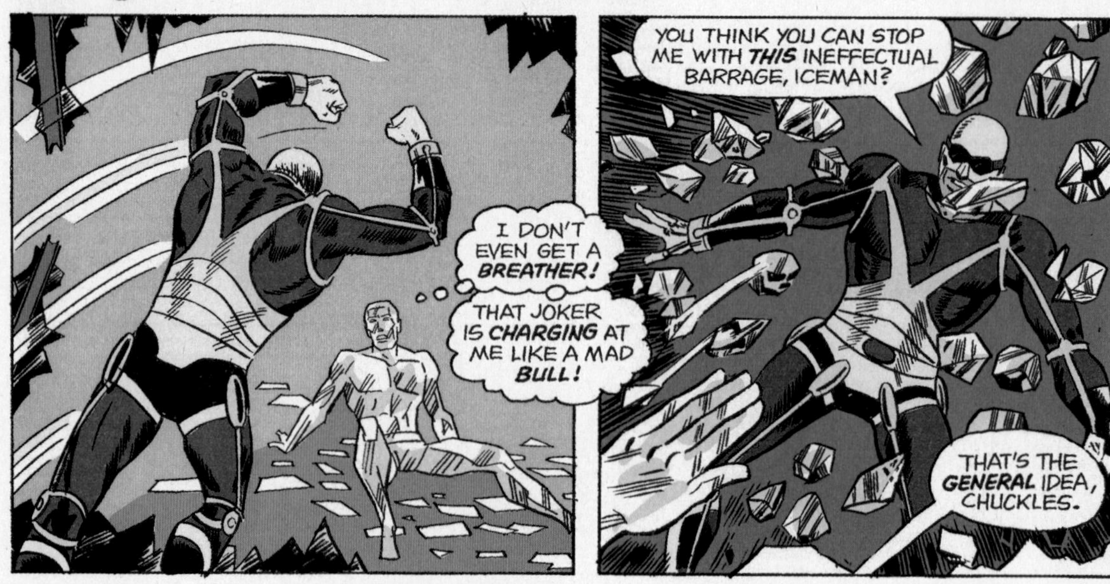

DON'T WASTE TIME TAKING IT TO THE PATENT OFFICE, LITTLE MAN.
BECAUSE AS IDEAS GO--
RENCH!

--IT ISN'T WORTH MUCH!
SWAT!
UHH!

MY HEAD FEELS LIKE A SOGGY MARSH-MALLOW.
IF HE CONNECTS AGAIN...

DIDN'T YOUR MOM AND I WARN YOU TO STAY AWAY FROM THE NEIGHBORHOOD BULLY, JUNIOR?
WARREN!
SLAM!
COMING TO YOU VIA THE COURTESY OF THE ONE EATERY IN L.A. THAT PLAYS NEWS BROADCASTS INSTEAD OF MUZAK!

THE ICEMAN'S EXTRA WEIGHT IS SLOWING YOU DOWN, ANGEL.
YOU'RE JUST GIVING ME TWO TARGETS FOR THE CUT-RATE PRICE OF ONE!

I THINK NOT, VILLAIN!
CLUNCH!
NOT WHILE HERCULES CALLS THEM COMRADES!

I'D HEARD THAT SEVERAL OF YOU "SUPERHEROES" HAD BANDED TOGETHER, BUT IT MAKES LITTLE DIFFERENCE TO ME.
ONE OR TEN--
SKRAKK
I CAN SMASH YOU ALL!

STARS! THOUGH THOU DOST HOWL LIKE A JACKAL--
--THY STRENGTH RIVALS THAT OF THE GOLDEN-CRESTED TITANS!
SKRRRR
STRENGTH ENOUGH TO CRUSH YOU, HERCULES!

I SAID THY MIGHT RIVALED THAT OF THE TITANS--
--NOT THAT OF THE PRINCE OF POWER!
YOU--YOU PULLED IT RIGHT OUT OF THESE MAGNETIC GRIPPERS!
BUT I'LL FINISH YOU OFF HAND-TO-HAND!
BY THE GODS, THE MAN IS CRAZED!

HARDLY, HERCULES.
COULD A MADMAN DEVELOP ARMOR POWERFUL ENOUGH TO FELL EVEN A SWAGGERING OLYMPIAN?
BRAKK!

MOMENTARILY, CRAZED ONE.

BUT ONLY MOMENTARILY!
THOOM!

OF ALL THE MYSTERIES THIS EARTH HOLDS, I SHALL NEVER UNDER-STAND--
--HOW A MORTAL CAN GAIN SUCH POWER AND THEN DO SO LITTLE WITH IT.

I SUPPOSE ARES IS A BOY SCOUT!
I WOULDN'T MAKE LIGHT OF HERCULES, ANGEL.
DON'T WORRY ABOUT IT, 'TASHA. HE'S TOO BUSY CON-GRATULATIN' HIMSELF TO TAKE OFFENSE.

ARES IS THE GOD OF WAR, MY FRIEND.
IT BE HIS NATURE TO ACT AS HE DOES.

HERCULES!

TOO LATE, LADY!
CLUBB!
YOU DIDN'T FIGURE ON THIS RIG'S--

--PROTECTIVE POWER!
SMASH!

HE'S CREAMIN' HERK!
COME ON, WINGS!
LET'S GET 'IM!

THOSE FOOL KIDS ARE GOING AFTER THAT JERK LIKE HE WAS THE ONLY SUPER-VILLAIN IN TOWN!
AND WITHOUT A BATTLE PLAN--
--THEY DON'T STAND A CHANCE!
PILE IT ON, BOBBY! HE'S STARTING TO BUST THROUGH THAT OVER-GROWN ICE CUBE ALREADY!
IT'S NOT GOING TO WORK, FLYBOY! GET OUT OF...

KRAK!

WOK!
AARGH!

HERK'S DOWN-- BOBBY'S DOWN-- AND I'M ONLY GONNA GET THIS ONE FREE SHOT BEFORE HE STARTS ON ME!

YOW!
IDIOT! MY HELMET'S MADE OF THE SAME INVINCIBLE ALLOY AS THE REST OF MY ARMOR!

BUT JUDGE FOR YOUR-SELF!
SWAT!
UGHN!
I'D BETTER GRAB WHATEVER MONEY I CAN, THEN GET OUT OF HERE. ONCE THEY'VE CLEARED THIS AREA, THE COPS'LL BE GETTING INTO THIS, TOO!

BUT BEFORE HE CAN RE-ENTER THE BANK...
THE BLACK WIDOW!
ZAT!

I HAVEN'T COME THIS FAR TO BE STOPPED BY A MERE WOMAN!
WHOOSH!

NO? THEN WHAT'LL YOU OFFER FOR HER PARTNER AND AN EXTREMELY IRRITATED DEMI-GOD?
GET THEE BACK, IVAN.

SORRY, HERK. FIRST COME, FIRST SERVERK!
THOU HAST STRUCK THY LAST COWARDLY BLOW, BASE ONE!
BOK!

WHAK

THE ANGEL'S STILL OUT, BUT THE OTHERS ARE REGROUPING! I'VE GOT TO STOP THEM!

WELL DONE, MY YOUNG ALLY! THY ICE SHIELD HAS PROTECTED NATASHA AND THYSELF FROM HARM!

BUT NOW HERCULES WILL PUT AN END TO THIS!

HERCULES! WAIT!
LISTEN TO THE LADY, HERK! THAT CREEP'S GOT US BY THE SHORT-HAIRS!
BACK OFF, MAN-GOD!

IF YOU COME ONE STEP CLOSER, I'LL SMASH THIS FIST RIGHT THROUGH THE ANGEL'S SKULL!
TO BE CONTINUED NEXT ISSUE!

STILL ONLY 25¢
MARVEL COMICS GROUP™
6 JUNE
CC 02112
HERCULES! BLACK WIDOW! ANGEL! GHOST RIDER! ICEMAN!
THE CHAMPIONS
™
APPROVED BY THE COMICS CODE AUTHORITY
THE HOUSE OF IDEAS DOES IT AGAIN! ANOTHER MAGNIFICENT MARVEL MAG!
MAYBE YOU CLOWNS JUST FORMED THE CHAMPIONS...
...BUT NOW RAMPAGE IS GONNA RIP YOUR TEAM APART!

The avenging ANGEL! The deadly BLACK WIDOW! Johnny Blaze, the GHOST RIDER! HERCULES, Prince of Power! The incomparable ICEMAN! Five fighters for justice united to battle for the common man...because the world still needs heroes!

Stan Lee PRESENTS: **THE CHAMPIONS**™

JV 270

...THEY COULD ALSO PROVE TO BE HIS LAST WORDS!

MAD DOGS and BUSINESSMEN

FEATURING: RAMPAGE--THE RECESSION-BORN SUPER-VILLAIN WHO COULD BE YOU!!

BACK OFF, HEROES! THE ICEMAN'S ALREADY SEEN MY FIST RIP THROUGH A STEEL VAULT!* BUT IF YOU COME ANY CLOSER--

--YOU'LL ALL GET TO SEE WHAT IT DOES TO THE ANGEL'S SKULL!

*LAST ISH--Marv.

A TRAGEDY OF TODAY BY: TONY ISABELLA, AUTHOR | GEORGE TUSKA & VINCE COLLETTA, ARTISTS | IRV WATANABE, LETTERER | PETRA GOLDBERG, COLORIST | MARV WOLFMAN, EDITOR

THOU HAST ISSUED THY FINAL THREAT, MORTAL!
COOL IT, BIG MAN!
THAT JOKER ISN'T KIDDING!

SKRAKK!
NICE TRY, IVAN, BUT IT LOOKS LIKE THE OLYMPIAN'S GON-NA BE STUBBORN!
SO I'LL JUST HAVE TO "COOL IT" FOR HIM!

THAT WASN'T TOO BRIGHT, SONNY!
THOU HAST STRUCK THINE OWN ALLY FROM BEHIND?!
THAT'S MY BEST FRIEND WITH A METAL MITT POINTED AT HIS PROFILE, WHISKERS.
THAT'S ENOUGH-- BOTH OF YOU!

TIME IS MONEY, HEROES--
--AND THE SECONDS YOU SPEND ARGUING COULD COST THE ANGEL HIS LIFE!

I THOUGHT THAT MIGHT QUIET YOU DOWN.
BY ALL THE GODS, FAIR NATASHA, THIS IS NOT THE WAY OF THE PRINCE OF POWER--
--TO TURN THUS AND WALK AWAY FROM AN AS-YET-UNDEFEATED FOE!
IT'S NOT MY WAY EITHER, HERCULES.
ICEMAN?

NOT TO WORRY, WIDOW. JUST BE READY TO MOVE WHEN I DO. AND, HERK--
--I'M SORRY ABOUT THE BACK SHOT, OKAY?
THE MATTER IS ALREADY FORGOTTEN.

THE LADY SURE DOESN'T ASK FOR THE EASY ONES. I'VE GOT TO CONCENTRATE AS NEVER BEFORE--
--LOWER MY BODY TEMPERATURE TO NEAR AB-SOLUTE ZERO!

AND WHEN I'VE REACHED THE LOWEST POSSIBLE DEGREE OF COLDNESS THAN EVEN I CAN WITHSTAND--
--I'VE GOT TO SPIN AROUND--

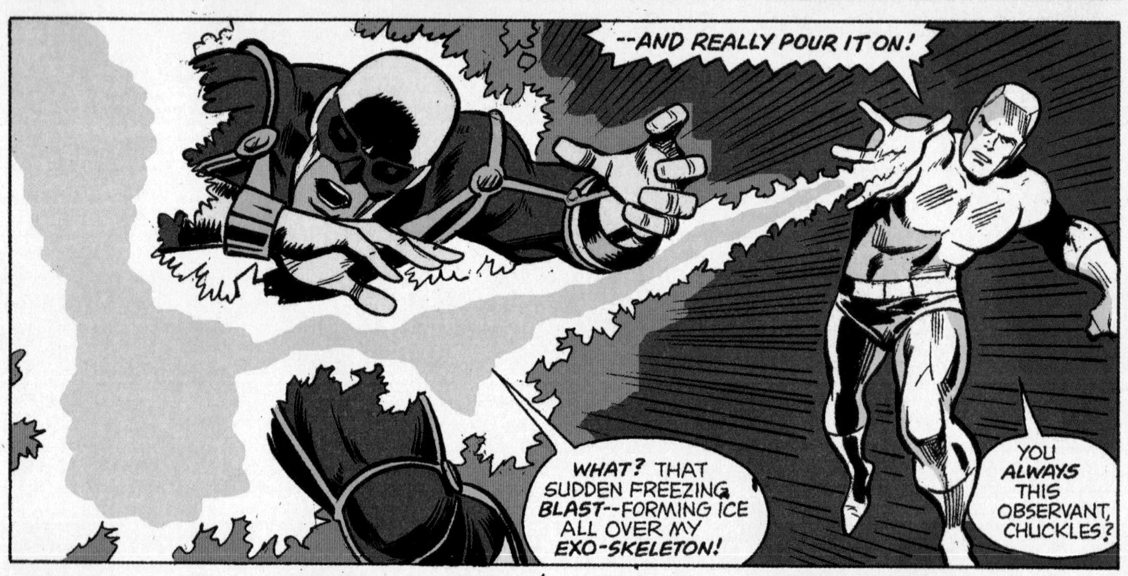
--AND REALLY POUR IT ON!
WHAT? THAT SUDDEN FREEZING BLAST--FORMING ICE ALL OVER MY EXO-SKELETON!
YOU ALWAYS THIS OBSERVANT, CHUCKLES?

THE YOUNG FOOL!
DOESN'T HE REALIZE I BROKE OUT OF ONE OF HIS OVER-GROWN ICE CUBES JUST MINUTES AGO?
BUT THIS AWFUL COLD--MY HEAD IS POUNDING LIKE A TRIPHAMMER--
--AND IT'S GETTING WORSE!

THY PLAN HAS BORN FRUIT, NATASHA.
THE ICE WON'T HOLD HIM FOR LONG--
--BUT WE WILL BE ABLE TO GET WARREN TO SAFETY!

MY BRAIN FEELS LIKE IT'S READY TO EXPLODE! I'VE GOT TO GET OUT OF THIS ICE TRAP!
BRAKKK!

STARS! YON VILLAIN HAS BURST FREE!
GET WARREN TO THE SIDE-LINES!
I'LL DELAY OUR PLAYMATE WITH MY WIDOW'S BITE!
'TASHA! NO!

SHE CAN'T HANDLE THIS BRUISER ALONE-- AND THE ICEMAN'S TOO EXHAUSTED TO HELP!
OVER HERE, FRIEND.

DON'T TRY TO STOP ME, WOMAN!
FSST
NO! THE "BITE" ISN'T WORKING!

THOOM!
UGHN!

IVAN!
HE--HE PUSHED ME OUT OF THE WAY-- AND TOOK THOSE BLOWS HIMSELF!

THERE WILL BE PAY-MENT EXACTED FOR THIS FOUL DEED, MORTAL!
WHAM
PAYMENT MOST DEAR!

CRUMP!
ARRGH! EVEN THROUGH MY PROTECTIVE COSTUME, I STILL FELT THAT PUNCH!
I MUST HAVE BEEN MAD TO CHALLENGE SUCH POWER!
FM-1
BUT I CAN'T SURRENDER TO THEM!

I MAY HAVE KILLED THAT MAN WHO RAN BETWEEN THE WIDOW AND MYSELF!
I'VE ALREADY LOST MY DREAM--

--I WON'T LOSE MY FREEDOM, TOO!
MAYBE THIS WILL HOLD HERCULES OFF LONG ENOUGH FOR ME TO ESCAPE!

BY THE SHATTERING SHAFTS OF APOLLO!
THE EARTHLY CONVEYANCE DOTH RUSH AT ME WITH A SPEED THAT DOTH RIVAL HERMES' OWN!
BUT I AM SWORN TO AVENGE THE LOYAL FRIEND WHO HATH BEEN MOST COWARDLY STRUCK DOWN--

CHOOM!
--AND I WILL NOT BE DETERRED FROM THAT VENGEANCE!

BUT WHEN THE SMOKE HAS CLEARED...
STYGIAN HORDES!
THE BASE VILLAIN HATH FLED!

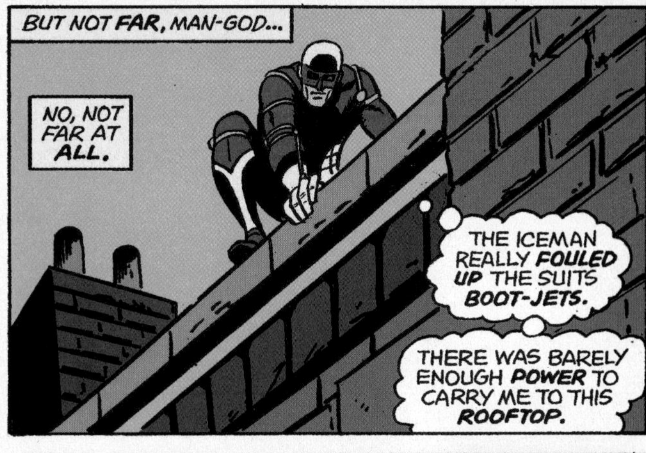
BUT NOT FAR, MAN-GOD...
NO, NOT FAR AT ALL.
THE ICEMAN REALLY FOULED UP THE SUITS BOOT-JETS.
THERE WAS BARELY ENOUGH POWER TO CARRY ME TO THIS ROOFTOP.

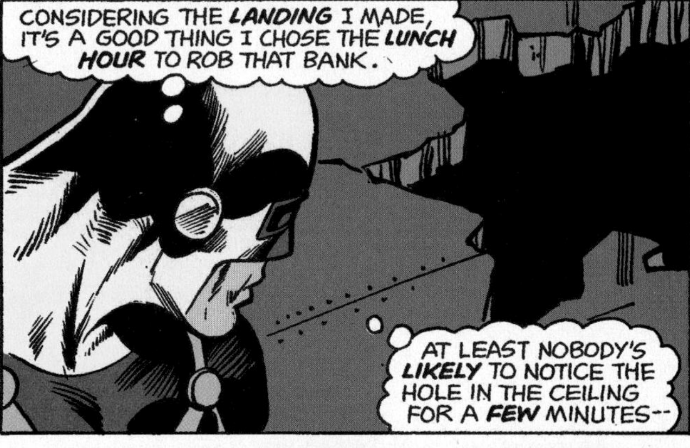
CONSIDERING THE LANDING I MADE, IT'S A GOOD THING I CHOSE THE LUNCH HOUR TO ROB THAT BANK.
AT LEAST NOBODY'S LIKELY TO NOTICE THE HOLE IN THE CEILING FOR A FEW MINUTES--

--AND THAT SHOULD BE ALL THE TIME I'LL NEED TO MAKE MY ESCAPE.
THIS ENTIRE BANK ROBBERY THING WAS THE SCHEME OF A MADMAN.

WELL, MAYBE THAT IS WHAT STUART CLARKE HAS BECOME --A MADMAN. BUT WITH THE HELP OF THIS OLD CRATE--
--I CAN WRITE A FINISH TO THE CRIMINAL PORTION OF MY SLOW JOURNEY INTO OBLIVION.

A COSTUMED BANK-ROBBER WOULDN'T STAND A CHANCE OF GETTING PAST THE POLICE THAT HAVE UNDOUBTEDLY GATHERED BELOW--
--BUT NOBODY'S GOING TO GIVE A SECOND GLANCE TO AN ORDINARY WORKMAN.

AND, WHEN HE REACHES THE **STREET**, RAMPAGE'S REASONING PROVES TO BE **CORRECT**.
YET EVEN WERE HE GARBED IN **FULL BATTLE REGALIA**, THE CHAMPIONS WOULD SCARCE NOTICE HIM...
...IN THEIR CONCERN OVER THE FALLEN **IVAN**.
MANY SEE IVAN AS MERELY THE BLACK WIDOW'S DRIVER, BUT METHINKS THE **BOND** BETWIXT THEM FAR **STRONGER**.
THAT'S HOW **I** READ IT, TOO, HERK.
YOU'VE **GOT** TO SAVE HIM, DOCTOR!
ADD **"NO MATTER WHAT THE EXPENSE"**, WIDOW.
THE **CHAMPIONS** TAKE CARE OF THEIR OWN.
HMM... LOOKS LIKE **LOS ANGELES** HAS HERSELF A **SUPERHERO** TEAM NOW--BACKED BY THE **WORTHINGTON FORTUNE**, NO LESS.

YOU'RE PLAYING "SEMANTICS" WITH ME, WARREN, BUT I SUPPOSE YOU'RE RIGHT. BLOODSHED WON'T SOLVE ANYTHING.
YOU KNOW HE'S RIGHT, WIDOW.
PAY ATTENTION, FROSTY. I'M ABOUT TO BE RIGHT FOR A RECORD SECOND TIME. WE GOT OUR TAILS KICKED JUST NOW BECAUSE WE ALL WENT OFF HALF-COCKED WITHOUT PLANNING OUR ATTACK.
PEOPLE...THE CHAMPIONS NEED A LEADER.
HERCULES DOES NOT DENY THY COURAGE, WINGED ONE, BUT T'WOULD BE UNSEEMLY FOR THE SON OF ZEUS TO FOLLOW THE COMMANDS OF A CALLOW YOUTH.
NOT ME, PAL. I HAVEN'T GOT THE EXPERIENCE TO COMMAND A BOY SCOUT TROOP!

NO, I WAS THINKING MORE IN TERMS OF--
--THE BLACK WIDOW!
WHAT?! ARE YOU SERIOUS, WARREN?

LOOK AT THE WAY YOU TOOK COMMAND DURING OUR BATTLE WITH PLUTO, NATASHA.*
YOU'VE GOT THE KNOW-HOW TO LEAD US, I'M CONVINCED OF THAT! WHAT DO YOU SAY, HERCULES?
*ISSUES #1-3 --MARV.

BY MY BEARD, ANGEL! I SAY:
AYE!
THERE BE NO QUEST HERCULES WOULD NOT DARE FOR A LEADER SUCH AS THIS!

HOW ABOUT YOU, ICEMAN?
IT'S FINE WITH ME, LADY. I'M PROBABLY A BETTER SPEAR-CARRIER THAN A GENERAL, ANYWAY.
WHY SHOULD I CARE WHO LEADS THE GROUP? AS SOON AS THE CHAMPIONS ARE RUNNING SMOOTHLY, THE ICEMAN IS GOING INTO RETIREMENT.

IT'S TIME FOR BOBBY DRAKE TO CHUCK THIS SUPERHERO TRIP AND START THINKING ABOUT HIS FUTURE!
I DON'T THINK THE GHOST RIDER'LL OBJECT*, WIDOW, SO I GUESS YOU'RE IN.
*HE'S MUCH TOO BUSY IN GHOST RIDER #18-- ON SALE EVEN AS WE SPEAK--MARV.

OUR FIRST STOP IS THE HOSPITAL.
CHECK. ONCE WE'RE SURE IVAN'S OKAY--
--WE WILL FIND THE VILLAIN WHO DID HIM INJURY. AND THEN, MY FRIENDS--
--THERE SHALL BE A RECKONING!

BUT BETWEEN THE PRESENT AND THE HOUR OF THAT INEVITABLE RECKONING, THERE MUST PASS SEVERAL HOURS... AND A MOST FATEFUL EDITION OF THE SIX O'CLOCK NEWS.
RAMPAGE IS THE NAME THE POLICE HAVE GIVEN THE ARMORED MARAUDER WHO ATTEMPTED TO ROB THE FIRST FEDERAL BANK EARLY THIS AFTERNOON--

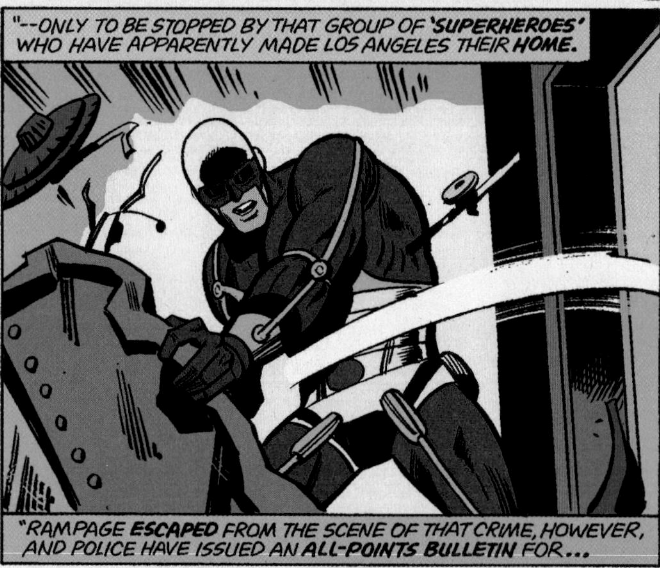
"--ONLY TO BE STOPPED BY THAT GROUP OF 'SUPERHEROES' WHO HAVE APPARENTLY MADE LOS ANGELES THEIR HOME.
"RAMPAGE ESCAPED FROM THE SCENE OF THAT CRIME, HOWEVER, AND POLICE HAVE ISSUED AN ALL-POINTS BULLETIN FOR...

...MY EX-CLIENT, STUART CLARKE!
HE ONCE SHOWED ME SKETCHES OF THE EXO-SKELETON HE'S WEARING.
SO THAT'S HOW THE HOT-SHOT SCIENTIST INTENDED TO PAY BACK HIS CREDITORS.

WELL, A CALL TO THE POLICE WILL PAY HIM BACK--FOR FIRING ME THIS MORNING.*
NEVER LET IT BE SAID THAT AMOS CRAWLEY ISN'T A PUBLIC-SPIRITED ATTORNEY.
*LAST ISSUE--MARV.

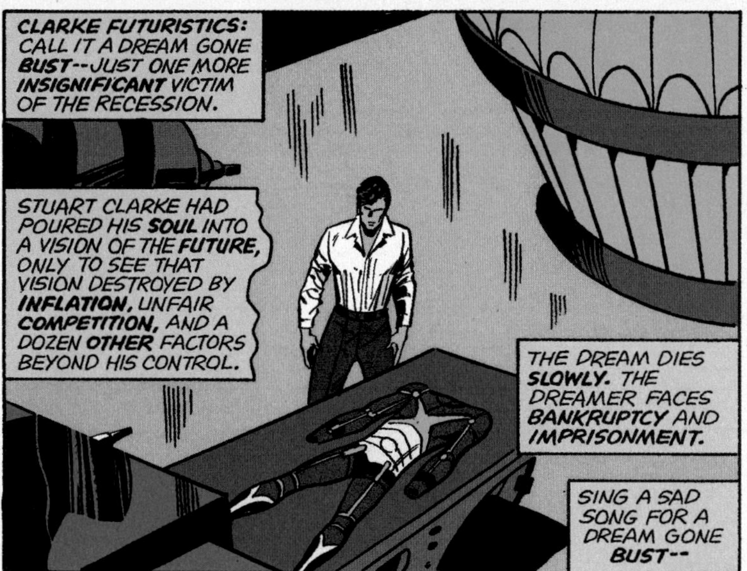
CLARKE FUTURISTICS: CALL IT A DREAM GONE BUST--JUST ONE MORE INSIGNIFICANT VICTIM OF THE RECESSION.
STUART CLARKE HAD POURED HIS SOUL INTO A VISION OF THE FUTURE, ONLY TO SEE THAT VISION DESTROYED BY INFLATION, UNFAIR COMPETITION, AND A DOZEN OTHER FACTORS BEYOND HIS CONTROL.
THE DREAM DIES SLOWLY. THE DREAMER FACES BANKRUPTCY AND IMPRISONMENT.
SING A SAD SONG FOR A DREAM GONE BUST--

--AND ADD A REFRAIN FOR THE DREAMER.
I'VE BEEN LUCKY SO FAR, BUT I'D BETTER TAKE THIS RIG APART BEFORE...
CLARKE! THIS IS THE POLICE!

GOOD LORD!
WE KNOW YOU'RE IN THERE, MR. CLARKE! COME OUT WITH YOUR HANDS UP!
MAKE IT EASY ON YOURSELF! YOUR LABORATORY IS SURROUNDED! YOU CAN'T ESCAPE!
POLICE

I CAN'T LET THEM PUT ME IN PRISON!
BUT I CAN'T FIGHT HALF THE POLICE FORCE, EITHER. AND MY BOOT-JETS ARE TOO DAMAGED TO FLY ME TO SAFETY!
UNLESS...

THERE'S BEEN NO RESPONSE FROM INSIDE, SIR.
SHOULD WE BREAK IN?
BLAST! I HATE TO DO IT THIS WAY.

"BUT I GUESS WE DON'T REALLY HAVE MUCH CHOICE, CONNERS. TELL THE MEN TO GO IN."
HOLD IT, GUYS. I THINK I HEARD SOMETHING IN THERE--
--LIKE AN ENGINE BEING WARMED UP.

NO!
KERAASH!
I DIDN'T REALIZE THEY'D BE STANDING THIS NEAR THE DOOR!
YRRGH!

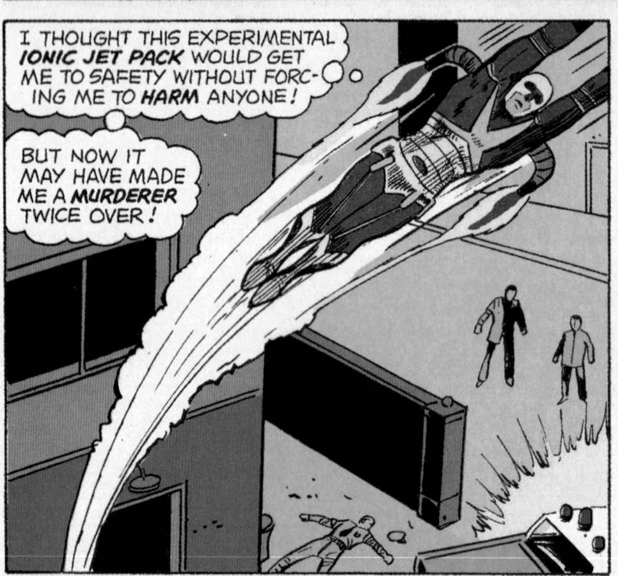
I THOUGHT THIS EXPERIMENTAL IONIC JET PACK WOULD GET ME TO SAFETY WITHOUT FORCING ME TO HARM ANYONE!
BUT NOW IT MAY HAVE MADE ME A MURDERER TWICE OVER!

THERE'S ONLY A SMALL AMOUNT OF FUEL IN THIS THING! I'LL HAVE TO LAND WITHIN MINUTES!
AND IF I HAVE KILLED THAT OFFICER, I DON'T STAND A CHANCE OF GETTING OUT OF THE CITY ALIVE!

QUICK-CUT: THE U.C.L.A. MEDICAL CENTER...
THEN THE VALIANT IVAN WILL RECOVER?
THE DOCTORS SAY HE WAS LUCKY, HERCULES.
IT'S AS IF RAMPAGE PULLED HIS PUNCHES AT THE VERY LAST SECOND.

AND JUST OUTSIDE IVAN'S ROOM...
IT'S A GOOD THING THE WIDOW STATIONED ME NEAR A RADIO!
WE'RE GONNA GET A SECOND CRACK AT RAMPAGE SOONER THAN WE FIGURED!
HE AND THE POLICE ARE HAVING A RUNNING BATTLE--

BLAM!
"--DOWN HOLLYWOOD BOULEVARD!"
KRAK!

MY GOD! IT'S LIKE A BATTLEFIELD!
HOW LONG CAN I HOLD THEM OFF BY THROWING THESE HUNKS OF CONCRETE?

"HOW LONG BEFORE I ACCIDENTALLY KILL AGAIN?"
WAM!
THERE ARE NO ANSWERS TO STUART CLARKE'S UNVOICED QUESTIONS, ONLY TO THE SEEMING THREAT HE POSES...

THEY ARE, OF COURSE, THE WRONG ANSWERS...
SPANGG!
PHWIING!
KWEE!
...BUT THOSE WHO GIVE THEM HAVE NO WAY OF KNOWING THIS.

WHY WON'T YOU LEAVE ME ALONE?
I DON'T WANT TO KILL ANY-BODY ELSE!

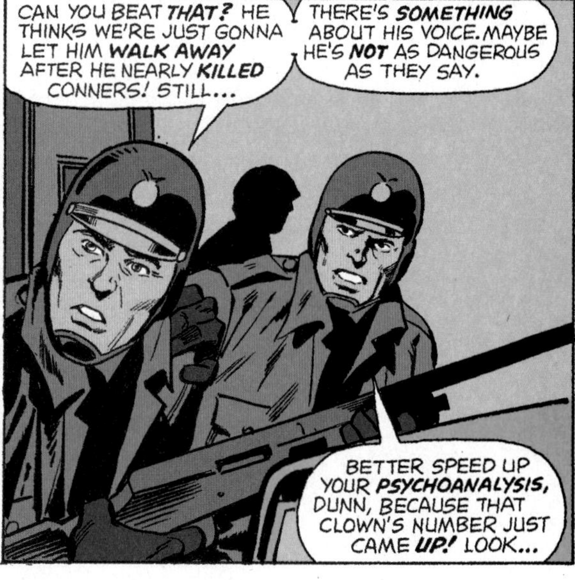
CAN YOU BEAT THAT? HE THINKS WE'RE JUST GONNA LET HIM WALK AWAY AFTER HE NEARLY KILLED CONNERS! STILL...
THERE'S SOMETHING ABOUT HIS VOICE. MAYBE HE'S NOT AS DANGEROUS AS THEY SAY.
BETTER SPEED UP YOUR PSYCHOANALYSIS, DUNN, BECAUSE THAT CLOWN'S NUMBER JUST CAME UP! LOOK...

HERE COME THE CHAMPIONS!
THERE'S OUR PIGEON, GROUP!
YOU LEAD THE ATTACK, WARREN.
AYE, ANGEL, AND MAKE GOODLY USE OF THE GOLDEN MACE THOU DOST WIELD!
IT WAS FASHIONED BY HEPHAESTUS HIM-SELF IN THE SACRED FORGE OF OLYMPUS!
NICE GOING, HERK. YOU'VE FOUND THE PERFECT GIFT FOR THE MUTANT WHO HAS EVERYTHING!

POOR, I'M NOT, FROSTBITE.
BUT AT LEAST I BELIEVE IN--

--SHARING THE WEALTH!
KLOM!

I OWED YOU THAT ONE, RAMPAGE.
BUT WE CAN END THIS BATTLE RIGHT HERE IF YOU'LL SURRENDER TO THE AUTHORITIES!
I JUST WANTED TO SLIP QUIETLY OUT OF TOWN, BUT IF I HAVE TO--

--I'LL FIGHT MY WAY OUT!
BAD MOVE, MISTER--AND YOU HAVE TO BE A LOT FASTER THAN THAT TO CATCH THE ANGEL ANYWAY...

...EVEN IF I WEREN'T BACKED UP BY THE ICEMAN.
ICE DAGGERS!

KEEP UP THE BARRAGE, ICEMAN.
HEY, I'M NOT EXACTLY NEW AT THIS, YA KNOW. I'LL MUDDLE THROUGH SOMEHOW!

HMM...PERHAPS I AM OVERPLAYING THIS LEADER ROLE.
I'D BETTER CONCENTRATE ON MY PART OF OUR ATTACK--

--AND STRIKE--

--AS ONLY THE BLACK WIDOW CAN!
BUNCH!
WHAT THE DEVIL?!

ALL RIGHT, HEROES. I DIDN'T WANT THIS, BUT IF I'M GOING TO BE TREATED LIKE A SUPER-VILLAIN--
--THEN I'LL ACT THE THE PART! AND I'LL BE THE DEADLIEST MENACE THE WORLD HAS EVER SEEN!

COME ON, HERCULES! I'VE KNOCKED YOU DOWN TWICE BEFORE. A THIRD TIME SHOULDN'T BE TOO DIFFICULT TO MANAGE!
HERCULES DIDST DEEM THOU MAD WHEN FIRST WE TWO CLASHED, MORTAL. BUT MAD OR NO--

--THOU MUST BE STOPPED!
POM!
UNNNH!

GIVE IT UP, MAN. YOU'VE LOST ALREADY.
AYE. I HAVE NO DESIRE TO HARM THEE FURTHER.
LISTEN TO THEM. YOU'VE BEEN LUCKY SO FAR.
BOTH MY CHAUFFEUR AND THE POLICEMAN WILL RECOVER. THE COURTS WILL BE...
THE COURTS WILL PUT ME BEHIND BARS!

AND I'D SOONER DIE THAN SPEND MOST OF MY LIFE IN A PRISON CELL!
HEADS UP, CHAMPS! HE'S MAKING HIS MOVE--
--FOR ALL THE GOOD IT'LL DO HIM!
SMASH!
THE SUIT'S POWER IS FAILING! I CAN'T KEEP MY BALANCE!

YOU HAD YOUR CHANCE TO COME PEACEFULLY, RAMPAGE. YOU SHOULD'VE TAKEN IT.
NOW WE'RE GOING TO DO IT THE HARD WAY!
KEK!
OOF!

THE SUIT'S COMPONENTS ARE BURNING OUT! IT CAN'T STAND MUCH MORE OF THIS PUNISHMENT!
IF I CAN JUST SQUEEZE A FEW MORE SECONDS OF FLIGHT OUT OF THE JET PACK...

SORRY, PAL.
NOBODY VIOLATES MY AIR SPACE!
WOK!
STAY OUT OF THE REACH OF THOSE ARMORED FISTS, WINGED ONE.

HERCULES SHALL END THIS UNFAIR BATTLE--
--WITH THE LEAST POSSIBLE DELAY!

PTOW!
ARRGH

I'M FINISHED! THE JET PACK IS HOPELESSLY SMASHED! BUT THERE'S STILL SOME FUEL LEFT IN IT--
--AND LIKE I TOLD THEM--

NEXT ISSUE: THE RETURN OF THE GHOST RIDER PLUS THE INCREDIBLE ENTRANCE OF THE MAN WHO CREATED THE BLACK WIDOW!

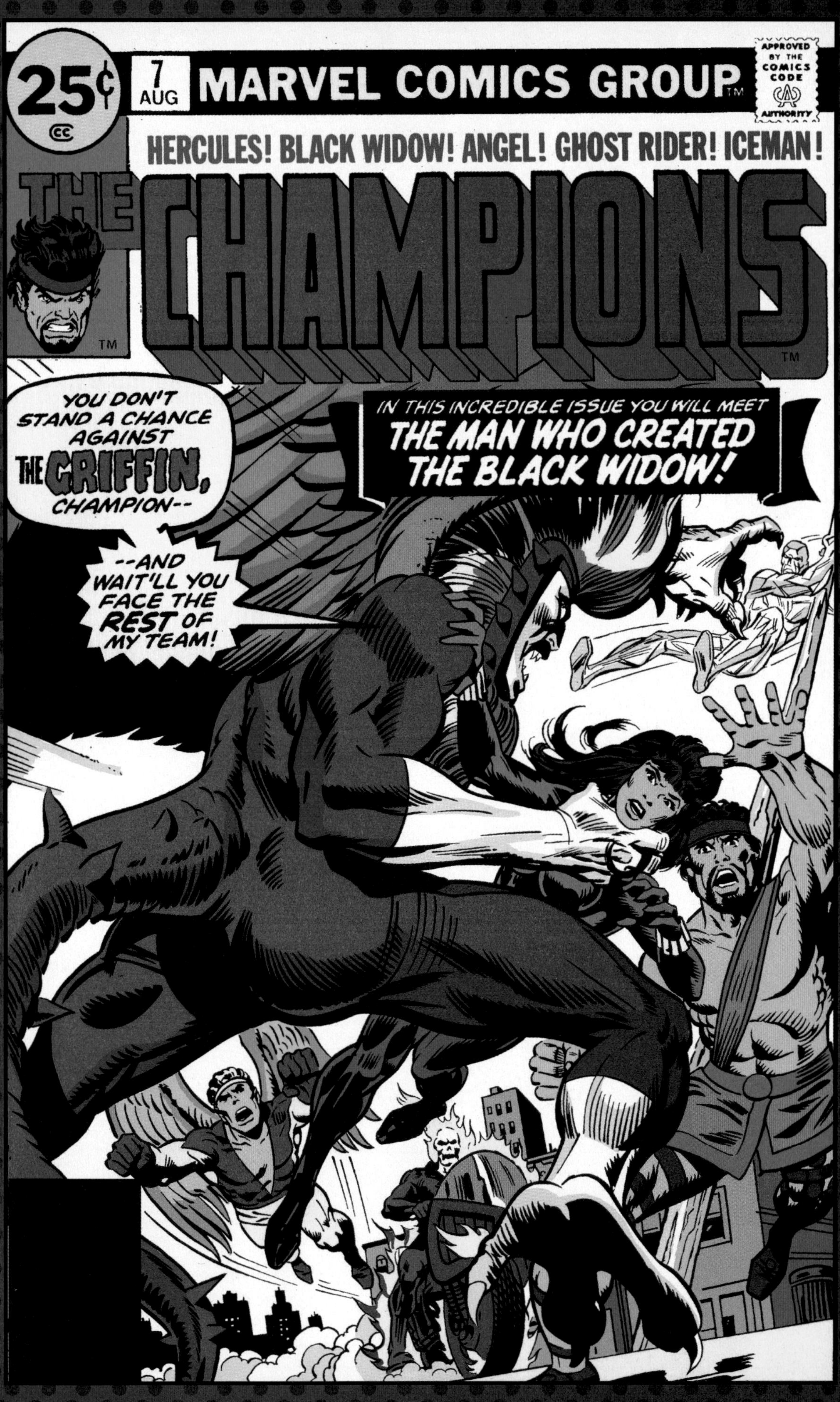
25¢
CC
7
AUG
MARVEL COMICS GROUP
APPROVED BY THE COMICS CODE AUTHORITY
HERCULES! BLACK WIDOW! ANGEL! GHOST RIDER! ICEMAN!
THE CHAMPIONS
YOU DON'T STAND A CHANCE AGAINST THE GRIFFIN, CHAMPION--
--AND WAIT'LL YOU FACE THE REST OF MY TEAM!
IN THIS INCREDIBLE ISSUE YOU WILL MEET
THE MAN WHO CREATED THE BLACK WIDOW!

The avenging ANGEL! The deadly BLACK WIDOW! Johnny Blaze, the GHOST RIDER! HERCULES, Prince of Power! The incomparable ICEMAN! Five fighters for justice united to battle for the common man...because the world still needs heroes!

Stan Lee PRESENTS:

THE CHAMPIONS™

TONY ISABELLA, WRITER | GEORGE TUSKA, ARTIST | VINCE COLLETTA, INKER | K. MANTLO, LETTERER | PHIL RACHE, COLORIST | M. WOLFMAN, EDITOR

WELCOME TO THE CHAMPIONS' TEMPORARY HEADQUARTERS, A PLUSH SUITE IN A TWENTY-THREE STORY TOP-DOLLAR LOS ANGELES OFFICE BUILDING WHOSE FIRST VISITOR HAS QUITE SURPRISINGLY TURNED OUT TO BE...

WHAM
BAH! IF I CANNOT SEIZE YON DEVICE--
--THEN I SHALL RENDER IT HARMLESS WITH BUT ONE SMASHING BLOW!

THAT'S STRIKE TWO, BIG FELLA.
LET'S SEE IF I HAVE ANY BETTER LUCK GOING AFTER IT FROM ABOVE!

YEOW!
IT REVERSED DIRECTION-- SHATTERED MY ICE SLIDE!

IT'S HEADING THIS WAY AGAIN!
FEAR NOT, FRIEND ICEMAN.
HERCULES HATH THOU!

DON'T LOSE YOUR "COOL" DICKIE-BOY!
I THINK I KNOW HOW TO HANDLE IT NOW!

"IT MUST BE PROGRAMMED TO AVOID ANYTHING THAT IT CAN'T BREAK THROUGH!
"SO THIS THICK, SUPER-HARD ICE CYLINDER SHOULD LEAVE IT WITH ONLY ONE WAY TO GO--

--RIGHT INTO HERK'S HOT LITTLE HANDS!
I STAND READY, MY YOUNG ALLY!
IT SHALL NOT ESCAPE ME A THIRD TIME!
WHAT'S GOING ON IN HERE?
WE HEARD THE COMMOTION, AND--
LOOK OUT HERCULES! HERE IT COMES!

FOOOMP!

THIS BE THE CAUSE OF ANY "COMMOTION", FAIR NATASHA-- ODD THOUGH IT MAY SEEM.
PERHAPS THY INVENTIVE COMPANION CAN SHED SOME LIGHT ON ITS PURPOSE.
TREAT IT WITH KID GLOVES, IVAN.
IT MIGHT BE DANGEROUS.

IVAN WAS HANDLING "TOYS" LIKE THAT BEFORE YOU OR I WERE BORN, MY FROZEN FRIEND. GIVE HIM A HALF-HOUR--
--AND HE'LL TELL YOU WHO MADE IT, WHY THEY MADE IT, AND, QUITE POSSIBLY, WHAT THEY HAD FOR BREAKFAST THE DAY THEY MADE IT.

I'M COUNTING ON IVAN'S SKILL, MY DEAR BLACK WIDOW. FOR WHAT IS THE GAME--
--WITHOUT WORTHWHILE ADVERSARIES?

HOW SAD THAT WHEN NEXT WE MEET--
--IT SHALL NOT BE FOR ANYTHING SO TRIVIAL AS MERE SPORT!

NO, I'M AFRAID WHEN NEXT THIS OLD SOLDIER HAS OCCASION TO FACE NATASHA ROMANOFF AND HER ENIGMATIC IVAN--
--THE THREE OF US WILL BE EMBROILED IN A DESPERATE STRUGGLE FOR--
--SURVIVAL!

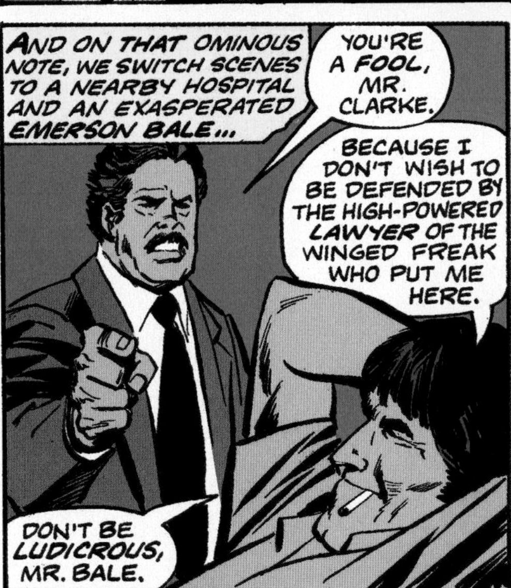
AND ON THAT OMINOUS NOTE, WE SWITCH SCENES TO A NEARBY HOSPITAL AND AN EXASPERATED EMERSON BALE...
YOU'RE A FOOL, MR. CLARKE.
BECAUSE I DON'T WISH TO BE DEFENDED BY THE HIGH-POWERED LAWYER OF THE WINGED FREAK WHO PUT ME HERE.
DON'T BE LUDICROUS, MR. BALE.

IT'S NO USE WARREN. HE WON'T ACCEPT MY AID-- AND WITHOUT IT--
--THE FINE SCIENTIFIC MIND OF STUART CLARKE SHALL UNDOUBTEDLY TO BE LEFT TO THE TENDER MERCIES OF THE PENAL SYSTEM.
57
THANKS FOR TRYING MR. BALE.

I WASN'T AROUND WHEN YOU AND OUR OTHER PARTNERS HAD IT OUT WITH THIS CLARKE FELLA, ANGEL.*
WHAT MAKES HIM SO DOWN-RIGHT SPECIAL?
*ISSUES #5 & 6--MARV.

"HE'S A GENIUS, JOHNNY-- DEVELOPED A SUIT OF EXO-SKELETON ARMOR THAT PUT HIM IN A LEAGUE WITH IRON MAN! BUT WHEN A RESEARCH COMPANY HE OWNED WENT BUST, HIS MIND SNAPPED. HE STARTED ROBING BANKS TO GET OUT OF DEBT. THAT'S WHERE WE CAME IN.

"WE HAD NO WAY OF KNOWING THAT RAMPAGE -- AS THE POLICE WERE CALLING HIM-- WAS A SICK MAN. OUR LAST BATTLE WITH HIM GOT PRETTY HAIRY...
"...AND ENDED WITH HIS ATTEMPTED SUICIDE.
"FOR A LONG TIME, THE DOCS HERE DIDN'T THINK HE WOULD RECOVER."

AS FOR WHY I'M TRING TO HELP HIM--
--ISN'T THAT WHAT THE CHAMPS ARE ALL ABOUT?
I DON'T DISAGREE WITH THE SENTIMENT, PAL.

BUT IT'S BEEN MY EXPERIENCE THAT NOBODY PASSES ON A SURE THING UNLESS THEY'VE GOT A SIDE BET GOING.
CLARKE'S UP TO SOMETHING.

SO SUPPOSE I TALK TO HIM--
--NOT AS JOHNNY BLAZE--

--BUT AS THE GHOST RIDER!

WHAT TH--!
UGHN!
WHAMP

SOMEBODY BLASTED THOSE GUARDS!
AND WHOEVER IT IS--
-- WANTS TO BUSHWHACK US, TOO!

SWEET JUMPING CATFISH!
WE CAN'T LET HIM PREVENT US FROM ESCAPING WITH OUR NEWEST TEAM MEMBER, GRIFFIN!
DON'T SWEAT IT, DARKSTAR. WHAT YOUR BLACK ENERGY COULDN'T DO--
--MY RAZOR-SHARP LION'S CLAWS WILL ACCOMPLISH QUITE NICELY!
I'LL RIP HIS HEART OUT!
UH-OH! FROM WHAT I REMEMBER READING OF THE GRIFFIN,* HE'S A HOMICIDAL MANIAC!
COWBOY, IT'S TIME FOR A HELLFIRE BLAST!
*AMAZING ADVENTURES #15 OR THE RECENT MARVEL TEAM-UP #38 --MARV.

HE'S STILL BREATHING, BUT NOT FOR LONG!
THAT'S ENOUGH GRIFFIN!
CLARK IS OUR ONLY OBJECTIVE FOR NOW!

LADY, THE ONLY GOOD SUPERHERO IS A DEAD ONE!
BUT IT'S NO SKIN OFF MY NOSE IF YOU WANT TO LET HIM LIVE A LITTLE LONGER!
I WANTED THE ANGEL, ANYHOW!

TOO BAD HE JUST TURNED TAIL AND RAN THE MINUTE IT GOT INTERESTING IN THERE!

GAKK!
FWOOSH
A GAS ATTACK! CAN'T... HOLD ON!
WHA--I'M FALLING!

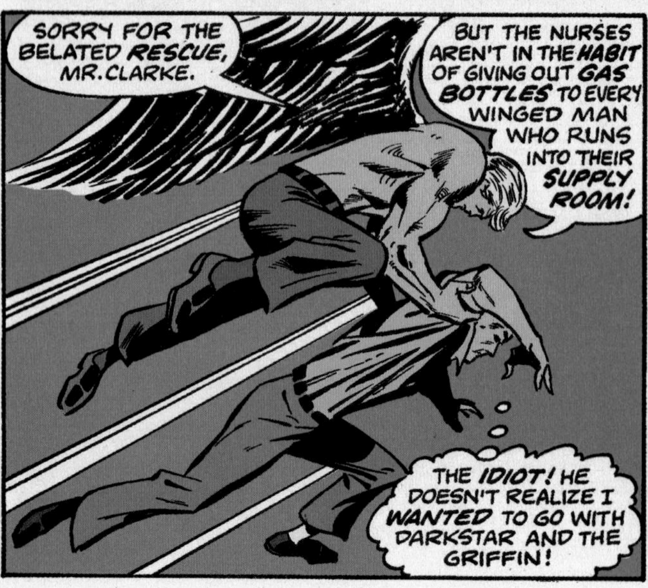
SORRY FOR THE BELATED RESCUE, MR. CLARKE.
BUT THE NURSES AREN'T IN THE HABIT OF GIVING OUT GAS BOTTLES TO EVERY WINGED MAN WHO RUNS INTO THEIR SUPPLY ROOM!
THE IDIOT! HE DOESN'T REALIZE I WANTED TO GO WITH DARKSTAR AND THE GRIFFIN!

I PROBABLY DISAPPOINTED THE GRIFFIN BY NOT GOING IN THERE SLUGGING--
--BUT WARREN WORTHINGTON HAS GROWN UP A LOT DURING THESE PAST FEW MONTHS.
I LIKE TO THINK I USE MY HEAD MORE THESE DAYS.
AL HOSPITAL

ARE YOU ALL RIGHT, MR. CLARKE?
HUH? OH... YEAH, KID.
I'M JUST FINE--

OOF!
--NOW THAT I'VE HAD A CHANCE TO USE THIS EXO-GLOVE DARKSTAR SMUGGLED INTO THE HOSPITAL FOR ME!
WHUD

AND THAT'S ONLY THE BEGINNING!
WRONG, MISTER!
I GAVE YOU THE BENEFIT OF THE DOUBT--

--NOT DUMP YOU OFF THE ROOF!
--BUT THE ANGEL IS NOBODY'S PUNCHING BAG!
CALM DOWN, FELLA. I'M JUST FLAPPING HARD ENOUGH TO TAKE YOU OUT OF ACTION--

YOU'LL DO NEITHER, ANGEL!
MY ENERGY BANDS WILL SQUEEZE THE LIFE OUT OF YOU!
THEY'RE ALREADY TIGHTENING!
IT'S GETTING HARD TO--

THE ANGEL IS FINISHED!
ACTUALLY, THE BANDS WILL LOOSEN AUTOMATICALLY WHEN WE LEAVE.
--BREATHE *WHUFF*

YURI'S PLAN CALLS FOR ALL THE CHAMPIONS--SAVE THE BLACK WIDOW AND IVAN--TO DIE AT THE SAME TIME.
IF OUR BLOODTHIRSTY GRIFFIN KNEW THAT THE ANGEL WAS STILL ALIVE--
--HE MIGHT KILL HIM NOW AND SPOIL EVCRYTHING!

AND WHILE YOU PONDER THE MEANING OF THAT STRING OF THOUGHTS, GENTLE READER...
THEY'RE FLYING OFF WITH CLARKE!
THAT MEANS THEY BEAT THE ANGEL!

I CAN'T DO WARREN ANY GOOD DOWN HERE--
--SO I RECKON ALL I CAN DO--
--IS KEEP THOSE BUZZARDS IN SIGHT!

I WARNED YOU ABOUT THIS, DARKSTAR!
THAT FLAME-FACED IDIOT IS FOLLOWING US!

JUST GET CLARKE TO HEADQUARTERS, GRIFFIN!
I'LL DEAL WITH THE GHOST RIDER.

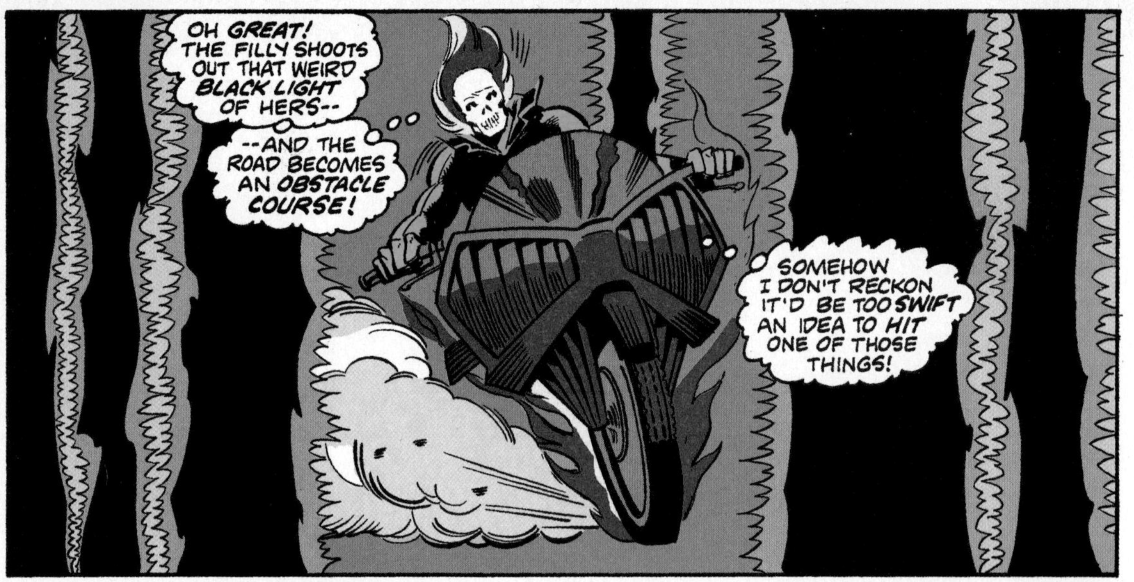
OH GREAT! THE FILLY SHOOTS OUT THAT WEIRD BLACK LIGHT OF HERS--
--AND THE ROAD BECOMES AN OBSTACLE COURSE!
SOMEHOW I DON'T RECKON IT'D BE TOO SWIFT AN IDEA TO HIT ONE OF THOSE THINGS!

COME ON SKULL-CYCLE! IT'S TIME TO DO SOME FANCY RIDING!
VRROOOM

BLAST! THIS STUNT JUST WENT FROM DIFFICULT TO IMPOSSIBLE!
THESE THINGS ARE MOVING CLOSER TOGETHER!

I'M NOT GOING TO MAKE IT!

WHOOM

ANGEL!
YOU PULLED ME OUT OF THE BLAST!
HECK, WHAT ARE PARTNERS FOR?

THE GRIFFIN AND HE OTHERS GOT CLEAN AWAY!
WE'LL SEE THEM AGAIN, JOHNNY.
I'VE GOT THIS NASTY HUNCH THAT WE'VE JUST FOUGHT THE FIRST BATTLE--

"-- OF AN ALL-OUT WAR!"
"SEARCH THE PLACE FROM TOP TO BOTTOM," HUH, FENSTER?
YOU GOT ANY IDEA HOW LONG THAT'LL TAKE THE THREE OF US?

IT CAN'T BE HELPED, ICEMAN. A LOT OF IMPORTANT PEOPLE WILL BE AT TOMORROW'S DEDICATION CEREMONIES.
PUBLICITY-WISE, WE CAN'T AFFORD ANY SURPRISES-- NOT LIKE THE ONE THAT FLEW THROUGH OUR WINDOW THIS MORNING.
IN TRUTH, I AM SORELY CONFUSED BY THE POMP AND CIRCUMSTANCE ATTENDING THE FOUNDING OF THE CHAMPIONS.
DO WE TRULY REQUIRE ALL THIS?

THESE ARE HIGH-POWERED TIMES HERCULES A HIGH-SPEED ORGANIZATION WITH PLENTY OF MANPOWER IS NEEDED TO ACCOMPLISH THE KIND OF JOB WE WANT TO DO!
PERHAPS, FRIEND FENSTER.
BUT HERCULES DOTH LONG FOR SIMPLER TIMES.

YOU AND ME BOTH, HERCULES.
I'M AFRAID MY BUDDY WARREN HAS TAKEN THIS WHOLE PROJECT WAY TOO FAR.
ACTUALLY--
ACTUALLY, DICKEY-BOY, THERE'S A REAL DANGER THE CHAMPS COULD LOSE SIGHT--

--OF THE COMMON JOES WE'RE SUPPOSED TO BE HELPING. THINK ABOUT IT.
I HAVE--AND IT'S JUST ONE MORE REASON-- THAT ONCE WARREN GETS THE GROUP RUNNING SMOOTHLY--
--THE ICEMAN IS CALLING IT QUITS!
IF THEY REMAIN HERE MUCH LONGER, THEY ARE CERTAIN TO DISCOVER ME!
I CANNOT RISK THAT!

I'LL HAVE TO ARRANGE A DIVERSION EVEN IF IT MEANS...
LOOK!

THERE'S SOMEBODY OVER THERE!
WHA--?
I CAN SEE YON INTRUDER'S, FORM--
--BUT THE DARKNESS DOTH CLOAK HIS IDENTITY!
HE'S ESCAPING INTO THE CORRIDOR!

IF HE REACHES THE STAIRWELL, WE'LL NEVER CATCH HIM!

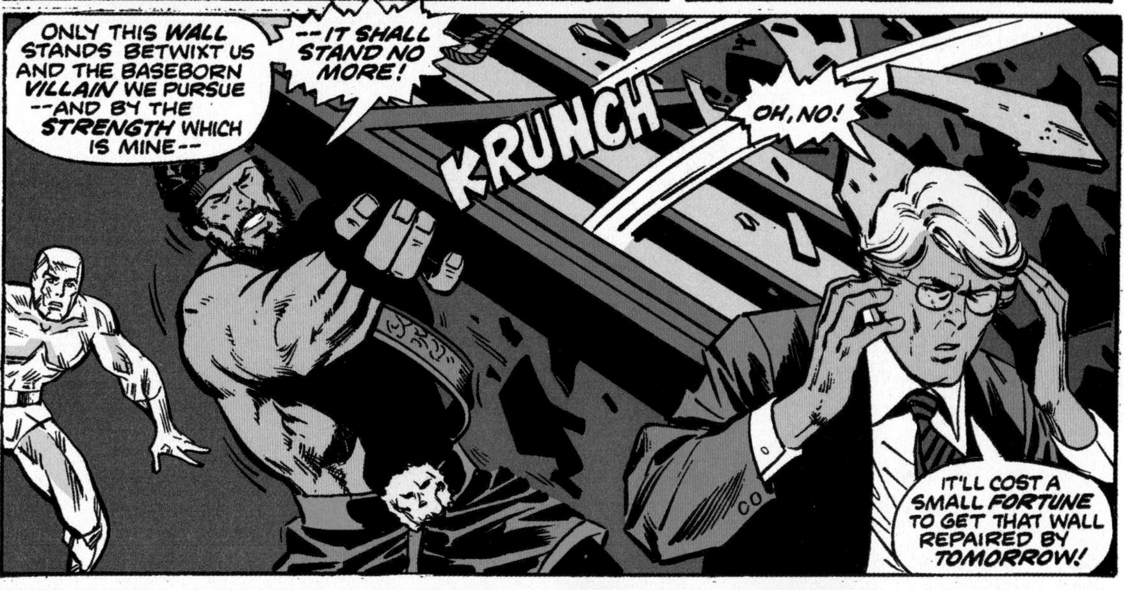
ONLY THIS WALL STANDS BETWIXT US AND THE BASEBORN VILLAIN WE PURSUE --AND BY THE STRENGTH WHICH IS MINE--
--IT SHALL STAND NO MORE!
KRUNCH
OH, NO!
IT'LL COST A SMALL FORTUNE TO GET THAT WALL REPAIRED BY TOMORROW!

BEFORE OUR SLIGHTLY OVER-EAGER OLYMPIAN RIPS THE WHOLE BUILDING APART--
--I THINK I'D BETTER STOP OUR FLEEING FRIEND MYSELF!
YEOWW!
FRIZZZ

I HAVE HIM, ICEMAN. I--
BY MY SOUL!

THOU ART BUT A CHILD!
I'M ⁝SOB⁝ SORRY I SNEAKED IN HERE, MISTER.
BUT I ⁝SOB⁝ HAD TO!

Y'SEE, I ⁝SOB⁝ HEARD ABOUT YOU AND YOUR FRIENDS ON ⁝SOB⁝ THE TELEVISION!
THE MAN SAID THAT IF PEOPLE WHO ARE IN ⁝SOB⁝ TROUBLE COME TO YOU-- --THAT YOU'RE S'PPOSE TO ⁝SOB⁝ HELP THEM.
AND, MISTER--

--I NEED HELP AWFUL BAD!

WHAT INCREDIBLE GOOD FORTUNE!
THE CHILD DISTRACTED THEM LONG ENOUGH FOR ME TO REACH THE OPPOSITE STAIRWELL. MOREOVER--

-- N. I SCOUTING MISSION WAS A SUCCESS.
I'VE LEARNED ENOUGH ABOUT OUR FOES TO INSURE US OF COMPLETE VICTORY.
SOON I WILL HAVE MY REVENGE--

--REVENGE ON THE MAN WHO MADE ME THE OUTCAST I AM--
-- THE MAN THE CHAMPIONS KNOW ONLY AS IVAN-- BUT WHO I KNOW AS--
--MY DEAR FATHER!

MEANWHILE IN A JURY-RIGGED LAB IN THE CHAMPION'S TEMORARY HQ...
OUR UNINVITED FLYING OBJECT BREAKS DOWN INTO THREE MAJOR COMPONENTS, 'TASHA--
--A HIDDEN AUDIO-VISUAL UNIT IN THE FRONT FOR COMMUNICATION AND GUIDANCE--
--A STORAGE UNIT IN THE CENTER--
--AND A PROPULSION UNIT AT THE END.
NOW THE BIG QUESTION, OLD FRIEND.
WHO SENT IT?

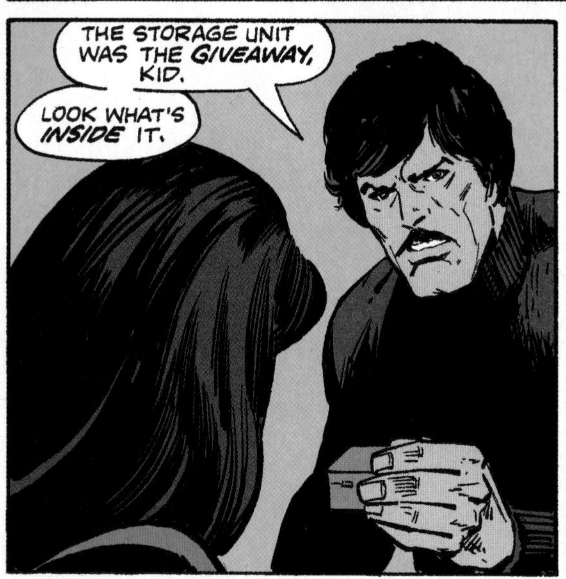
THE STORAGE UNIT WAS THE GIVEAWAY, KID.
LOOK WHAT'S INSIDE IT.

A BLACK PEARL!
IVAN THERE'S ONLY ONE MAN IN ALL THE WORLD WHO WOULD SEND THIS!

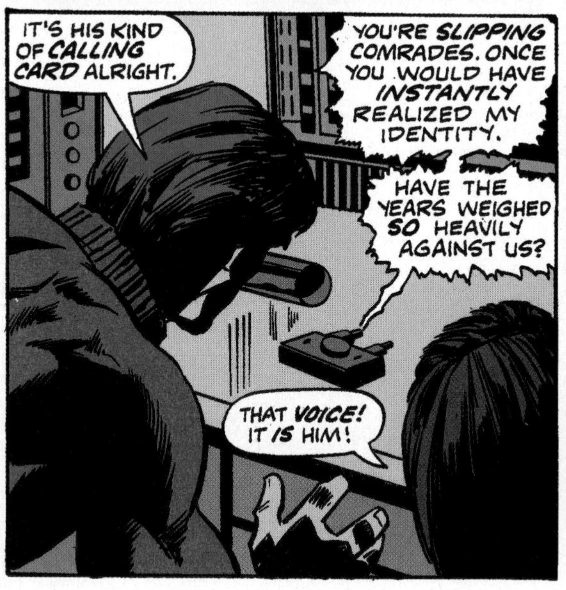
IT'S HIS KIND OF CALLING CARD ALRIGHT.
YOU'RE SLIPPING COMRADES. ONCE YOU WOULD HAVE INSTANTLY REALIZED MY IDENTITY.
HAVE THE YEARS WEIGHED SO HEAVILY AGAINST US?
THAT VOICE! IT IS HIM!

NATURALLY, MY LITTLE TSARINA, AND SHOULD YOU DESIRE FURTHER VERIFICATION, YOU HAVE BUT TO JOIN ME.
I SHALL BE WAITING.
I CAN SEE HIM, IVAN.
HE'S ON THE ROOF ACROSS THE STREET.

THERE'S ONLY ONE WAY TO LEARN WHAT HE WANTS.
NATASHA-- WAIT!
IT MIGHT BE A TRAP!

TRAP? YES, IT COULD BE.
BUT WHY WOULD COMMISSAR BRUSKIN COME AFTER US NOW?

IT'S BEEN YEARS SINCE IVAN AND I DEFECTED TO AMERICA.
THEY ONLY TRIED TO GET ME ONCE--*
*AVENGERS #16--MARV.

--AND THAT ATTEMPT WAS SO CLUMSILY DONE I COULD NEVER BELIEVE BRUSKIN HAD A PART IN IT.
NOT THAT I HAVEN'T HAD AN OCCASIONAL ALTERCATION WITH MY FORMER SOVIET MASTERS IN THE PAST--*
*AVENGERS # 44, FOR ONE --MARV.

--BUT, FOR A LONG TIME NOW, IVAN AND I HAVE STAYED AS FAR REMOVED FROM POLITICS AS POSSIBLE.
CARRYING ON OUR OWN PERSONAL DÉTENTE WITH THOSE WE ONCE SERVED.

WHICH BRINGS US FULL CIRCLE TO THE QUESTION THAT STARTED THIS REVERIE.
WHY DOES ONE OF THE SOVIET UNION'S HIGHEST-RANKED INTELLIGENCE CHIEFS--
--COME TO AMERICA TO SEE THE TWO PEOPLE WHO USED TO BE HIS TOP AGENTS?

HE DUCKED OUT OF SIGHT WHILE I WAS SWINGING OVER HERE.
THIS IS LIKE ONE OF OUR OLD TRAINING EXERCISES.

OH, THERE YOU ARE.
YOU ONCE PLAYED THIS GAME WITH A TOUCH MORE SUBTLETY, OLD TEACHER.
BUT THERE'S SOMETHING YOU SHOULD KNOW.

I DON'T PLAY GAMES ANYMORE!

EXCELLENT-- EXCELLENT!
THAP

HAD I NOT BEEN PREPARED, YOU WOULD HAVE DISARMED ME AND QUITE POSSIBLY BROKEN MY WRIST!
SO IT IS YOU.
AFTER ALL THESE YEARS...

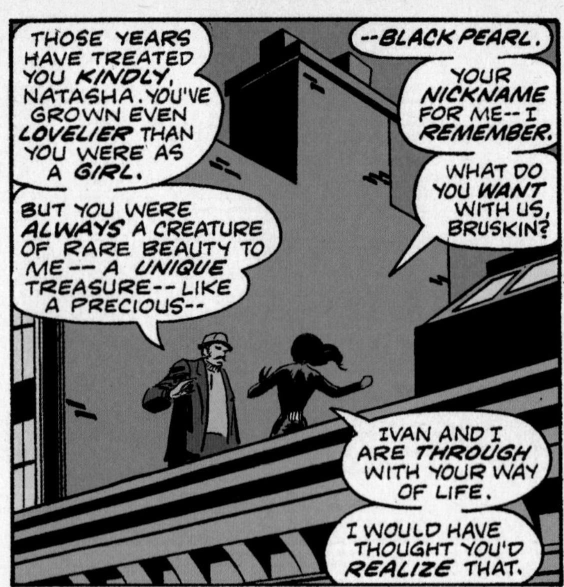
THOSE YEARS HAVE TREATED YOU KINDLY, NATASHA. YOU'VE GROWN EVEN LOVELIER THAN YOU WERE AS A GIRL.
BUT YOU WERE ALWAYS A CREATURE OF RARE BEAUTY TO ME -- A UNIQUE TREASURE -- LIKE A PRECIOUS--
--BLACK PEARL.
YOUR NICKNAME FOR ME-- I REMEMBER.
WHAT DO YOU WANT WITH US, BRUSKIN?
IVAN AND I ARE THROUGH WITH YOUR WAY OF LIFE.
I WOULD HAVE THOUGHT YOU'D REALIZE THAT.

I TRAINED YOU, NATASHA.
NO ONE KNOWS YOU BETTER THAN I.
AND YOU KNOW YOU AND IVAN HAVE ALWAYS BEEN MORE THAN AGENTS TO ME.

IT'S GOOD TO SEE YOU AGAIN--
--OLD FRIEND.
WE WILL HAVE A FIT REUNION LATER, TSARINA.

BUT NOW I MUST WARN YOU OF--
ARRGH!
BRUSKIN!

THE TITANIUM MAN!
DON'T WASTE TIME WORRYING ABOUT HIM, WIDOW.
YOUR TROUBLES ARE JUST BEGINNING.
NEXT ISSUE: DARKSTAR-- the GRIFFIN-- the OUTCAST-- RAMPAGE-- AND THREE SUPER-SHOCK SURPRISES! YOU DARE NOT MISS!

THE CHAMPIONS MARVEL COMICS GROUP™

APPROVED BY THE COMICS CODE AUTHORITY

30¢ 8 OCT 02112

HERCULES! BLACK WIDOW! ANGEL! GHOST RIDER! ICEMAN!

THE CHAMPIONS

™

The avenging ANGEL! The deadly BLACK WIDOW! Johnny Blaze, the GHOST RIDER! HERCULES, Prince of Power! The incomparable ICEMAN! Five fighters for justice united to battle for the common man...because the world still needs heroes!
Stan Lee PRESENTS: THE CHAMPIONS
DIVIDE AND CONQUER!
BY THE SILVER BOW OF APOLLO! WHAT MANNER OF BASE TRICK--??
BETTER TAKE ANOTHER LOOK, OLYMPIAN!
BASE THEY SURE AS BLAZES MAY BE-- BUT THIS HERE COWBOY IS LAYIN' ODDS THEY'RE FOR REAL!
WHY DON'T YOU SAY IT, BOY? THEY'VE GOT HER!
JOHNNY'S RIGHT, HERCULES! MUCH AS I HATE TO ADMIT IT--
--IT'D BE PRETTY HARD TO FAKE A BUNCH OF SHOTS LIKE THAT!
BILL MANTLO WRITER / BOB HALL PENCILLER / B. PATTERSON INKER / K. MANTLO LETTERER / D. WARFIELD COLORIST / ARCHIE GOODWIN EDITOR

THEY'VE TAKEN THE BLACK WIDOW!
YEAH, IVAN. PHOTOGRAPHS CAN GIVE YOU THAT KIND OF INFORMATION...
... BUT WHAT DO THEY TELL YOU OF THE DESPERATION INVOLVED IN AVOIDING BURST AFTER BURST OF SEARING ENERGY?
THEY CAN TELL YOU THAT THE UNCONSCIOUS MAN WITH NATASHA IS AN OLD COMRADE--ALEXI BRUSKIN, THE COMMISSAR...

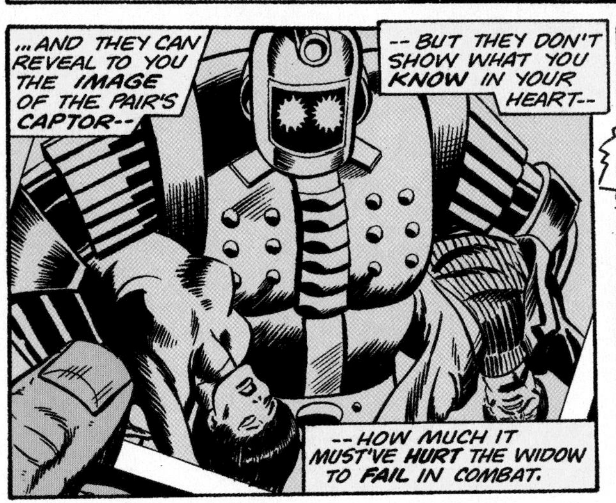
...AND THEY CAN REVEAL TO YOU THE IMAGE OF THE PAIR'S CAPTOR--
--BUT THEY DON'T SHOW WHAT YOU KNOW IN YOUR HEART--
--HOW MUCH IT MUST'VE HURT THE WIDOW TO FAIL IN COMBAT.

HERCULES HATH SEEN ENOW!
THERE IS KNAVERY HERE STILL TO BE DEALT WITH!

IF YOU MEAN ME, WHISKERS, YOU MIGHT AS WELL SAVE YOUR BREATH!
'CAUSE RAMPAGE DOESN'T SCARE!
AT LEAST NOT WHILE I'M HOLDING ALL THE ACES!
METHINKS, MORTAL--THAT THOU DOST PLACE TOO MUCH TRUST IN THY POSITION AS COURIER--
--AND THAT ONCE THINE ARMOR IS PEELED OFF --THOU WILT SPEAK MORE CIVILLY TO THY BETTERS!
EASE OFF, HERCULES! THE WIDOW AND ME ARE REAL CLOSE, PAL--

--SO I'M TELLIN' YA TO LEAVE THIS CLOWN TO ME!
WHERE IS SHE, CLARKE?
I WAS GETTING TO THAT, RUSSKI! DON'T RUSH ME OR I MIGHT JUST UP AND LEAVE--
--AND THEN YOU'LL NEVER KNOW HOW TO GET HER BACK--

--OR WHY THE TITANIUM MAN KIDNAPPED HER IN THE FIRST PLACE!
WHY YOU--!

COME ON THEN, LITTLE MAN! I ALMOST PULPED YOU ONCE--*
--I GUESS I CAN DO IT AGAIN!
BY MY MACE!
FENSTER! YOU AND BALE STAY BACK!
*CHAMPIONS #6--ARCHIE.

IVAN! THE POWER IN THAT EXO-SKELETON SUIT OF HIS'LL TURN YOU INTO PUDDING!
THE MAN AIN'T UP FOR LISTENIN', FROSTY!
NOT WITH THE WIDOW AT STAKE!

I KNOW YOU AIN'T THE BRAINS BEHIND THIS CAPER, CLARKE! ALL YOU EVER CARED ABOUT WAS THE DOUGH!
AN' I AIN'T PUT TOGETHER ALL THE PIECES YET-- BUT THE ONES I HAVE ALL COME OUT SPELLIN' "MOTHER RUSSIA!"
I'M NOT GETTING PAID TO KNOW, RUSSKI--

--BUT AS LONG AS I GET PAID-- I COULD CARE LESS!
BUT I DO KNOW ONE THING! THE DUDE WHO'S RUNNING THIS IS REALLY HOT TO MEET YOU!
I DON'T KNOW WHO HE IS, CHUM --BUT HE CALLS HIMSELF--

--THE OUTCAST!

LIAR!!
WHA-TAM!

BY ZEUS, FRIEND -- T'WAS QUITE A BLOW!
NEARLY BROKE MY BLASTED HAND, "FRIEND"--
--BUT IT WAS WORTH IT!

MAYBE--BUT LAUGHIN' BOY'S SHAKIN' IT OFF LIKE IT WAS NUTHIN'!
LET HIM, BLAZE!
WE'VE TAKEN ABOUT ALL WE'RE GOING TO TAKE FROM YOU, CLARKE!
AT FIRST I THOUGHT YOU WERE MISGUIDED--

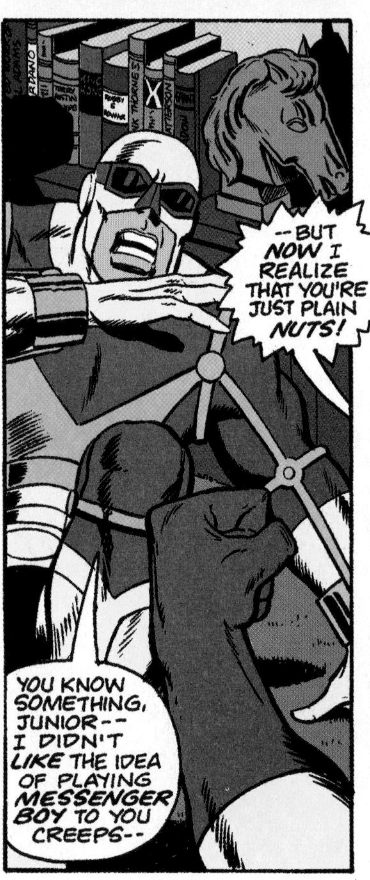
--BUT NOW I REALIZE THAT YOU'RE JUST PLAIN NUTS!
YOU KNOW SOMETHING, JUNIOR-- I DIDN'T LIKE THE IDEA OF PLAYING MESSENGER BOY TO YOU CREEPS--

--BUT NOW I'M BEGINNING TO THINK OF WAYS TO TURN IT INTO--

--FUN!!
CRUNCH
BUT FIRST THINGS, FIRST!
I ALWAYS WAS A BUSINESSMAN--

--AND I ALWAYS LET MY PLEASURE WAIT UNTIL THE END OF A TRANSACTION!
WHEN IT'S SWEETEST!
STAY TUNED, CHAMPIONS! ONCE I PRESS THIS STUD--
--YOU'RE GONNA HAVE YOUR FIRST VERBAL CONTACT WITH MY EMPLOYER! DIRECT FROM--
--HELL!
BJH-TWOOM!
YEEARGHHH!
BY ALL THE GODS THERE BE--
--THE MAN IS MAD!!
SEEMED TO ME THAT HE LOOKED AS STUNNED AS WE ARE!
HERC'S BODY SHIELDED IVAN--
--AND THIS ICE-SCREEN'LL KEEP THE REST OF US ALIVE--

"--BUT WHY IN HEAVEN'S NAME WOULD SOMEBODY JUST BLOW HIMSELF UP??!"
IT IS DONE!
SO MUCH FOR OUR POOR MR. CLARKE!
WHY FEEL SORRY FOR RAMPAGE, LADY?

THE LITTLE TWERP GOT THE MONEY HE WAS AFTER! THAT'S ALL HE EVER WANTED!
HOW WAS HE TO KNOW HE WASN'T GONNA LIVE TO ENJOY IT?
'LESS ONE OF US WAS TO'VE TOLD HIM--AN' RUINED EVERYTHING!

I'M NOT AS COLD AS YOU, GRIFFIN--OR AS DESIROUS OF ANOTHER'S DEATH--
--UNLESS IT IS ABSOLUTELY NECESSARY!
OH, BUT IT WAS, LADY! IT WAS!

LEASTWAYS THAT'S WHAT OUR "MASTER" KEEPS TELLIN' US, AIN'T IT?
PERHAPS. BUT YURI ONLY COMMANDS MY OBEDIENCE, GRIFFIN--
--NOT MY CONSCIENCE. THAT ALONE HAS BEEN LEFT TO DARKSTAR... MAY HEAVEN HELP ME!

AND WHILE WE PONDER THE MEANING OF THE MYSTERIOUS LADY'S PARTING WORDS, LET US RETURN TO...
GET OUT OF HERE, ALL OF YOU!--BEFORE THE FLAMES BLOCK THE EXITS!
FIRE AND FUMES DON'T BOTHER ME! I'LL RECOVER RAMPAGE'S BODY!

NO! STAND FAST! WE CAN'T LET THIS BUILDING DO A TOWERING INFERNO!
I'LL HANDLE THIS--

-- WITH AN INSTANT INDOOR SNOWSTORM!
FSSST
NICE WORK!

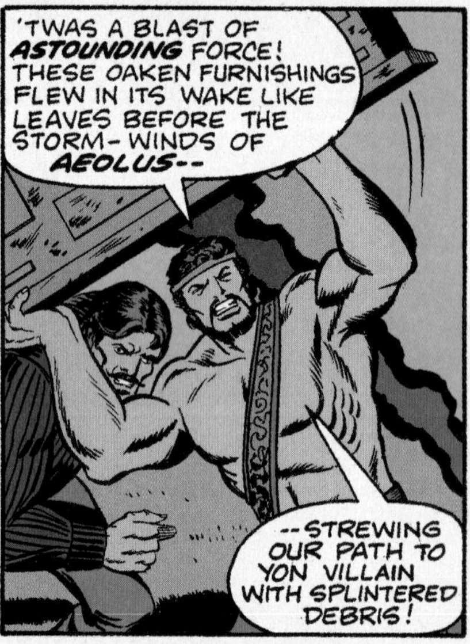
'TWAS A BLAST OF ASTOUNDING FORCE! THESE OAKEN FURNISHINGS FLEW IN ITS WAKE LIKE LEAVES BEFORE THE STORM-WINDS OF AEOLUS--
--STREWING OUR PATH TO YON VILLAIN WITH SPLINTERED DEBRIS!

IS IT SAFE FOR US MERE MORTALS NOW, WARREN?
I BELIEVE SO, MR. FENSTER.
I DIDN'T REALIZE BEING THE CHAMPION'S LAWYER WOULD INVOLVE THIS KIND OF... DANGER!

FROSTY! RAMPAGE IS STILL BREATHING!
DON'T MOVE HIM! HE PROBABLY HAS INTERNAL INJURIES!
FENSTER! FIND A PHONE THAT STILL WORKS AND CALL AN AMBULANCE!

WHAT A WASTE! THIS GUY BUILDS A SUIT CAPABLE OF MIRACLES--
--AND AN INSANE OBSESSION FOR MONEY BRINGS HIM TO THIS.
YOU DON'T KNOW WHAT IT'S LIKE TO BE BROKE--WHAT IT CAN DO TO YOU!
I... GUESS NOT!

TABLEAU: FIVE BEINGS OF GREAT SKILL AND POWER --IN ONLY A MOMENT RENDERED TOTALLY HELPLESS--
--SILENCED, AS ANOTHER BEING LIES DYING IN THEIR MIDST.

BUT ONE OF THOSE FIVE REFUSES TO ALLOW EVEN DEATH TO CHEAT HIM OF THAT WHICH HE MUST KNOW.
THE OUTCAST, CLARKE! WHO IS HE?? WHAT'S HE DONE WITH THE WIDOW??
YOU'RE NOT GONNA DIE WITHOUT TELLIN' ME, BLAST YOU!!
BIG... WORDS, RUSSKI.

I'M FINISHED... AN' I... KNOW IT. I... STUPID! LET 'EM ... DOUBLE-CROSS... ME!
IT WAS... OUTCAST WHO... DID IT... ALL.
SAID YOU AN' HIM WERE... TIGHT! ... SAID YOU'D... KNOW WHO HE WAS--
--FROM A LONG WAY ... BACK...

CLARKE!!
I CAN STILL FEEL A PULSE ...WEAK, BUT HE'S ALIVE!

ALIVE AND USELESS! THE LADY'S STILL GONE--
--AND WE'RE LEFT WITH NOTHING BUT RIDDLES!
TRAM
RELAX, IVAN! THE PLACE DOESN'T NEED TO BE BUSTED UP ANY MORE--
--AND BEATING UP WALLS ISN'T GOING TO GET US TO THE WIDOW ANY FASTER!

THE WINGED YOUTH DOTH SPEAK ARIGHT, FRIEND IVAN! FORTH-WITH, OUR ENERGIES SHALL BE FULLY DEVOTED TO RESCUING THE BEAUTEOUS BLACK WIDOW! SO VOWS THE PRINCE OF POWER!
YA THINK ANY OF YA KNOW WHAT THE WIDOW MEANS TO ME!
YA THINK KNOWIN' HER FOR A FEW WEEKS EVEN GIVES YA THE RIGHT TO CARE--
--THE WAY I'VE CARED FOR YEARS?!?

I DON'T THINK IT MUCH MATTERS!
THE LADY JOINED THIS TEAM --
-- AN' IN MY BOOK OUR CARIN' COMES WITH THE JOB!
BUT I'M THROUGH WAITIN' AROUND, FRIENDS! CLARKE, HERE, ISN'T GONNA LAST TILL THAT AMBULANCE COMES! I'M TAKIN' HIM TO THE HOSPITAL NOW!

-- AND WHEN I COME BACK, WE GO TO FIND THE WIDOW -- OR I GO ALONE!
WAIT, BLAZE! I'LL TAKE HIM! I'M FASTER!

I'LL RACE YOU SOME-TIME, WINGS, BUT FOR NOW, STAY OUTTA MY WAY!

GOOD LORD! I -- I JUST REALIZED SOMETHING!
THAT SKULL! IT'S NOT A MASK!!
WHY DO YOU THINK I HAD TO SIT DOWN, MR. FENSTER?
FRIGHTENING. MOST FRIGHTENING.

AND AFTER A SOMEWHAT RATTLED EMERSON BALE HAS LEFT TO RESUME THE MORE DOWN-TO-EARTH TASK OF PRACTICING LAW...
ALL RIGHT, PEOPLE-- LISTEN UP! JOHNNY BLAZE HAS TAKEN CARE OF OUR MOST IMMEDIATE PROBLEM--
--BUT AS YOUR PAID-TO-PRODUCE PUBLIC RELATIONS MAN, I THINK I'D BETTER REMIND YOU OF ANOTHER YOU SEEM TO HAVE FORGOTTEN!
NAMELY THAT IN TWO HOURS THE PARK OUTSIDE THIS BUILDING IS GOING TO BE THE SCENE OF A GALA OCCASION!
THE OFFICIAL INAUGURATION OF THE SPANKING NEW SUPER-GROUP CALLED THE CHAMPIONS!
AND LET ME TELL YOU, FRIENDS-- BOTH YOU AND YOUR TEMPORARY H.Q. LOOK A MESS.
MAYBE WE'D BETTER CANCEL, DICK! WITH THE WIDOW AND GHOST RIDER BOTH GONE--
-- THE GLAD TIDINGS JUST DON'T SEEM TO MAKE ALL THAT MUCH SENSE ANYMORE!

YOU SURE GOT A ROTTEN SENSE OF TIMIN', FLY-BOY! JUST WHEN I WAS ABOUT TO UP AN' ADMIT THAT MAYBE NATASHA WAS RIGHT IN JOININ' THIS GROUP--
--YOU WANNA THROW IN THE TOWEL AN' DISSOLVE IT!

YOU GUYS MAKE ME LAUGH!
IVAN! WAIT!
NOT A CHANCE, BUB!

HOW COME I SUDDENLY FEEL LIKE A LEPER?
'TIS NOT US, STRIPLING--BUT RAGING AGAINST HELPLESSNESS THAT DOTH DRIVE IVAN FROM US!
FAR BE IT FROM ME TO ADVISE A GOD, HERCULES--
--BUT I THINK IVAN'S OLD ENOUGH TO TAKE CARE OF HIMSELF!

AND WHILE HE COOLS OFF IN THE LAB, FIGURING OUT A WAY TO TRACK DOWN THE WIDOW--
--I SUGGEST WE MAKE LIKE WHITE TORNADOES AND GET THIS PLACE IN SHAPE!
REMIND ME, FRIEND FENSTER, TO TELL THEE SOME TIME OF ONE OF MY MANY LABORS--
--INVOLVING THE CLEANSING OF A KING'S STABLE!
SOUNDS LIKE A LOT OF MANURE IF YOU ASK ME!

AND I'M BEGINNING TO THINK THIS K.P. SCENE IS FOR THE BIRDS!
IF YOU DON'T MIND GROUP--I THINK I'LL GO AND GIVE OUR RESIDENT RUSSIAN A LITTLE MORAL SUPPORT!
GO AHEAD, BOBBY. I'M SURE OUR "HONORED GUESTS" AND GENTLEMEN OF THE PRESS--
--WILL BE JUST AS BORED WITH ONLY HERCULES AND I AS THEY WOULD BE BY THE PRESENCE OF THE WHOLE GROUP!

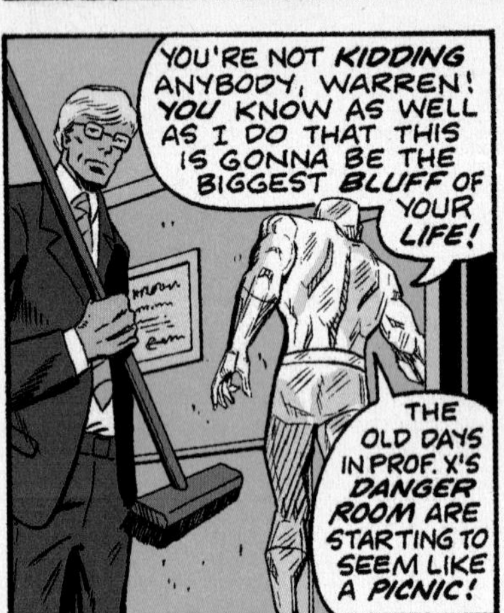
YOU'RE NOT KIDDING ANYBODY, WARREN! YOU KNOW AS WELL AS I DO THAT THIS IS GONNA BE THE BIGGEST BLUFF OF YOUR LIFE!
THE OLD DAYS IN PROF. X'S DANGER ROOM ARE STARTING TO SEEM LIKE A PICNIC!

HE'S RIGHT, YOU KNOW.
BELIEVE ME, DICK --I KNOW!
AND EVEN REPLACING THIS RUINED COSTUME WITH A NEW ONE ISN'T GOING TO THROW A HORDE OF DISASTER-HUNGRY NEWSMEN OFF THE SCENT WHEN THEY START TO SMELL TROUBLE
YOU RECKON WITHOUT THE PRINCE OF POWER, LAD!

WITH HERCULES AT THY SIDE THE MORTALS WILL GIVE NOT A THOUGHT TO ANYTHING BUT THE MAGNIFICENCE OF OUR PRESENCE!
ESPECIALLY IF THERE BE LADIES IN THE AUDIENCE.

FORGIVE US NOW AS WE TRAVEL ACROSS LOS ANGELES TO THE SEA-SIDE OLDER SECTION KNOWN AS VENICE...
...AND FOCUS IN ON A ONCE-ABANDONED WAREHOUSE...

...ABANDONED NO LONGER.
THE WOMAN IS NATASHA ROMANOFF -- BETTER KNOWN TO THE WORLD AS THE BEAUTEOUS BLACK WIDOW.
THE MAN IS ALEXI BRUSKIN --EX-RUSSIAN KGB CHIEF KNOWN AS THE COMMISSAR...
...AND ALSO THE WIDOW'S TEACHER.*
*LAST ISH--ARCH.

TOO BAD THAT TEACHING WASN'T ENOUGH TO ENABLE HER TO DEAL WITH THE ENERGY-BLASTS OF AN ARMOR-CLAD FOE.
AH. SO YOU ARE AWAKE MADAME NATASHA!
WHO--?

I AM CALLED DARKSTAR, TZARINA --AND THE OTHERS HAVE MADE ME YOUR JAILER.
DO YOU REQUIRE ANYTHING, MADAME?
ONLY ANSWERS, MY FRIEND. WHO ARE THESE OTHERS?

THERE ARE ONLY THREE BESIDES MYSELF, TZARINA. COMRADE BULLSKI-- THE TITANIUM MAN-- YOU HAVE ALREADY MET--
--WHICH LEAVES ONLY THE GRIFFIN--
--AND YURI!

BUT YOU AND THE COMMISAR WILL MEET US ALL. SOON!
IS BRUSKIN ALL RIGHT!
HE WAS HIT SO HARD--

ONLY AS HARD AS WAS NECESSARY, COMRADE WIDOW!
SO! MY CAPTOR RETURNS!
WHAT NEWS, COMRADE?

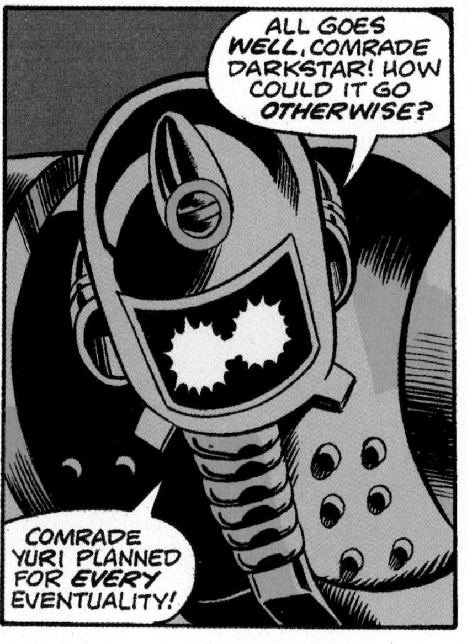
ALL GOES WELL, COMRADE DARKSTAR! HOW COULD IT GO OTHERWISE?
COMRADE YURI PLANNED FOR EVERY EVENTUALITY!

BUT IT SEEMS INAPPROPRIATE TO SPEAK OF SUCH THINGS IN FRONT OF OUR GUESTS!
I... SUPPOSE SO, COMRADE! BUT SHE MUST KNOW WHAT IS TO BECOME OF HER--

--AND WHY SHE IS WANTED--
--HOME!
JUST ONE WORD... YET IT IS THE PREFACE TO DESPAIR.

DO I DETECT CONCERN IN YOU FOR AN ENEMY OF THE STATE, COMRADE?
YURI WOULD NOT BE... PLEASED!
THAT IS FOR YURI TO SAY, TITANIUM MAN!
AND I SENSE THERE IS MORE IN YURI'S ATTACK ON THE FAMOUS BLACK WIDOW THAN A MERE DESIRE TO SERVE HIS COUNTRY!
SHE IS... BEAUTIFUL, COMRADE!

TALK! THAT'S ALL YOU RUSSKIES EVER DO--AN' THE GRIFFIN IS GETTIN' SICK OF IT!
WHEN DO WE TEAR INTO THEM, TIN MAN? WHEN DO I MAKE THE ANGEL CRAWL?
WHEN WE GIVE THE WORD, IMPATIENT ONE!
TZRAK!
WHAT--??
WRONG, COMRADE!

IT IS NOT WHEN "WE" GIVE THE WORD, MY FRIEND--
BUT WHEN I GIVE IT!
IT IS THE CRIMSON DYNAMO WHO LEADS!

THE NEW CRIMSON DYNAMO! I--YURI PETROVITCH!
GIVEN BY THE STATE THE HONOR OF RETURNING THREE EMBARRASSING DEFECTORS! THE BLACK WIDOW... THE COMMISSAR...
...AND ONE OTHER...

"...IVAN PETROVITCH!"
"MY FATHER!!"
OKAY, IVAN--I GIVE UP! I'VE WATCHED YOU TINKER IN THAT LAB FOR THE PAST HOUR--
--AND I STILL HAVEN'T GOT THE FAINTEST IDEA WHAT YOU'VE ACCOMPLISHED!

IT'S A TRACKING SCOPE, KID!
FINE. ONLY WHAT IS IT SUPPOSED TO TRACK?
THIS!
LOOKS LIKE A BLACK PEARL!

IT IS! AND OF A KIND CARRIED BY ONLY ONE MAN IN THE WORLD! ALEXI-BRUSKIN -- THE COMMISSAR!
SEE! ALREADY FREQUENCY IS SHOWING UP ON THE SCOPE! THE PEARL HAS A COMPANION NEARBY.
AND WHERE BRUSKIN IS --THAT'S WHERE I'M BETTIN' WE'LL FIND THE WIDOW!

THEN WHAT'RE WE WAITIN' FOR, FRIEND?
A QUICK ICE-SLIDE WILL HELP US BEAT THE L.A. TRAFFIC SITUATION--

--AND AN ICE-RIGGED SLED WILL ENABLE YOU TO KEEP UP WITH ME!
KID-- I APPOLOGIZE FOR THE WAY I BUSTED UP BEFORE!
YOU GET ME TO THE WIDOW-- AND I'LL SEE THAT YOU'RE KEPT IN POPSICLES FOR A YEAR.
YOU'RE ON! AS LONG AS YOU KNOCK IT OFF WITH THE "KID" STUFF... GRAMPS!

AND ACROSS TOWN, YET ANOTHER CHAMPION HAS FOUND A WAY TO BEAT THE RUSH HOUR.
LOS ANGELES HOSPITAL IS JUST UP AHEAD--
--BUT I LOST TRACK OF CLARKE'S HEARTBEAT ABOUT TEN MINUTES AGO!
I HOPE I HAVEN'T OUT-EVILED KNIEVEL FOR NOTHING!
NO. UNH-UNH. NO WAY.
MUST BE THE SMOG IN MY EYES!
YEAH. IT'S GOTTA BE!

MADE IT!
AND PROBABLY SET A RECORD FOR FLAMING SKULL-CYCLES AROUND THE WORLD!
WHAT THE BLAZES--
I BRING YOU A FELLOW MORTAL IN NEED OF AID, HUMAN!
HOSPITAL
SPEEEE

HEY! YOU JUST CAN'T BARGE IN LIKE THIS AND DUMP A DEAD MAN ON US!
NOT WITHOUT AN EXPLANATION!
NO PARK
SUCH AN EXPLANATION WOULD MEAN THIS MORTAL'S DEATH--

--AND YOU, FOOL, WOULD BE HELD ACCOUNTABLE FOR IT!
SEE TO IT THAT HE IS CARED FOR--
--OR I WILL RETURN AND SEEK YOU OUT!

HUH? OH, YEAH!
SURE!
WHATEVER YOU SAY!
QUIT YAMMERIN'! WE GOT US A PATIENT!
EXIT
EMERGENCY
AMBULANCE

AND...
I THOUGHT I DITCHED THIS OUTFIT WHEN I LEFT THE X-MEN!
IT WAKES UP A LOT OF MEMORIES, DICK!
I WISH YOU'D TOLD ME THAT BEFORE YOU POINTED OUT THAT I'D GOT THE COLORS WRONG!

I CAN LIVE WITH IT!
YOU'RE GONNA HAVE TO, FLY-BOY!
BECAUSE WE'VE JUST RUN OUT OF TIME!
HUH?

TAKE A LOOK!
THEY'RE HERE!!
MOST OF LOS ANGELES!
HERE'S WHERE YOU MAKE HISTORY, WARREN--

"-- AND BELIEVE ME, I WISH YOU LUCK!!"
CANST THOU TASTE THEIR ADORATION, WINGED ONE?
'TIS AS SWEET AS THE AMBROSIA ON HIGH OLYMPUS!
AND MAYBE TOO SWEET FOR A MERE MORTAL, HERCULES!
TODAY IS A DAY OF HISTORY AS THE WHOLE WORLD WATCHES THE DEDICATION OF A NEW SUPER-TEAM--
I REMEMBER THE DAY THE FANTASTIC FOUR GOT STARTED! IT'S THE SAME FEELING NOW!

I UNDERSTOOD THERE WERE FIVE OF THEM, PIERRE.
THERE ARE RUMORS, GOVERNOR, THAT--
WELCOME CHAMPS
GOVERNOR BROWN! THIS IS AN HONOR!
HERE COMES THEIR P.R. FLACK, GOVERNOR!
WE CAN BEGIN NOW, ANGEL!

AND MOMENTS LATER...
SPEAK TRUE, FRIEND ANGEL-- FOR THOU DOST SPEAK FOR HERCULES!
I'LL DO MY BEST, TEAMMATE!
LADIES AND GENTLEMEN! TODAY I GIVE YOU THE START OF A DREAM! THE EMERGENCE ON THE AMERICAN SCENE OF A GROUP OF INDIVIDUALS--
--DEDICATED TO FIGHTING FOR EVERY INDIVIDUAL'S RIGHT TO BE FREE!
I WROTE IT, ANGEL--BUT YOU'RE MAKING ME BELIEVE IT!
I GIVE YOU... THE BIRTH OF THE CHAMPIONS!!

NEXT: THE BATTLE OF LOS ANGELES!

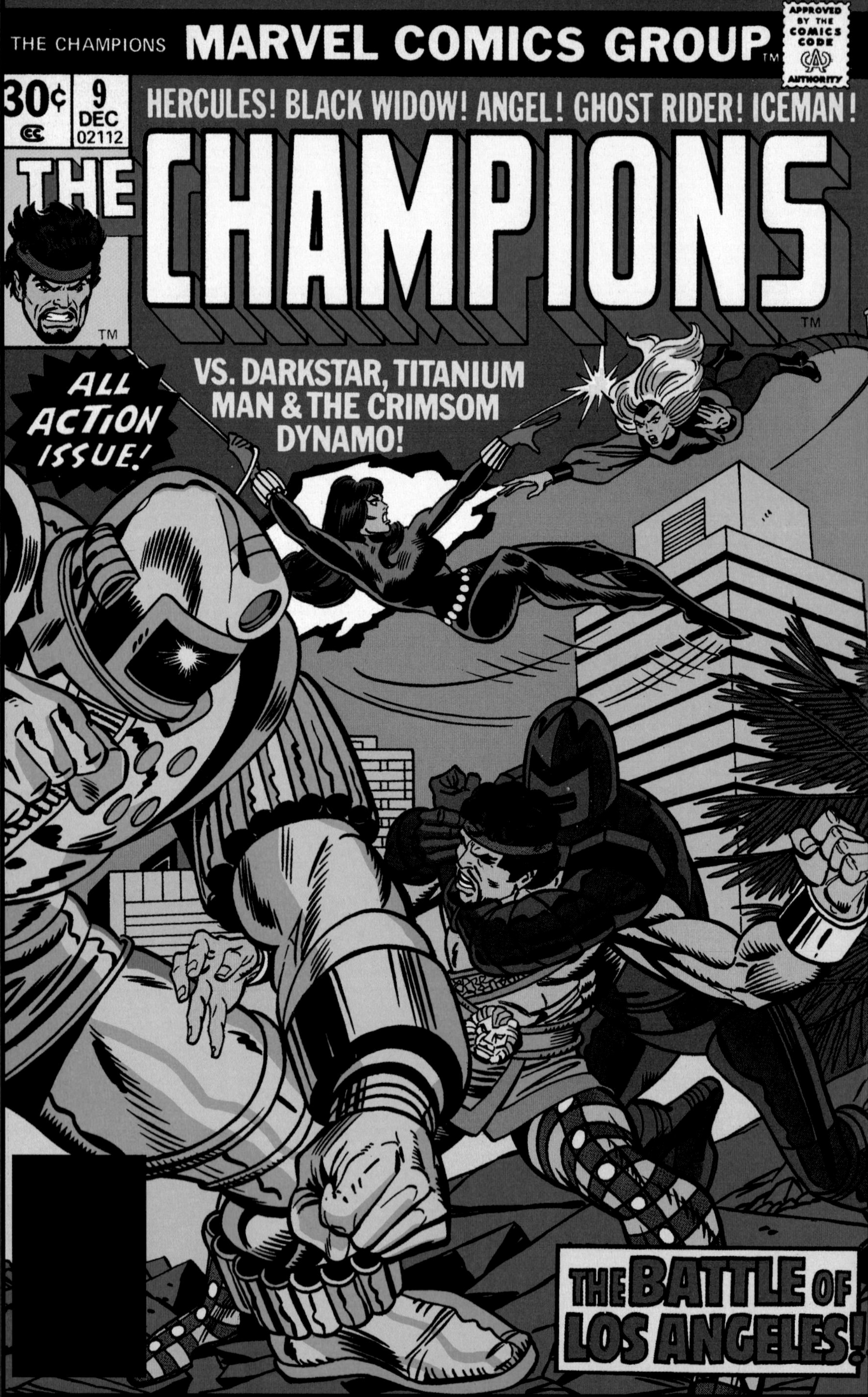

THE CHAMPIONS **MARVEL COMICS GROUP**™

APPROVED BY THE COMICS CODE CA AUTHORITY

30¢ 9 DEC 02112

HERCULES! BLACK WIDOW! ANGEL! GHOST RIDER! ICEMAN!

THE CHAMPIONS™

ALL ACTION ISSUE!

VS. DARKSTAR, TITANIUM MAN & THE CRIMSOM DYNAMO!

THE BATTLE OF LOS ANGELES!

The avenging ANGEL! The deadly BLACK WIDOW! Johnny Blaze, the GHOST RIDER! HERCULES, Prince of Power! The incomparable ICEMAN! Five fighters for justice united to battle for the common man...because the world still needs heroes!

Stan Lee PRESENTS: # THE CHAMPIONS

C-112 TM

BILL MANTLO WRITER / BOB HALL ARTIST / BOB LAYTON INKER / KAREN MANTLO LETTERER / DON WARFIELD COLORIST / A. GOODWIN EDITOR

WE'VE BEEN SET UP! THE TITANIUM MAN ... THE GRIFFIN ... AND THE CRIMSON DYNAMO! HOW CAN JUST THE TWO OF US STAND AGAINST THEM?
THIS IS THE END OF YOUR INANE ORGANIZATION, ANGEL! THIS WILL BE YOUR FINAL BATTLE!
FORGET THE SPEECHES RUSSKI! POWER THE ONLY THING THAT MATTER NOW!

STRIKE UPON MY ORDER COMRADES!
THEN COME YE, VILLAINS ALL! STAND FORTH AND FACE THE FURY OF HERCULES-- THE PRINCE OF POWER!!
ONLY A FAST AND DECISIVE VICTORY WILL PREVENT TOTAL CHAOS!
AND THAT IS TO BE DENIED YOU, FOOL!
WE HAVE ALREADY TAKEN THE BLACK WIDOW, AND IT IS ONLY A MATTER OF MOMENTS BEFORE YOU AND THE WINGED ONE FALL TO US!

WANNA BET, DYNAMO?
YOU'RE TALKING TO A GUY WHO USED TO BE KNOWN AS THE AVENGING ANGEL, MISTER!
I TOOK EVERYTHING THAT WAS THROWN AT THE X-MEN--

--AND STILL CAME UP ACES!
WHAP
AND I DIDN'T FORM THE CHAMPIONS BECAUSE I THOUGHT THEY WERE A LOSING PROPOSITION!

OFFICER! GET GOVERNOR BROWN TO SAFETY, MAN!
THEY'RE ATTACKING THE PODIUM, GOVERNOR!
HAVE THE NATIONAL GUARD ALERTED! IF THIS ESCALATES INTO A FULL-SCALE BATTLE, I'LL DECLARE A STATE OF EMERGENCY.

STAND THEE BEHIND ME, DICK FENSTER!
YOU SHOULD GIVE LESS THOUGHT TO OTHERS--

--AND MORE TO DEFENDING YOURSELF!
WA-TOOOM

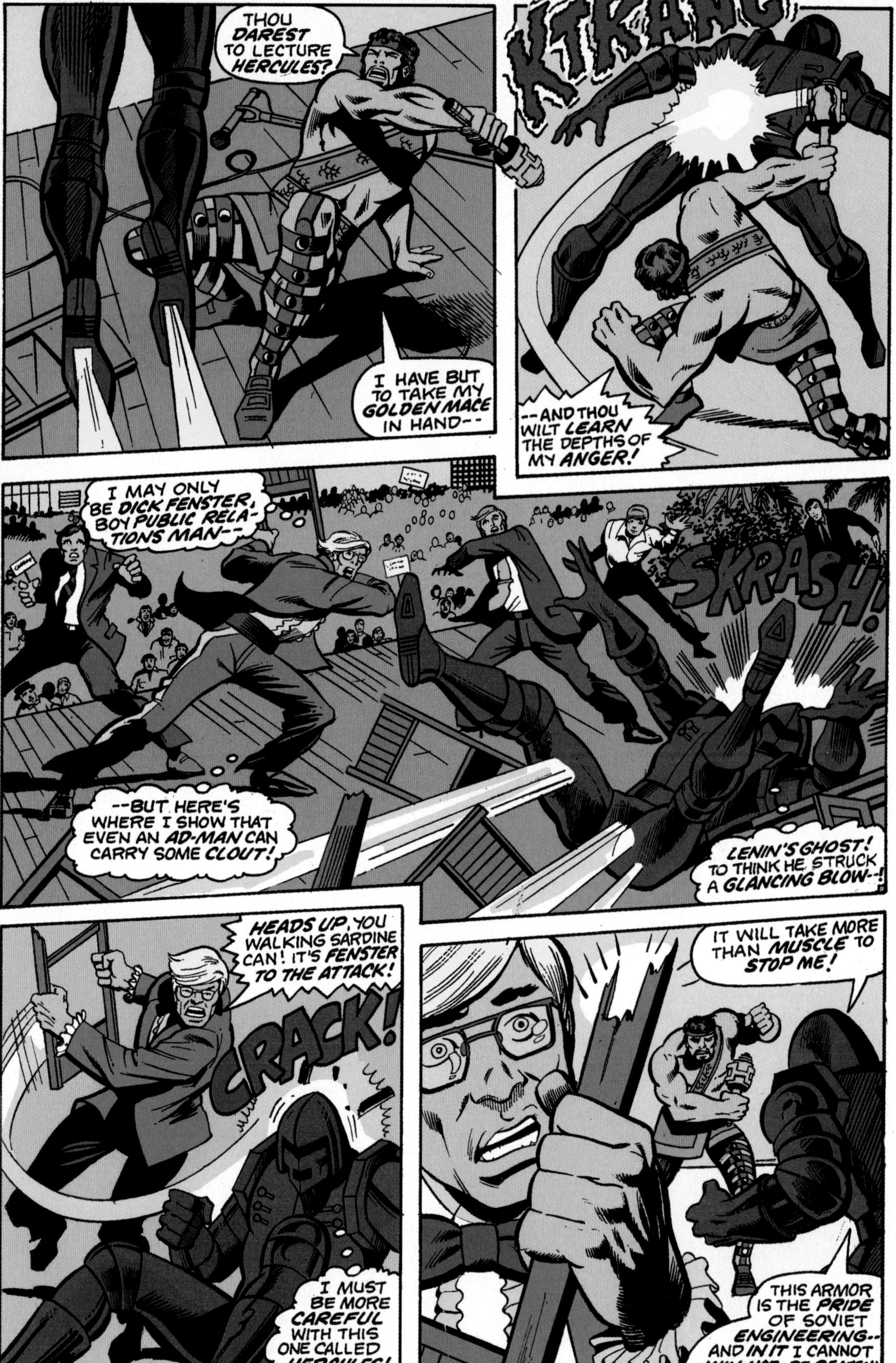

THOU *DAREST* TO LECTURE *HERCULES?*

I HAVE BUT TO TAKE MY *GOLDEN MACE* IN HAND--

KTRANG

--AND THOU WILT *LEARN* THE DEPTHS OF MY *ANGER!*

I MAY ONLY BE *DICK FENSTER,* BOY *PUBLIC RELATIONS MAN*--

SKRASH!

--BUT HERE'S WHERE I SHOW THAT EVEN AN *AD-MAN* CAN CARRY SOME *CLOUT!*

LENIN'S GHOST! TO THINK HE STRUCK A *GLANCING BLOW*--!

AND AT THAT MOMENT...
RAMPAGE IS IN THE HANDS OF THE DOCS NOW-- BUT THEY WEREN'T LAYIN' ODDS ON HIS SURVIVAL!
WHOA! THERE'S A CROWD UP AHEAD-- AROUND OUR TEMPORARY HEADQUARTERS!
THERE! IT'S THE STUNT-RIDER!
THE ONE THAT ALMOST STOPPED ME AT THE HOSPITAL!*
THE GRIFFIN! HERE!?
OF COURSE! THE INAUGURATION MUST'VE STARTED ALREADY! I MIGHT HAVE MADE IT BACK IN TIME IF I HADN'T HAD TO STOP AT THE STUDIO TO PICK UP MY REAL BIKE. COULDN'T SHOW UP HERE AS JOHNNY BLAZE ASTRIDE A MYSTIC FLAME CYCLE!
SKREEEEEE
*CHAMPIONS #7--ARCH.

SO THAT'S WHY THEY SENT RAMPAGE TO BLOW HIMSELF UP!
THEY MUSTA FIGURED ON DIVIDING US--
--AN' THEN PICKIN' OFF THE PIECES!
YOU'RE GONNA BE THE EASIEST TO GET RID OF, COWBOY!
WORDS, CREATURE!

NOW, GRIFFIN! STRIKE NOW WHILE HE IS SURROUNDED BY THE CROWD!
THE GHOST-LIKE YOUTH--HE WHO DOTH SEND A COLD CHILL THROUGH MY BEING!
HE IS IN DANGER!

"--YET I DID NOT ALLY MYSELF WITH SOME OF THE CHAMPIONS...BUT WITH ALL!"
KEEP YOUR EYES OPEN, DYNAMO--
--AN' YOU'LL SEE THE GRIFFIN DO IT--
--HIS WAY!
OH, MAN! HERE IT COMES!

NO! IT SHALL NO BE!
FOOL! YOU MISJUDGED YOUR THROW!
YOUR MACE HAS BOUNCED OFF MY ARMOR!

IT WAS NO MISTAKE, MORTAL!

IT WAS MORE A CASE OF GETTIN' THE RIGHT ANGLE SO I'D CATCH IT AND USE ITS MOMENTUM TO LIFT ME ABOVE THE CROWD--
--TO WHERE I CAN BLAST TOE NAILS HERE WITHOUT ZAPPING THE GOOD PEOPLE OF LOS ANGELES!
YAARRR!
CHTAASH

TOUCHDOWN! SAFE, SOUND-- AND AWAY FROM THE MOB!
I OWE THE SON OF ZEUS FOR THAT ONE!

NOW LET'S SEE IF I CAN REPAY IT!
THOR-STYLE!!
GO, MACE--

WHAM!
--GO!

HERCULES THANKS THEE, TEAMMATE!
AND NOW, WITH MACE IN HAND--
ZAAT!

STRANG!
--METHINKS 'TIS TIME TO END THIS FRAY!
BUT WHAT OF THE ONE CALLED ...ANGEL?

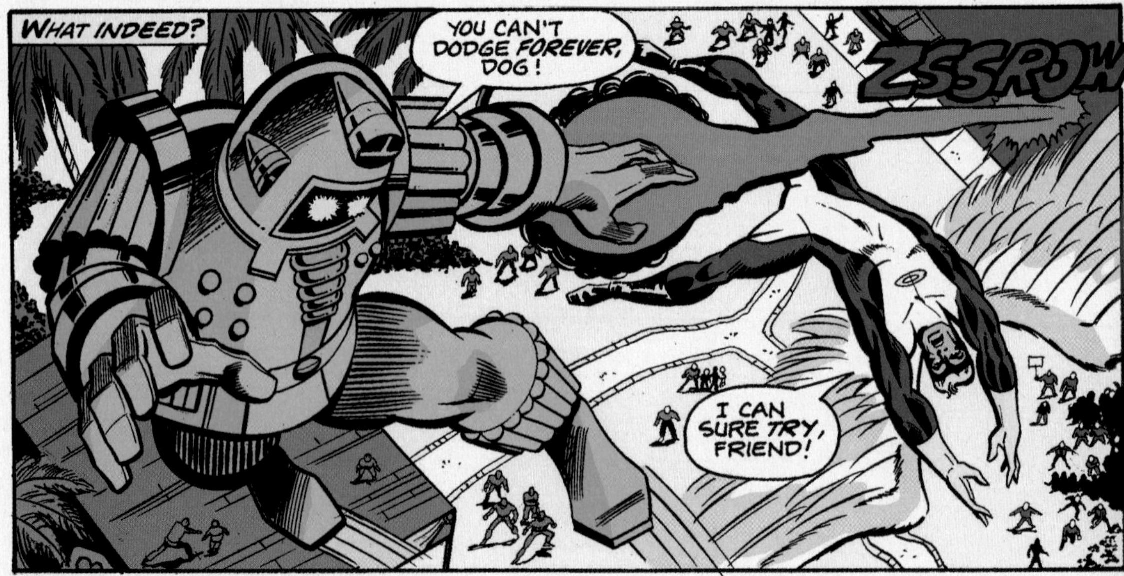
WHAT INDEED?
YOU CAN'T DODGE FOREVER, DOG!
ZSSROW
I CAN SURE TRY, FRIEND!

BUT, SINCE THAT WOULD EVENTUALLY GET BORING, I THINK I'LL SHOW YOU THAT POWER DOESN'T AMOUNT TO BEANS--
--WHEN YOUR OPPONENT'S LIGHTER AND FASTER THAN YOU ARE!
NO! YOU ARE UPSETTING MY CENTER OF BALANCE!

MY OWN BOOT-JETS ARE DRIVING ME EARTHWARDS!

THAT'S JUST GREAT--
--EXCEPT FOR THE FACT THAT HE'S FALLING RIGHT TOWARDS--

"--HERCULES!"
BY ZEUS!

KA-TRAM!

HERC!!
THE JERK! HE'S FORGOTTEN ABOUT ME!
AND TURNED HIS BACK!

SKRIIITT
YEAAGH!

WHAT'S WITH THIS GUY? YA KNOCK HIM OUT AN' HIS MASK DISAPPEARS??
GRIFFIN! IF YOU'VE HURT HIM, I'LL--

YOU WILL DO NOTHING, ANGEL--
STRAMM!

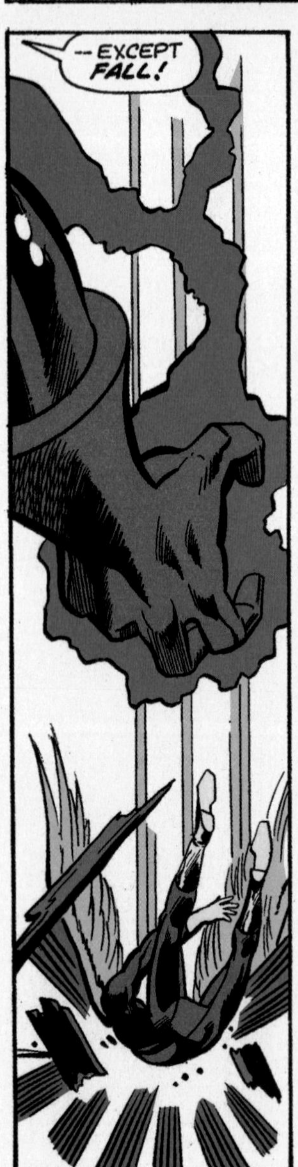
--EXCEPT FALL!

HEY! WE DONE IT!
WE POLISHED OFF THE CHAMPIONS!
ALL SAVE THE ICEMAN!
HE CAN BE DEALT WITH, COMRADE! ALL THAT CONCERNS US IS THAT IVAN PETROVITCH IS NOW UNGUARDED--
--AND HIS DAY OF RECKONING IS AT HAND!!
WELCO
CHA

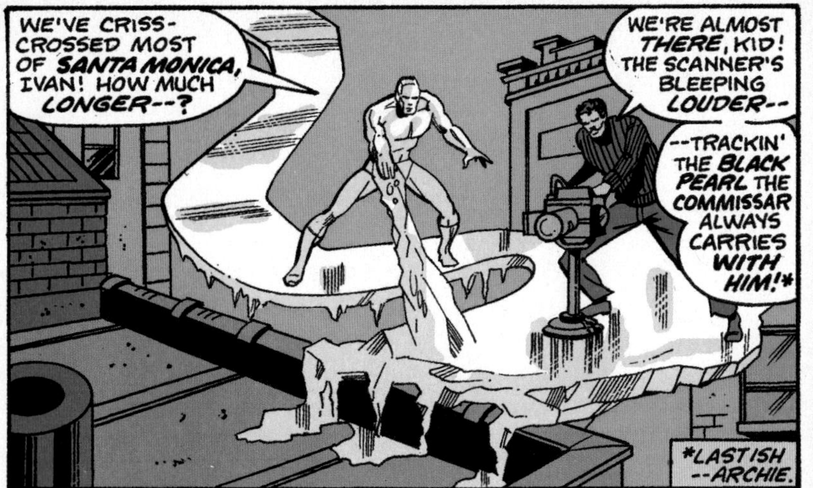
WE'VE CRISS-CROSSED MOST OF SANTA MONICA, IVAN! HOW MUCH LONGER--?
WE'RE ALMOST THERE, KID! THE SCANNER'S BLEEPING LOUDER--
--TRACKIN' THE BLACK PEARL THE COMMISSAR ALWAYS CARRIES WITH HIM!*
*LAST ISH --ARCHIE.

THERE!!
VENICE BEACH, KID! WE'VE HIT THE JACKPOT!

THAT WAREHOUSE IS WHERE WE'LL FIND THE WIDOW!
OR MAYBE A WELCOMING-COMMITTEE!
LET'S JUST SLOW DOWN AND THINK THIS OUT BEFORE--

THINK?? WITH NATASHA IN DANGER??

LISTEN, KID--ME AN' THE WIDOW'VE BEEN TOGETHER A LONG TIME. I'VE SEEN THE LADY UP--
--AN' I'VE SEEN HER DOWN! WE'VE BEEN THROUGH A LOT OF CHANGES TOGETHER--
--BUT NEITHER OF US EVER RUN OUT WHEN THE OTHER NEEDED HELP!

WHY YOU PIG-HEADED OLD RUSSIAN! WHO SAID ANYTHING ABOUT RUNNING OUT?
I WAS JUST TRYING TO POINT OUT TO YOU THAT THERE'S A THIRTY FOOT JUMP BETWEEN THIS ROOF AND THE OTHER ONE--
-- BUT NOW I'M BEGINNING TO WISH I'D LET YOU JUMP AND FIND OUT FOR YOURSELF!

I SWEAR--SOMETIMES I THINK US MUTANTS ARE THE ONLY ONES WITH ANY BRAINS ON THIS PLANET!
HERE! IT AIN'T THE LINCOLN TUNNEL--

--BUT IT'LL GET US ACROSS!
AND WHILE YOU'RE WALKING --TRY GIVING A THOUGHT TO THE IDEA OF TEAM-WORK!
WE'RE ALL ON THE SAME SIDE, POPS --WHICH YOU SEEM TO FORGET!
YOU BETTER SAVE THE SPEECHES FOR LATER, KID--

HOW CONVENIENT! OUR NEXT TARGETS HAVE SAVED US THE TROUBLE OF LOOKING FOR THEM--
--BY COMING TO US!
I WILL REMOVE THE BOY, COMRADES!

LOOKS LIKE THEY'VE ACED YOUR PARTNERS, JUNIOR! AND WE'RE NEXT!
DO ME A FAVOR, POPS! GO FIND THE WIDOW AND LEAVE THESE SUPER-TYPES TO ME!

AGGHH! MY ARMOR SUDDENLY FREEZES ABOUT ME, DYNAMO!
YOU WERE CARELESS, TITANIUM MAN-- YOU KNEW THE YOUTH'S POWERS!

STRAKK!
KID!
THEY GOT HIM!
I'LL PAY'EM BACK FOR YOU, JUNIOR! EVEN THOUGH I DON'T THINK MUCH OF YOUR SUPER-TEAM --YOU WERE ONE OF THE BEST!
BUT ALL THAT MATTERS NOW IS FINDIN'--

"--THE BLACK WIDOW!"
IT IS TIME FOR YOUR MEAL, TZARINA!
SHE IS ASLEEP, YOUNG ONE!
THOUGH HOW SHE CAN SLEEP AT SUCH A TIME-- I CANNOT SAY!
STILL, SHE MUST EAT...

TZARINA, I APOLO-- YOU LIED--!
CLICK
MADAM NATASHA IS--
ABOVE YOU, MY FORMER PUPIL!

BUT NOT FOR LONG!!
SLAM!
WELL DONE, STUDENT!
YOU MAKE AN OLD MAN PROUD!

YOU FORGET, COMRADE BRUSKIN--
--THAT I WAS YOUR PUPIL AS WELL--
--AND WHILE THE AGILITY OF THE FAMED BLACK WIDOW FAR SURPASSES MY OWN--

--DARKSTAR HAS OTHER POWERS AT HER COMMAND!
POWER SUCH AS--

--THIS!

ALEXEI! SOME KIND OF FORCE COMING FROM HER HAND!
LEAVE ME, CHILD!
SAVE YOURSELF!

I WOULD BE UNTRUE TO YOUR TEACHING WERE I TO DO THAT, ALEXI BRUSKIN!
AND I WOULD BE UNTRUE TO THAT SAME TEACHING WERE I TO ACT ANY DIFFERENTLY, MADAM WIDOW!
THOUGH I CANNOT SAY WHICH OF US IS RIGHT!
ZAP!
NOTHING! EVEN THOUGH I RECOVERED MY WIDOW'S--BITE--IT HAS NO EFFECT!
NATASHA! ABOVE YOU! ON THE SKYLIGHT!!
HAVE YOU SO SOON FORGOTTEN ME, OLD ONE?
SAME AS EVER, ALEXEI! BUT WE'LL CHAT AFTER MY TRANQUILLIZER-BULLETS HAVE TAKEN CARE OF YOUR JAILER!
SKRASH
IVAN!!
TO DO THAT THEY FIRST MUST HIT ME, IVAN PETROVITCH!
AND THAT THEY SHALL NOT DO!
I TRAINED HER, IVAN! SHE IS FAST!

AH, BUT CAN SHE SEE IN TWO PLACES AT ONCE?
HOW'VE YOU BEEN, 'TASHA?

FINE, OLD FRIEND!
UNHH!
STOOM!
JUST FINE!

LAYNIA!
CHILD! ARE YOU--?
I AM... ALL RIGHT, TEACHER.
SAVE FOR ...MY DIGNITY!

THAT AIN'T THE ONLY SPOT THAT'S GONNA BE HURTIN', LITTLE GIRL!
NOW SUPPOSE YOU TELL ME WHERE THE OTHERS ARE BEFORE...

UNHAND HER, TRAITOR!
WHO IN BLAZES?!

IT IS THE "OTHERS" WHOM YOU SOUGHT, IVAN PETROVICH!
THEY ARE HERE!
STAND WHERE YA ARE, WIDOW--OR THE CHAMPS GET IT!
WHO ARE YOU? THE REAL CRIMSON DYNAMO IS DEAD?
WHAT DO YOU WANT OF US?
NOT "US," WIDOW! JUST YOU, IVAN-- AND THE OLD MAN!

THE CHAMPIONS **MARVEL COMICS GROUP**™

APPROVED BY THE COMICS CODE AUTHORITY

30¢ 10 JAN 02112

HERCULES! BLACK WIDOW! ANGEL! GHOST RIDER! ICEMAN!

THE CHAMPIONS™

ASIDE, SATAN-SPAWN! THE SONS OF ZEUS *MUST* BREAK FREE!

BACK, HERCULES! YOU'LL FEEL THE FULL FURY OF *HELL*--

--BEFORE I LET YOU *ESCAPE* THIS *ROOM!*

CHAMPION VS. CHAMPION!

THE DEMON AND THE DEMI-GOD!

The avenging ANGEL! The deadly BLACK WIDOW! Johnny Blaze, the GHOST RIDER! HERCULES, Prince of Power! The incomparable ICEMAN! Five fighters for justice united to battle for the common man...because the world still needs heroes!

Stan Lee PRESENTS: THE CHAMPIONS™

ONE MAN'S SON IS ANOTHER MAN'S POISON!

YOU ARE GOING TO *DIE*, CHAMPIONS-- *AND YOU'LL NEVER EVEN KNOW WHY!!*

COMRADE, I-- THEY ARE *WAKING!* I CAN'T MAINTAIN THE *DARKFIELD* MUCH *LONGER!*

BAH! LET THEM *AWAKE!* THE *TITANIUM MAN* FEARS THEM *NOT!*

THE END OF AN *EPIC*, AND MAYBE THE END OF THE *CHAMPIONS*, BROUGHT TO YOU BY:

BILL MANTLO - WRITER
BOB HALL - ARTIST
FRANK GIACOIA - INKER
RAY HOLLOWAY - LETTERER
DON WARFIELD - COLORIST
ARCHIE GOODWIN - EDITOR

THE MORTAL FEMALE-- DARKSTAR! SHE HOLDS US IN SOME MANNER OF ENERGY FIELD!
LAST THING I REMEMBER IS THE BATTLE AT OUR INAUGURATION, BUT THAT WAS IN LOS ANGELES!
WHERE IN BLAZES ARE WE NOW??
YURI! I--
WE WILL NOT BE MUCH LONGER, LAYNIA! JUST LONG ENOUGH TO ENJOY THEIR HELPLESSNESS!

BASE VILLAIN!
NO MERE POWER OF DARKNESS CAN HOLD THE SON OF ZEUS!

BY ACHILLES' SHIELD!
NOTHING! THE FIELD DEFIES YOU, OLYMPIAN!

ALL RIGHT THEN, SPOOK-STUFF! LET'S SEE IF THE COMBINED POWER OF ICEMAN AND THE GHOST RIDER CAN DO ANY BETTER!
THAT IS-- IF YOU CAN DROP THE BELA LUGOSI ROUTINE LONG ENOUGH TO GO INTO ACTION!
IF YOU KNEW THE SOURCE OF MY POWER, FROZEN ONE--YOU WOULD NOT QUESTION ITS MANIFESTATION!

LAYNIA!!
IT IS... TOO MUCH, YURI!
I CAN'T HOLD THEM!!

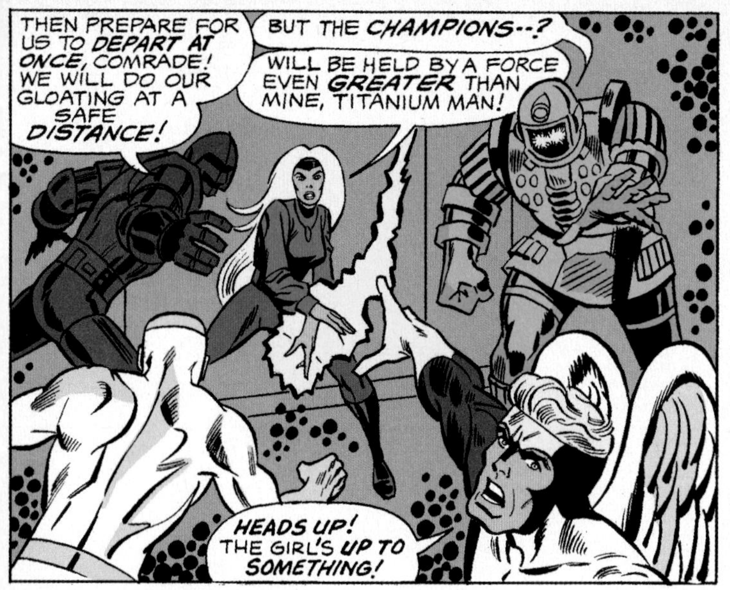
THEN PREPARE FOR US TO DEPART AT ONCE, COMRADE! WE WILL DO OUR GLOATING AT A SAFE DISTANCE!
BUT THE CHAMPIONS--?
WILL BE HELD BY A FORCE EVEN GREATER THAN MINE, TITANIUM MAN!
HEADS UP! THE GIRL'S UP TO SOMETHING!

IT IS DONE! NOTHING CAN STAY OUR DEPARTURE NOW!

GOOD LORD! THEY-- THEY'RE FADING OUT!
THE FIELD AROUND THEM IS GONE--

"--BUT SO ARE THEY!!"
WE ARE ON THE SURFACE ONCE MORE!
WHILE THE ACCURSED, INTERFERING CHAMPIONS LANGUISH IMPRISIONED IN A PLACE YET UNKNOWN TO THEM!

GONE! AND THEY'VE LEFT US INSIDE SOME KIND OF STEEL CUBICLE!
IF THEY THINK THEY'VE TRAPPED US-- THEN THEY'VE RECKONED WITHOUT HERCULES, ANGEL!
THOU SPEAKEST TRUE!

THERE BE NO METAL-- WHETHER FORGED BY GOD OR MAN-- THAT MAY HOLD AGAINST THE PRINCE OF POWER!
BY ZEUS! THERE BE NAUGHT BUT STONE BEYOND THE STEEL!

WHAT IN SATAN'S NAME--?!
EARTHQUAKE!! IT STARTED JUST AS HERCULES STRIPPED AWAY THE WALL!
RRUMMMBLE!
BUT WHY!?? AND WHERE ARE WE THAT WE'RE SURROUNDED BY SOLID ROCK!??

HAVE YOU NOT YET GUESSED, YOUTH?
THERE! THE VISUAL-SCAN IS SET SO THEY CAN SEE AND HEAR US AS WE HAVE OBSERVED THEM!
THEY WERE WATCHING THE WHOLE TIME!
QUIET, BOBBY! HEAR THEM OUT!

YOU ARE ENCASED IN A VAULT SET DEEP IN THE SAN ANDREAS FAULT!
THERE IS NO WAY OUT, SAVE BY DARKSTAR'S POWERS OF SPATIAL DISPLACEMENT! ANY MOVE ON YOUR PART TO ESCAPE WILL ACTIVATE THE FAULT, AND CAUSE A SERIES OF EARTHQUAKES WHICH WILL LEAVE LOS ANGELES NO MORE THAN A MEMORY!
HERC! WHAT--?!!
STOP HIM, BOBBY! IF HE HITS THAT WALL--!

WHOM!
TOO LATE, WARREN!
NOT THAT I COULD HAVE HELD BACK A GOD EVEN IF I'D WANTED TO!

AGAIN THE EARTH MOVES! AS IF THE TITANS IMPRISONED IN ITS DEPTHS SOUGHT ONCE MORE THE SUN!
WHAT MADNESS RULES HERE?!

HERCULES! TAKE IT EASY! THERE'S MORE THAN US AT STAKE! THERE'S THE WHOLE STATE OF CALIFORNIA!
THOU SPEAKEST TO HERCULES, WINGED ONE--WHOM EVEN ZEUS ONCE FEARED!
BUT HERCULES WILL NOT BE SHACKLED!!

YOU WILL IF IT MEANS MY HOME TOWN'S AT STAKE, MUSCLES!
AND I DON'T NEED MY SPOOK-ACT TO STOP YOU--
--NOT WHEN I'VE GOT HELLFIRE!!

NEVER DID HERCULES TRUST THEE, FOR IN TRUTH DIDST THY POWER SEEM TO BE A GIFT OF PLUTO AND THE STYGIAN DEPTHS OF HADES!
BUT IF THE LORD OF THE DEAD FAILED TO HOLD ME-- WHAT HOPE HAST THOU?!!

STOP IT! BOTH OF YOU! NO MATTER WHAT YOU THINK OF EACH OTHER, WE'RE A TEAM NOW!
CALM DOWN, HERC!
MAYBE BLAZE JUMPED THE GUN, BUT YOU GOTTA ADMIT YOU DO HAVE A TENDENCY TO ACT BEFORE YOU THINK!

AND INSIDE THE HOVERING SUPERSONIC CRAFT...

IVAN!!

IT IS NO USE, NATASHA! HE HAS NOT SPOKEN SINCE THE CRIMSON DYNAMO WAS REVEALED AS HIS SON! *

A SON HE ABANDONED! A SON HE LEFT FOR DEAD! YOU REMEMBER THAT, DON'T YOU, FATHER!??

YURI! MUST YOU--?

YES, LAYNIA! I MUST! MY DEAR FATHER WILL BE MADE TO REMEMBER--

*LAST ISSUE-- ARCHIE.

-- AND I HOPE THE MEMORY KILLS HIM!
BUT NOT TOO QUICKLY! I WANT HIM TO SUFFER AS I HAVE BEEN MADE TO SUFFER!

YURI PETROVITCH! I HAVE KNOWN IVAN FOR YEARS-- EVEN BEFORE WE DEFECTED! I KNOW THAT HE HAD A SON--
--BUT BOTH THE BOY AND IVAN'S WIFE ARE DEAD! KILLED IN A MOTOR ACCIDENT!
THAT IS THE STORY MY FATHER FED THE WORLD! BUT IF YOU WISH TO KNOW THE TRUTH, MADAME NATASHA, THEN HEAR THE STORY OF IVAN PETROVITCH, BEGINNING IN MOSCOW--

"--NINETEEN YEARS AGO!"
WE GO TO ZOO TODAY, POPPA?
LITTLE YURI WILL SOON BE AS BIG AS HIS FATHER!
LENIN'S BEARD, THE BOY IS ONLY FIVE!
"BUT EVEN THOUGH JUST A BOY, I STILL REMEMBER THE DAY EVERYTHING... CHANGED!"
THE DAYS OF THE REVOLUTION ARE PAST, IVAN PETROVITCH! COMMUNISM IS DEAD!
YOU ARE A SCIENTIST! A MASTER TECHNICIAN! THE WEST NEEDS YOU, PETROVITCH!
NO! GET OUT!!
MOTHER? WHAT--?
I FROZE IN THE SNOWS OUTSIDE LENINGRAD FIGHTING HITLER TO SAVE THIS LAND! RUSSIA IS MY HOME! IF THERE IS WRONG IN IT-- IT MUST BE CHANGED! NOT DESTROYED!
HUSH, YURI! YOUR FATHER IS ANGRY!

"AND A SHORT TIME LATER..."
YOU AND LITTLE YURI MUST LEAVE MOSCOW FOR A WHILE, MY WIFE! STALIN'S DEATH HAS MADE THINGS...UGLY HERE!
I...UNDERSTAND, IVAN! I WILL... WRITE TO YOU FROM THE MOUNTAINS!
STAY, LENYA! STAY WITH FATHER!

"BUT WE NEVER REACHED THE MOUNTAINS."
BRATTA-TAT-TATTA-TAT-TAA!!
"I HEARD MY MOTHER SCREAM ONLY ONCE--OVER THE ROAR OF THE MACHINE-GUN--

"--AND THEN I KNEW SHE WAS BEYOND SCREAMING."
M-MOTHER? MOTHER!!
I HAVE THE BOY, BRACKETT!
LET'S GO!!

"I COULD IMAGINE MY DEAR FATHER'S GRIEF!
"AFTER ALL, THE MEN WHO'D TAKEN ME HAD JUST OFFERED HIM A FORTUNE TO LEAVE RUSSIA, HAD THEY NOT?
"WHAT BETTER WAY TO TO SEVER ALL TIES, EH?"

ARE YOU MAD? HOW CAN YOU POSSIBLY BELIEVE THAT OF--
THERE IS MUCH YOU DO NOT UNDERSTAND, TZARINA. MUCH EVEN THE BOY DOES NOT KNOW.
LET HIM... FINISH.

COMRADE! WE HAVE JUST PICKED UP WHAT CAN ONLY BE THE AMERICAN AIR FORCE ON THE RADAR!
YEAH, "COMRADE!" AN' THEY'RE CLOSIN' FAST!!
TITANIUM MAN! YOU AND DARKSTAR FLY OUT AND STOP THEM!
YOU'RE IN COMMAND, JUNIOR! GOT ANY ORDERS?
NOT I, YURI! I WILL NOT WORK ANY FURTHER WITH THAT... BUTCHER!

HAH! THAT IS THE NAME THEY CALLED ME IN THE CAMPS, FAIR ONE!
IT IS A NAME I RELISH, AS THE AMERICAN PILOTS WILL SOON SEE!
SHALL I GO ON, FATHER? OR DO YOU STILL PRETEND NOT TO KNOW--?
"THAT THE AMERICAN AGENTS-- FOR SUCH WERE THEY WHO HAD KIDNAPPED ME, HELD ME IN WEST BERLIN FOR NINE YEARS!
"TRAINING ME! EDUCATING ME! BRAINWASHING ME TO WORK AGAINST THE STATE--
"BUT TO NO AVAIL!"
THIS IS CAGED BIRD TO HOME PERCH! I FEAR THAT SOON THEY WILL DISCOVER THIS RADIO I HAVE BUILT!
IF I AM TO BE RESCUED-- IT MUST BE SOON!
TONIGHT, THEN, CAGED BIRD!
"HOME PERCH WAS TRUE TO HIS WORD!"
YOU ARE SAVED, BOY! THESE SCUM WILL NEVER HURT YOU AGAIN!
YOU CAN'T-- GNNN!
PTOW!
QUIET, AMERICAN!
CLEAN UP THIS DEN OF THIEVES, BORIS--WHILE I TAKE THE YOUTH BACK ACROSS THE WALL--
--AND HOME!
"HOME."
HOME TO A GRAVE BEARING MY MOTHER'S NAME AND THE DISGRACE OF LEARNING THAT MY FATHER HAD DEFECTED!
MY SUSPICIONS WERE CONFIRMED! MY FATHER HAD SOLD US OUT! IVAN PETROVITCH WAS A TRAITOR!
THERE IS ANOTHER SIDE, BOY! ONE WHICH--
HEY, DYNAMO! YOU OUGHTTA SEE WHAT YER COMRADE'S DOIN' TO THEM PLANES!
AND TAKIN' HIS OWN SWEET TIME WHILE WE HOVER LIKE SITTIN' DUCKS UP HERE!

LENIN'S GHOST! I ORDERED HIM TO STOP THE PLANES--
--NOT DESTROY THEM!!
BULLSKI! RETURN TO THE COMMAND SHIP! AT ONCE!!
WHY NOT? THAT WAS THE LAST OF THE SWINE!

AND BACK IN THE SHIP...
YOU SAID THERE WAS ANOTHER SIDE, BRUSKIN! WHAT DO YOU KNOW?
SO! NOW THAT THE BOY IS GONE YOU CHOOSE TO SPEAK?
VERY WELL, IVAN PETROVITCH! KNOW THEN--

"--HOW YOU AND YOUR SON WERE... BETRAYED!"
HOW GOES IT, MEDVEDEV?
AS PLANNED, BRUSKIN! THE BOY BELIEVES HIMSELF HELD BY THE AMERICANS! HE HAS NEVER GUESSED THAT IT IS HIS OWN PEOPLE WHO KIDNAPPED HIM!

"WHEN THE BOY HATED THE WEST ENOUGH, A 'RESCUE' WAS FAKED!"
HE'S READY! HE'LL BELIEVE ANY LIES BRUSKIN FEEDS HIM! AND WHEN THE TIME IS RIGHT-- HE'LL EVEN HUNT DOWN HIS DEFECTOR FATHER!

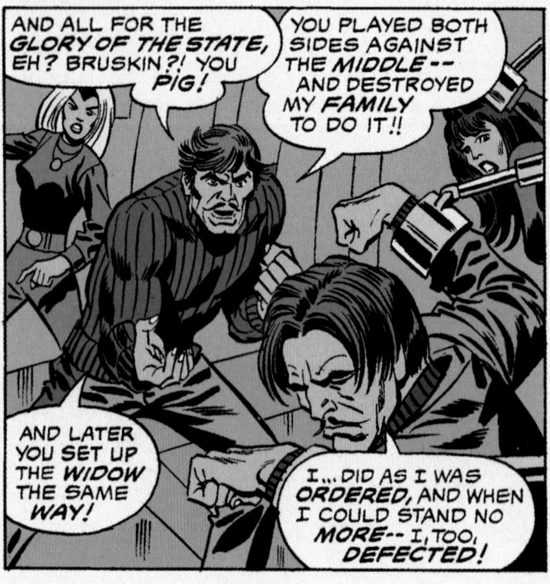

AND ALL FOR THE GLORY OF THE STATE, EH? BRUSKIN?! YOU PIG!
YOU PLAYED BOTH SIDES AGAINST THE MIDDLE-- AND DESTROYED MY FAMILY TO DO IT!!
AND LATER YOU SET UP THE WIDOW THE SAME WAY!
I... DID AS I WAS ORDERED, AND WHEN I COULD STAND NO MORE-- I, TOO, DEFECTED!

THE PLANES ARE... GONE, LAYNIA! TELL THE GRIFFIN TO PROCEED!
YURI, NO! THERE IS SOMETHING YOU MUST HEAR-- ABOUT YOUR FATHER!

I HAVE NO FATHER!
AND I FORBID YOU TO TALK TO THIS WITCH AGAIN! I'LL NOT HAVE YOU LISTENING TO HER LIES!
WHAP!
'TASHA!!
YURI!! NO!!

YOU SEE WHAT YOU'VE DONE, BRUSKIN?! YOU'VE MADE MY SON A KILLER!!
LISTEN TO YOUR TEACHER, YURI! LET HIM TELL YOU HOW HE MURDERED YOUR MOTHER!!
LIAR!!

HE'S TELLING THE TRUTH, YURI!
NO! NO!
UNNHH!

SKRIT!
SKRAK!
IF YOU WILL NOT LISTEN OF YOUR OWN WILL--
--THEN YOU MUST BE MADE TO HEAR!!

STOP HER!
YOUR WRETCHED FEMALE IS JEOPARDIZING THE WHOLE OPERATION!
SKROW!
DARKSTAR!!
I DO NOT NEED TO BE TOLD MY DUTY, TITANIUM MAN!

I AM... UNHURT, MADAME NATASHA! YURI WOULD NEVER TRY TO HURT ME!
BUT HE MUST BE MADE TO HEAR THE TRUTH-- BEFORE THE LIE HE HAS BEEN LIVING...
...DESTROYS HIM!
AND WHILE WE LACK THE STRENGTH TO FORCE HIM TO HEAR US--

--THANK THE STARS THERE ARE OTHERS WITH SUCH STRENGTH!

YOUR MYSTIC FLAMES SHALL RESTRAIN ME NO LONGER!
HERCULES WILL BE FREE!
BUT THERE'S A CITY AT STAKE--!

--MAYBE THE WHOLE STATE!
LIES! OUR CAPTORS DECEIVE US, HOPING TO KEEP US PRISONERS OF FALSE WORDS!
NO! WE CAN'T TAKE THE CHANCE!
I AM HERCULES-- I HAVE KNOWN THOUSANDS OF GENERATIONS OF MEN AND MANY TIMES MET SIMILAR DECEIT! I WILL TAKE THIS "CHANCE"!
WAIT! SOMETHING IS...

...HAPPENING.
GRASS! ROCKS! TREES! I DON'T KNOW HOW, BUT-- WE'RE OUT!
SO WE ARE. BUT I'M STILL NOT FINISHED WITH OUR SELF-APPOINTED GOD!

LATER, BLAZE! NOW ALL WE'VE GOT TO DO IS--
HUH?
MAKE IT TO THE AIRBASE ABOUT A MILE FROM HERE, COMMANDEER A PLANE AND HEAD COASTWARD!
DON'T ASK ME, WARREN! IT JUST POPPED INTO MY HEAD-- LIKE THE OLD DAYS WHEN PROFESSOR X WOULD CONTACT US TELEPATHICALLY!

CUT ONE LAST TIME TO...
ACCURSED WITCH OF A TRAITORESS!
YOU'LL NOT LIVE TO STAND TRIAL!!
YOU HAVE A LOT TO LEARN, MY FRIEND! FIRST, THAT IT TAKES MORE THAN ARMOR TO MAKE A WARRIOR!
ZIT!
STROW!
THERE ARE THINGS YOU'VE YET TO MASTER!
LIKE TACTICS! NO GOOD COMMANDER WOULD LEAVE HIS PILOT UNCOVERED!
CRIPES! SHE SHOT OUT THE MASTER CONTROL!
WE'RE GOING INTO A DIVE!!
I HAVE THE WIDOW, GRIFFIN! RADIO THE SUBMARINE THAT AWAITS US AND TELL THEM TO SURFACE AND PICK US UP HERE!
I'LL DO IT, BUT I DON'T LIKE IT! WE'RE STILL INSIDE THE THREE-MILE LIMIT--
--AN' WHILE I DON'T MIND FIGHTIN' SUPER-HEROES, THE FEDS ARE SOMETHIN' ELSE!!

YOU HAVE DONE YOUR WORK WELL, CAPTAIN! I WILL SEE YOU ARE CITED FOR IT!
SPARE ME, COMRADE! I ONLY DO AS I AM ORDERED--
--BUT I DISAPPROVE OF THESE WITCH-HUNTS INSTIGATED BY FORCES WITHIN OUR GOVERNMENT!

CAPTAIN ANDREYIVICH! AN AMERICAN FIGHTER!
IT HAS SEEN US!

LOOK OUT, BOBBY! THEY'RE FIRING AT US!
WHOOM!

THIS THING IS SLOWER THAN THE X-PLANE-- BUT IT STILL MOVES!
IT GOT US HERE-- BUT WE BETTER GET DOWN THERE BEFORE THE SUB DIVES!

HERCULES! YOU SURE YOU KNOW WHAT YOU'RE DOING?
AYE, LAD--

--HERCULES IS SURE!!
FTASHT!
THEY'VE ESCAPED! THE CHAMPIONS ARE HERE!!
KEEP THEM BUSY-- BUT FIND THE WIDOW!!
BLANG!

'TWAS THOU, ARMORED ONE, THAT DIDST FELL HERCULES IN THE BATTLE PAST! *
*LAST ISSUE-- ARCH.

THERE SHE IS! THE DYNAMO'S GOT HER!
AND THE DYNAMO SHALL KEEP HER, FOOL!
SKTOW!
SOME HEROES! THIS IS LIKE SHOOTIN' FISH IN A BARREL!

TEACHER! THEY DARE NOT FIGHT AT FULL STRENGTH WHILE YURI HOLDS THE WIDOW!
WOK!
THEN YURI MUST BE MADE TO LET HER GO, STUDENT!
EXCUSE ME, SAILOR--

--BUT I HAVE NEED OF YOUR WEAPON!
BRIP-BRIP-BRIP!
KTANG!
CLANG!
BRUSKIN, YOU ARE A FOOL,

AND SOON YOU WILL BE A DEAD FOOL!
STRAM!

YURI! HAD YOU KNOWN THE TRUTH, I WOULD HAVE UNDERSTOOD THE ACT YOU JUST COMMITTED!
BUT KNOWING YOUR IGNORANCE-- I KNOW NOW THAT YOU ARE NO MORE THAN A COLD-BLOODED MURDERER!
AND THOUGH WE TWO HAVE SHARED LOVE-- NOW WILL YOU FACE THE POWER OF DARKSTAR!!
LAYNIA! MY LOVE, NO!!

BA-TOOM!

THE WIDOW AND IVAN SEEMED TO KNOW HIM, ICEMAN--BUT THEY DON'T LOOK LIKE THEY WANT TO TALK ABOUT IT JUST NOW!

I DON'T GET IT-- WHO WAS THAT GUY?

'TWOULD APPEAR, MY FRIENDS, THAT THE BLACKGUARDS ARE ALL BUT VANQUISHED!

THE LION-MANED ONE IS HELPLESS, ICEMAN!

THE DYNAMO IS DOWN, IVAN PETROVITCH!

TELL ME WHAT I AM TO DO WITH HIM!

KID, I--

BACK TO THE SPOOK-ROUTINE, HUH? OH, WELL, IT'S YOUR SCENE! I WON'T KNOCK IT!

COMRADE! YOU MUST DECIDE! I AM HIS... LOVER! HOW CAN I--?
YOU'RE GONNA HAVE TO, KID! I DON'T EVEN KNOW HIM! IT'S BEEN TOO MANY YEARS.
IF HE'S GOT ANY GOOD POINTS, YOU KNOW 'EM BETTER'N I EVER WILL.
DO WHAT YOU WANT WITH HIM, KID.
I JUST DON'T CARE ANY MORE.
FOOLS! YOU HAVEN'T SEEN THE LAST OF THE CRIMSON DYNAMO!
LATER...
I HOPE SOMEBODY'S GOT AN EXPLANATION FOR WHAT WENT ON BACK THERE, AND FOR WHY THE CRIMSON DYNAMO WAS ALLOWED TO ESCAPE!
THERE WAS A SIDE OF THIS BATTLE KNOWN ONLY TO A FEW OF US, ANGEL! YOU MUST TRUST THAT WHAT WE DID WAS RIGHT--
--AND MAYBE SOMEDAY YOU WILL LEARN ALL!
I...THANK YOU, MADAME NATASHA. I HOPE I WILL PROVE WORTHY OF THAT TRUST!
SWELL! THE TEAM FOR THE "COMMON MAN" NOW EVEN KEEPS SECRETS FROM ITSELF! MAYBE YOU WERE RIGHT, IVAN! MAYBE THE CHAMPIONS ARE A BUST!
IVAN PETROVITCH SAYS NOTHING, BUT HIS EYES ARE HOODED BY A MASK IT WILL TAKE YEARS TO DRAW AWAY. THE TRIP BACK TO LOS ANGELES IS MADE... IN SILENCE.
NEXT:
THE CHAMPIONS MOVE INTO THEIR NEW HEADQUARTERS IN A POWER-PACKED ISSUE CHOCK-FULL OF GUEST-STARS AS THEY FACE...
The SHADOW FROM THE STARS!!

THE CHAMPIONS MARVEL® COMICS GROUP™

APPROVED BY THE COMICS CODE AUTHORITY

30¢ 11 FEB 02112

HERCULES! BLACK WIDOW! ANGEL! GHOST RIDER! ICEMAN!

THE CHAMPIONS™

GUEST STARRING BLACK GOLIATH!*

KANE & LAYTON

*PROVIDING HE LIVES THAT LONG!

The avenging ANGEL! The deadly BLACK WIDOW! Johnny Blaze, the GHOST RIDER! HERCULES, Prince of Power! The incomparable ICEMAN! Five fighters for justice united to battle for the common man...because the world still needs heroes!

STAN LEE PRESENTS: THE CHAMPIONS™

SCRIPT by BILL MANTLO / INKS by BOB LAYTON / LETTERS by PATTERSON / COLORS by D. WARFIELD / EDITING ARCHIE GOODWIN / AND INTRODUCING THE PULSE-POUNDING PENCILS OF JOHN BYRNE--ARTIST

BUN LIKE THIS...
DO SOMETHING, LADV! PULL BACK ON THE STICK! KICK IT! ANYTHING!
BUT DO SOMETHING!!
I...AM TRYING, ANGEL! DESPITE YOUR SENSELESS COMMANDS--

--I AM TRYING!!
THERE! WE'RE STRAIGHTENING OUT!

OKAY, WE'VE GOT THE STEERING BACK! HOW ABOUT THE LANDING CONTROLS?
WHY DON'T YOU LAY OFF ON THE WIDOW, WARREN! I MEAN, NOT ALL OF US WERE BORN TO FLY!

JUST WHAT WE NEED-- ADVICE FROM THE PEANUT GALLERY!
HOLD ON! WHO MADE YOU BOSS-MAN OF THIS TEAM?
QUIET! BOTH OF YOU! I'M TRYING TO LAND!
HERE THEY COME! AND FAST!

WIDOW! YOU'VE GOT TO SLOW DOWN OR YOU'LL OVERSHOOT THE ROOF!
SHE'S TRYING! HEY! COME BACK HERE, YOU COWARD!

I'M NOT BAILING OUT-- I'M CLEARING THE WAY!
HEY, FRIEND! MOVE IT! THIS COULD BE A ROUGH LANDING!
I'D LIKE TO OBLIGE YOU, WINGS, BUT YOU SEE--I DESIGNED THAT THING--

--AND I DON'T AIM TO SEE IT CRASH!!
HOLY SMOKES!
BY MY TROTH-- A GIANT!
GIANT OR NOT, HE'S JUST MADE HIMSELF A BIGGER TARGET-- AND WE'RE GONNA HIT HIM DEAD CENTER!

I WOULDN'T WORRY TOO MUCH ABOUT THAT, SON! YOU SEE, A CERTAIN AMOUNT OF POWER GOES ALONG WITH THE SIZE!

METHINKS 'TIS NOT ENOUGH, GIANT!
UNHH! IT'S GOT MORE MOMENTUM THAN I THOUGHT!
METHINKS YOU'RE RIGHT, HERC!

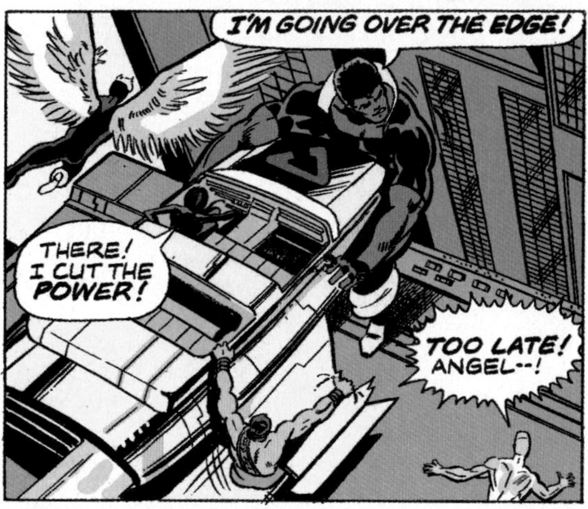
I'M GOING OVER THE EDGE!
THERE! I CUT THE POWER!
TOO LATE! ANGEL--!

NEED A LIFT, BOBBY?
TEAMWORK DOES IT AGAIN! JUST LIKE THE OLD DAYS IN THE X-MEN!
ALL IS FORGIVEN, WARREN-- THIS TIME!
I DON'T BELIEVE IT! A PLATFORM OF SOLID ICE!
PONDER IT LATER, MY FRIEND! AFTER YOU'RE BACK ON THE ROOF!

AND SOME MINUTES LATER...
WELL, WARREN? ANY IDEA WHY TWO MILLION DOLLARS WORTH OF AIRCRAFT DOESN'T WORK?
NOT A ONE, WIDOW-- THOUGH MAYBE OUR LARGE FRIEND HAS A COUPLE!

SPEAKING OF WHOM-- JUST WHO ARE YOU, BIG FELLA! I MEAN, YOU'RE SURE NOT THE ORIGINAL GIANT-MAN I MET WHILE I WAS WITH THE X-MEN!*
*AN X-MEN CLASSIC FROM ISSUE #9 -- ARCHIE

AYE, IN TRUTH THOU ART NEITHER HENRY PYM NOR CLINT BARTON! THE PRINCE OF POWER HATH FOUGHT BESIDE BOTH-- AND THY SKIN COLOR DOTH MARK THEE AS ANOTHER!

I'D THINK SO! BUT LISTEN, SINCE MY COVER WENT THE WAY OF MY CLOTHES-- THE NAME'S BILL FOSTER--
--OR BLACK GOLIATH! L.A.'S HARDEST-TO-MISS, SPANKING-NEW SUPER-HERO--
--WHO ALSO HAPPENS TO BE TONY STARK'S WEST COAST REP! NO APPLAUSE, JUST THROW MONEY!

OUR THANKS FOR YOUR HEROIC EFFORT-- BUT IF IT WAS YOU WHO BUILT THE SHIP...
HE JUST DESIGNED IT, 'TASHA! IT WAS BUILT BY A CREW HIRED BY OUR LAWYER, EMERSON BALE!
WHICH ISN'T HALF AS INTERESTING AS WHO JUST DROPPED IN!

WELCOME, DARKSTAR. I TRUST THE CUSTOMS AUTHORITIES WERE NOT... TOO HARD ON YOU?*
NO! THANKS TO THE INTERVENTION OF YOUR FRIEND NICK FURY!
DARKSTAR THANKS YOU, MADAME WIDOW... FROM MY HEART!
AND SPEAKING OF HEARTS...
*DARKSTAR DESERTED HER SOVIET SUPER-AGENT TASK FORCE AND DEFECTED TO THE WEST LAST ISSUE -- ARCH.

WHILE BOBBY DRAKE RENEWS A RECENT ACQUAINTANCE, LET US SHIFT EASTWARD TO THE DESERTS OF ARIZONA AND CATCH UP WITH A CERTAIN CYCLIST CALLED...
GHOST RIDER!
MAN, WHAT A MESS OF TROUBLE I'VE HAD SINCE I PICKED UP THAT HANDLE!

BUT THE CHAMPS DON'T SEEM TO MIND THE GHOST RIDER-- 'CEPT MAYBE FOR HERC, WHO SOMEHOW EQUATES MY POWERS WITH DEMONS OR SOMETHING!
MOST FOLKS OUTRIGHT PANIC WHEN MY SKULL STARTS BLAZING!

IT'S... STRANGE! I'M JUST NOT USED TO GETTING SO MUCH UNDERSTANDING!

HMPH! IT'D BE JUST LIKE ME TO BLOW IT JUST WHEN I'M BEGINNING TO FEEL LIKE I BELONG--
HEY! I'M CHANGING! THAT MEANS DANGER!

--AND THERE IT IS!
COMIN' FAST AND ON THE HOOF!
STAMPEDE!

THEY'RE RUNNIN' BLIND-- PANICKED-- AND MY FLAMIN' HEAD ISN'T GONNA MAKE 'EM ANY CALMER!
MY REAL BIKE'S SQUASHED FLATTER'N A FLAPJACK-- ONLY CHANCE IS TO WHIP UP A FAST FLAME-CYCLE--

--AND HIGHTAIL IT OUTTA HERE--
--BY RIDIN' RIGHT UP THE SIDE OF THE CANYON WALL!

AND AS THE GHOSTLY CYCLIST GUIDES HIS MYSTICAL BIKE ABOVE THE HORNS OF THE FEAR-MADDENED STEERS...
BUH-WHOOM!
AN EXPLOSION!? BUT WHAT--??

QUESTION ANSWERED! AN ARROW--
--AND IT'S HEADED RIGHT AT ME!

NO, IT HIT BEHIND ME!!
WHOEVER'S PLAYIN' ROBIN HOOD HAS SEALED THE CATTLE IN--

--BY CAUSIN' A LANDSLIDE AT EITHER END OF THE RAVINE! PRETTY FANCY SHOOTIN'!

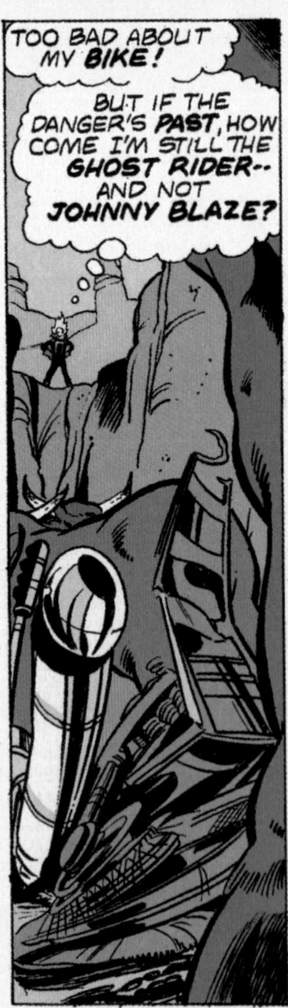

TOO BAD ABOUT MY BIKE!
BUT IF THE DANGER'S PAST, HOW COME I'M STILL THE GHOST RIDER-- AND NOT JOHNNY BLAZE?

PAST, DID YOU SAY, G.R.?
HOLD IT RIGHT THERE, MISTER SPOOK! THIS LITTLE DARLIN'S LOADED--
--AND I'D SURE AS SPIT LIKE T'SEE IF YOU'RE REALLY THE GHOST Y'PRETEND T'BE!
UH-OH! BETTER GO INTO MY ACT!
HAVE A CARE, MORTAL, FOR MY POWER IS NOT TO BE SNEERED AT!

MAYBE NOT... BUT YOUR DIALOGUE IS A DOWNRIGHT SCREAM! HE'S OKAY, MARSHAL!
WELL, IF YOU SAY SO, MISTER...
YOU! I SHOULD HAVE KNOWN!

HAWKEYE! WHAT'S GOING ON OUT HERE BIG ENOUGH TO BRING IN THE AVENGERS?
WHERE'VE YOU BEEN, GHOST RIDER? I LEFT THE AVENGERS-- THE PAPERS WERE FULL OF IT-- AND TEAMED UP WITH THE MASKED MAN YOU SEE BEHIND ME!*
SAY HELLO TO A LIVING LEGEND-- MATT HAWK, THE TWO-GUN KID!
HOW DO, HOMBRE?
* AVENGERS #143-- Arch.

THE TWO-GUN--!?? YOU'VE GOTTA BE KIDDING!!
NOPE. IT ALL STARTED WHEN KANG--LOOK, I DON'T FEEL LIKE REELING IT OFF AGAIN!
LET'S JUST SAY WE'RE HERE, AND THESE RANCHERS NEED OUR HELP!
MAYBE YOU'D BETTER TELL HIM WHY, HAWKEYE!

RIGHT! THERE'S SOMETHING-- STRANGE OUT HERE, HOT-STUFF-- SOMETHING THAT'S GOT THESE PEOPLE SPOOKED!
THAT STAMPEDE YOU JUST SQUEAKED OUT OF WAS A PRIME EXAMPLE!

AND, LIKE ANY GOOD SCI-FI STORY, IT STARTED WITH FUNNY LIGHTS OUT IN THE DESERT-- NEAR A PLACE THE LOCALS CALL LA MESA DE LAS ALMAS PERDIDAS!
THE MESA OF LOST SOULS!
WE WERE JUST HEADIN' OVER THERE TO--

HAWKEYE! LOOK AT--
I SEE IT! A FLYING SAUCER!
LET'S GET TO THAT MESA FAST!

MEANWHILE...
THE OTHERS HAVE ACCEPTED DARKSTAR WITHOUT QUESTION! PERHAPS IT IS THAT SHE IS SO LIKE A YOUNGER BLACK WIDOW THAT CAUSES ME TO WORRY--!
I... HOPE HER DEFECTION WILL BE... EASIER!
I'VE FOUND THE PROBLEM, CHAMPIONS! THE BASIC DESIGN IS FLAWLESS, BUT THE ACTUAL METAL USED IN CONSTRUCTION SEEMS TO HAVE JUST CRUMBLED UNDER STRESS!
YOU'RE SAYING WE PAID A COOL TWO MILLION FOR A STRUCTURALLY UNSOUND AIRCRAFT?
WHAT I'M SAYING IS-- YOU'VE BEEN ROBBED!

AN UNCONFIRMED REPORT CLAIMS THAT THOSE RANCHERS NEAREST THE MESA HAVE ALL BEEN AFFLICTED BY SOME FORM OF MANIA--
--SAVAGELY ATTACKING PEOPLE THEY'VE KNOWN ALL THEIR LIVES, AS IF CONTROLLED BY SOME UNKNOWN FORCE!
LIVE FROM NEW MEXICO

WE HAVE HEARD ENOUGH! GOLIATH -- WILL THIS SHIP GET US THERE?
IF YOU KEEP IT TO WITHIN FIVE TIMES THE SPEED LIMIT, YEAH, IT SHOULD!
THEN LET'S HEAD OUT, PEOPLE! TOO BAD WE DON'T HAVE A CATCHY ASSEMBLY CALL!
Y'KNOW, LIKE "CHAMPIONS CONVENE," OR SOMETHING!

HEY, PRETTY LADY! MY HAND'S WAITING!
I APPRECIATE YOUR OFFER, ROBERT DRAKE! MOST SINCERELY--

--BUT DARKSTAR PREFERS HER OWN MODE OF TRANSPORT!
YEAH, I SEE!
ICEMAN, I WILL NEED A NAVIGATOR-- AND WHERE IS HERCULES?

HEY, MUSCLES! WHERE--?
DIDST THOU FORGET THAT OUR CRAFT NEEDS BE LAUNCHED FROM THE ROOF?
--AND THAT ONLY HERCULES DOTH POSSESS THE STRENGTH TO BEAR IT HENCE?

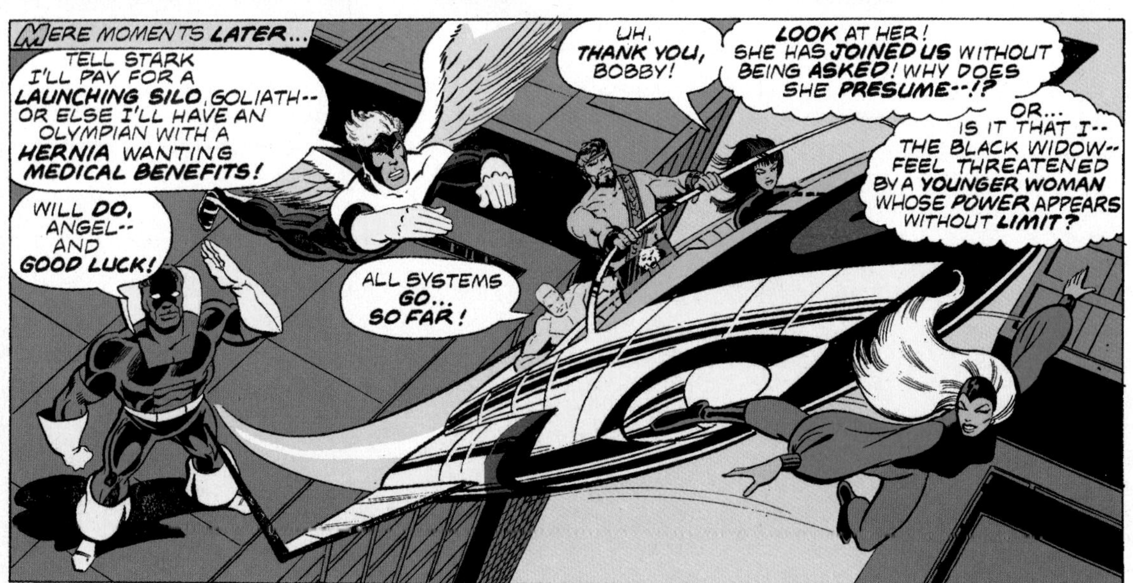
MERE MOMENTS LATER...
TELL STARK I'LL PAY FOR A LAUNCHING SILO, GOLIATH-- OR ELSE I'LL HAVE AN OLYMPIAN WITH A HERNIA WANTING MEDICAL BENEFITS!
WILL DO, ANGEL-- AND GOOD LUCK!
UH, THANK YOU, BOBBY!
ALL SYSTEMS GO... SO FAR!
LOOK AT HER! SHE HAS JOINED US WITHOUT BEING ASKED! WHY DOES SHE PRESUME--!?
OR... IS IT THAT I-- THE BLACK WIDOW-- FEEL THREATENED BY A YOUNGER WOMAN WHOSE POWER APPEARS WITHOUT LIMIT?

AND AT THE MESA OF LOST SOULS...
WE CAN'T HURT THESE RANCHERS, TWO-GUN! SOMETHING IS MAKING THEM ATTACK US!
I RECKON YOU'RE RIGHT, HAWKEYE-- BUT THAT WON'T STOP THEM FROM HURTIN' US!
KILL!
KILL!

THEY'RE STOPPIN'! JUST STANDIN' THERE-- NOT MOVIN'!
ALMOST LIKE THEY WERE WAITIN' FOR SOMETHIN' TO HAPPEN!

BUT WHAT COULD THEY--?
KILL! KILL!
WHAT IN THUNDERATION--!?

THAT SHADOW! MOVIN' BY ITSELF!!
AS SOON AS IT MET UP WITH HIS OWN-- HE CHANGED BECAME AS LOCO AS THE REST!

THAT FIRE O' YOURS IS KEEPIN' IT AWAY, MISTER MUCH OBLIGED!
WE NOW KNOW THE REAL ENEMY! BE ON YOUR GUARD, MORTAL!

GHOST RIDER'S HELLFIRE IS HOLDIN' THEM OFF!
IF IT'S LIGHT THEY DON'T LIKE-- LET'S SEE HOW A BLINDING FLARE ARROW GRABS 'EM!
THE SHAFT FLIES FROM HAWKEYE'S BOW, GLOWING BRIGHTER AS IT GAINS ALTITUDE--

--CASTING ITS EERIE LIGHT ON THE SCENE BELOW...
VERY RESOURCEFUL, HUMANS--
--BUT THIS WILL NOT KEEP US AT BAY FOR LONG!
BEHOLD, MORTALS! REVEALED IN THE GLARE--THE TRUE ENEMY!
THE SHADOWS!

OF COURSE, FOOL! THE SHADOWS-- SOLDIERS OF WARLORD KAA!
KAA!? THE ALIEN SHADOW BEING! I REMEMBER HIM FROM AVENGER FILES!
HE'S ATTACKED EARTH TWICE BEFORE-- AND JUST BARELY BEEN DRIVEN OFF!
THAT IS PAST, FOOL! EACH TIME I HAVE COME BACK STRONGER!

THE SECOND TIME, OUR SCIENCE HAD ENABLED ME TO BECOME A SHADOW DUPLICATE OF THE HULK! I DEFEATED HIM, BUT OUR BATTLE HAD CARRIED US INTO A MILITARY BASE, WHERE...
NO! THERE ARE FLOODLIGHTS ALL AROUND US! I'M FADING!

BUT THE LIGHTS HAD NOT BEEN BRIGHT ENOUGH TO DISSIPATE ME ENTIRELY...
AFTER MANY MONTHS I WAS ABLE TO REFORM!

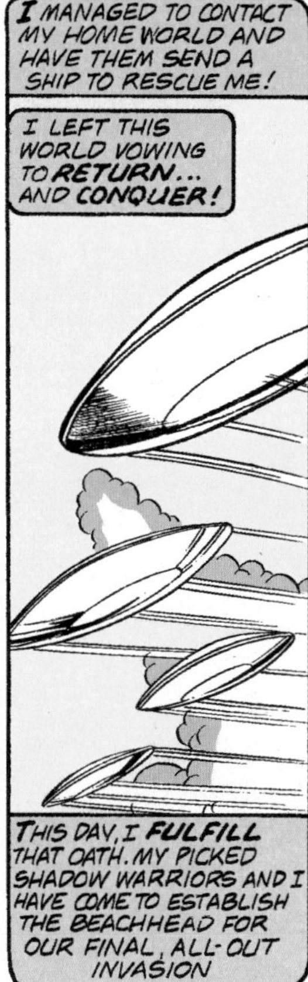
I MANAGED TO CONTACT MY HOME WORLD AND HAVE THEM SEND A SHIP TO RESCUE ME!
I LEFT THIS WORLD VOWING TO RETURN... AND CONQUER!
THIS DAY, I FULFILL THAT OATH. MY PICKED SHADOW WARRIORS AND I HAVE COME TO ESTABLISH THE BEACHHEAD FOR OUR FINAL, ALL-OUT INVASION

WE HAVE DEVELOPED A NEW POWER--THE POWER TO POSSESS HUMANS' MINDS BY INHABITING THEIR SHADOWS!
THIS TIME, NOTHING CAN STOP US!

--AND KAA WILL RULE SUPREME!
NO! YOU WILL BE DEFEATED-- BY HELLFIRE!!
WOULD YOU HARM YOUR OWN PEOPLE, HUMAN? I THINK NOT!

AND THEREIN LIES THE KEY TO OUR VICTORY--
--FOR WE WOULD SACRIFICE ALL OUR HUMAN SLAVES TO DEFEAT YOU, AND NEVER RISK ENDANGERING OURSELVES!
HERE IT COMES, GANG! GET READY TO--

WIDOW!
YOU SHOULD LEARN TO FINISH A SENTENCE, HAWKEYE! IT'S IMPOLITE TO TO LEAVE A LADY DANGLING!

HEY, SHE'S NOT HERE ALONE, YOU KNOW!
FOR HAWKEYE SHE IS, WINGS! THEY USED TO KNOW EACH OTHER!
WHAT GETS ME IS NOT EVEN A WORD OF WELCOME FROM SPOOK-STUFF, HERE!
YOU HAVE DONE NOTHING YET WORTHY OF MY NOTICE!

THESE ARE THE RANCHERS THE NEWS REPORT SAID HAD BEEN POSSESSED OF SOME FORM OF MADNESS!
A SIMPLE DARKFIELD SHOULD SUFFICE TO--

BUT, TO THE YOUNG RUSSIANS SURPRISE...
SOMETHING-- PENETRATES THE FIELD!
FOOLISH FEMALE! HOW CAN DARKNESS SHACKLE BEINGS WHOSE ESSENCE IS DARKNESS!?

AND AS DARKSTAR STARES IN UNCOMPREHENDING HORROR...
THE BEING APPROACHES MY OWN SHADOW! HIS FINGERS REACH FOR IT--
--AND, AS HE TOUCHES IT, MY SOUL BEGINS TO SCREAM WITHIN ME!
POWER SUCH AS YOURS WILL SERVE US WELL, WOMAN!

MAYBE, CREEP-- AND MAYBE NOT!
WHAT? THE WOMAN'S SHADOW IS GONE! THERE IS NOTHING TO POSSESS!
ICEMAN!!

AH, MY HEART MELTS TO HEAR MY NAME SLIP FROM YOUR LOVELY LIPS, FAIR MAID!
NOW, IF YOU'LL JUST STAY BENEATH MY ICE-SHADE, WE'LL FIGURE OUT HOW TO PUT OUR WOULD-BE CONQUERORS ON ICE-- IF YOU'LL PARDON THE PUN!
HOW WE'LL DO IT, ONLY DA SHADOW KNOWS-- NYAH HAH HA!

THOU HAST STRUCK UPON A SOLUTION, YOUNG ONE! IF YON BEINGS CANNOT WORK THEIR EVIL LEST THERE BE LIGHT--
-- THEN I SHALL KEEP THEM FROM THE LIGHT BY BURYING THEM BENEATH THIS MOUNTAIN OF STONE!

BUT AS THE MIGHTY OLYMPIAN HEAVES THE MASSIVE WEIGHT ABOVE HIS HEAD...
SMASH US, BRAGGART? IS THAT WHAT YOU HOPED TO DO?
NOW THAT YOUR SHADOW AND YOUR MIND HAVE MERGED WITH MINE, PERHAPS YOU'LL FEEL MORE LIKE SMASHING--

--THE BLACK WIDOW!
THY TIME HAS COME TO DIE!
FIGHT BACK, HERCULES! THEIR HOLD ON YOU CAN'T BE AS STRONG AS THAT THEY ACHIEVE OVER A MORTAL!

HE... IS HESITATING-- AS IF HE BATTLES WITH HIS OWN SOUL!
WIDOW! GET OUT OF THE WAY! HURRY!

NO! HE MUST SEE ME, AND KNOW THAT IF HE LETS THEM POSSESS HIM IT WON'T ONLY BE A FRIEND HE'S DOOMED--BUT PERHAPS A WORLD AS WELL!

IF THE SON OF ZEUS UNDERSTANDS THOSE WORDS, THE ONLY SIGN OF IT IS THE SWEAT THAT BEGINS TO DRIP FROM HIS BROW AND THE KNOTTING OF MIGHTY SINEWS BENEATH HIS SUN-BRONZED SKIN.
GET THEE... FROM ME, DEMON! 'TIS HERCULES THOU DOST FACE-- NOT SOME SON OF MAN--

--BUT HERCULES! HE WHO IS CALLED PRINCE OF POWER-- SON OF ZEUS, ALL-SEEING!

AND I WILL NOT SHAME MY BIRTHRIGHT!!

DEPART, VILE SHADOW-- AND POSSESS YON STONE, IF THOU CANST!
AND BEHIND HIM, THE BLACK WIDOW... SMILES.

WHILE, ELSEWHERE...
I HOPE THIS PLAN OF YOURS WORKS, GHOST RIDER!
WE MAY NOT BE ABLE TO TO GET THIS CLOSE TO THE MOTHER-SHIP, AGAIN!

THEN WE SHOULD BEGIN, HAWKEYE-- ONCE I GRIP YOUR ARROW WITH THE TOUCH OF... HELL FIRE--
--CAUSING IT TO GLOW WITH A LIGHT FROM WHICH NONE MAY HOPE TO HIDE!

WHY DON'T YOU KNOCK OFF THE SPOOK ROUTINE AND GET ON WITH IT! KAA COULD RETURN AND SECOND AND"

KAA IS HERE, FOOLS! AND YOU THREE WILL BE THE FIRST TO DIE!!
N-NOOOO!

CEASE STRUGGLING, HUMAN! KAA NOW INHABITS YOUR SHADOW! YOUR WILL IS MINE!
NO!

I...WON'T LET YOU!
MUST... RESIST!

I DIDN'T SPEND ALL THOSE YEARS WITH PROFESSOR X WITHOUT LEARNING SOMETHING ABOUT CLOSING MY MIND TO OUTSIDERS!
AND, WHILE I MAY NOT BE ANYWHERE NEAR AS GOOD AT IT AS MARVEL GIRL WAS--
--I'M STILL THE AVENGING ANGEL, KAA, AND YOU'VE MESSED WITH THE WRONG CHAMPION!

THE ANGEL SOARS SKYWARD, AND KAA FEELS HIS POWER WANING...

...AS THE SHADOW HE FOOLISHLY DARED POSSESS GROWS SMALLER...
...UNTIL FINALLY IT IS TOO SMALL TO PRESERVE HIS LIFE ESSENCE.

THERE IS A TERRIFIED SHRIEK INSIDE THE ANGEL'S MIND...THEN KAA AND HIS EVIL ARE... GONE!

FLEW TOO--
HIGH! STRAINED MY WINGS!
GOT TO KEEP GOING! JUST ENOUGH STRENGTH TO FINISH THE JOB!

DON'T STOP, WINGS! I CAN TELL BY THE WAY YOU'RE FLUTTERING THAT WE'RE ONLY GONNA GET ONE SHOT AT THIS!

THEN YOU'D BETTER NOT MISS, AVENGER!
EX-AVENGER, X-MAN! I WISH YOU PEOPLE WOULD REMEMBER THAT!

AND NOW WE'LL FIND OUT WHETHER YOUR RESIDENT DEMON'S GOT ROCKS IN HIS SKULL--
THWANG!
--OR WHETHER A CRAZY STUNT LIKE THIS'LL WORK!!

THEY HAVE SLAIN THE WARLORD KAA-- AND THEY ATTACK THE COMMAND SHIP!
ALL UNITS REGROUP! REACH THEM BEFORE IT IS--

TOO LATE!!
HAWKEYE'S MOST POWERFUL BLAST ARROW--IMBUED WITH THE FULL, SEARING BRILLIANCE OF HELLFIRE--BLOWS THE ALIEN SHIP APART IN A BLINDING FLASH--
--AND A VIRTUAL TIDAL WAVE OF DEADLY INCANDESCENCE SWEEPS THROUGH THE SHADOW WARRIORS' RANKS-- ENDING THEIR THREAT.

*BLACK GOLIATH #3 & 4-- --Archie

--THE STRANGER!!

WHAT CAN WE SAY? JUST, BE HERE!!

Original unused cover to *Champions* #7